GALVESTON:1900
INDIGNITIES

Book Five:
The Arrangement

N.E. BROWN

Galveston: 1900 – Indignities
Book 5: The Arrangement

Copyright © 2015 by N. E. Brown.
All rights reserved.

ISBN:13-978-0-9968510-0-8

Library of Congress Control Number: Pending

Book Cover Design: Anya Kelleye Designs
www.AnyaKelleye.com

OTHER BOOKS BY AUTHOR, N. E. BROWN

Galveston-1900-Indignities, The Arrival,
Book One ISBN: 978-0-9894748-8-7
Galveston-1900-Indignities, The Aftermath,
Book Two ISBN: 978-0-9897168-6-4
Galveston-1900-Indignities, The Atonement,
Book Three ISBN: 978-0-9898820-4-0
Galveston-1900, Indignities, The Affirmation,
Book Four ISBN: 978-0-9903626-0-9
Carson Chance, PI, Over the Edge
ISBN: 978-1-63122-333-4

If you enjoyed reading The Arrangement, the author would appreciate it if you would leave a review on Amazon.com.

GALVESTON, 1900, INDIGNITIES, THE ARRANGEMENT, BOOK FIVE

Prologue

Liverpool, England, 1901

It was like taking candy from a baby. The tall, dark-haired man scratched the week old stubble on his square jaw. His deep-set charcoal eyes gazed over the sea of travelers disembarking from the ships. Tired, eyes glazed over, arms filled with their children and carpet- bags, the unsuspecting travelers were immune to potential threat and danger.

This is where he worked. He silently moved through the crowd with the grace and ease of a fast-moving vessel. Making eye contact with no one, his focus was on today's agenda.

While maneuvering through the crowd, his hands quickly reached into pockets, carpetbags and purses, fetching his daily bounty. Ladies' necklaces slid from their necks and pocket watches were easily extracted from men's waist chains.

He moved with the grace of a circus magician. He was the stranger. He was nobody.

By the time anyone noticed an item had been taken, the stranger disappeared like a shooting star in the night leaving no clues.

1

Rosenberg, Texas- 1906

The barn was dank and smelled of wet decaying hay. Catherine's arms were tied tightly above her head. The foul odor of whiskey exhaled through her abductor's clenched teeth as he continued to rape her. She was screaming and sobbing. Her nightmares were taking her deeper, deeper, into a cavern of pain and sorrow.

"Catherine, Catherine! Wake up." Her husband, Trent, was shaking her. "You're having a nightmare."

Catherine pushed Trent away from her without waking. A loud clap of thunder followed by blazing flashes of lightning blasted through the curtains in their bedroom. Startled by the sounds, she woke and fell languishing into Trent's arms, sobbing uncontrollably as he stroked her hair and coddled her.

This wasn't the first time these nightmares interrupted their sleep. In the eight months they had been married their nights were frequently interrupted with crying and screaming. Trent had the patience of a saint and never demanded that Catherine tell him what the dreams were about. He'd told her, when they were first married, her past was inconsequential, and unless she really wanted to share the details with him, it wasn't necessary.

This time was different and Trent decided it was time for Catherine to tell him who her demons were.

After a while Catherine finally settled down as she relaxed in her husband's loving arms.

"Would you like to talk about it, Catherine?"

She stiffened and wiped her nose with the sleeve of her linen nightgown. Fully awake now, she released her hold from around his neck, sat up in their bed, and rested her hands on her pregnant belly. She was six months pregnant, but the baby was a mere bump in her delicate small-shaped figure.

Swallowing the huge lump that had settled in her throat, she took a deep breath trying to think of how she could tell him about the indignities of her past life. Would he still love her if she told him the truth? She wondered. Having to relive the pain she'd endured when she was captured by David Brooks several years ago and taken to Beaumont as his mail-order bride was unthinkable and appalling. It frightened her that the emotional trauma she'd suffered would be too much for Trent to understand. Maybe that was why she was having the nightmares again.

Catherine had been pregnant with Daniel when Brooks captured her. During the year and a half he kept her, she gave birth to his son, Adam. The thought of having to confess these sins she bore was overwhelming, and she put her arms around Trent's wide shoulders and clung to him, shutting her eyes tightly.

As Trent softly rubbed her back, she tried to compose herself as she listened to his soft words.

"I know I told you I never needed to know anything about your past, but it is having a terrible effect on you and now our unborn child. Perhaps if you shared some of it with me, it would make you feel better."

"I'm afraid you won't understand and will leave me. I couldn't bear that, Trent. I love you too much."

Biting his lower lip, he pressed on. "Nothing you could tell me would ever make me love you less. I know you've had a really difficult time since you arrived in America, but maybe if I could share some of that burden with you, it might ease your pain. It grieves me that you won't let me help you. What's done is done and you can't go back and change anything. Perhaps sharing some of it with me will help release the guilt and hurt that you're feeling. If you won't talk to me, perhaps you could talk to one of your doctor friends."

Catherine reached over, turned on the light, and gave Trent an incredulous look. "Do you think I am crazy?"

Trent took a deep breath and released it.

"You are anything but crazy, Catherine. These dreams are causing you an insurmountable amount of stress. Don't you think your stress affects our child?"

Catherine was at a loss for words. It was the first time since their marriage that a disagreement of this magnitude had interrupted their life, and she hated to admit he was right. Even though she was a doctor, it had not occurred to her that her nightmares and insomnia would affect their unborn child.

"You're right." She barely whispered. "I do know someone who could help me and I'll make an appointment."

Trent pulled her closer and held her. He lifted her hair back over her shoulder and bent down gently kissing her neck. "You are everything to me, Catherine. Your pain is my pain and I want more than anything to make you happy."

She leaned back and gazed at him. "Oh, Trent, I don't think I've ever been this happy. I don't think about my past anymore and I'm sorry I can't control what I dream about, but I will get some help. I know it's important to you and it is to me, too."

Trent kissed her on her forehead and looked at his timepiece, which he kept beside the bed. It was 2:25 in the morning. He laid it back on the table and reached over Catherine to turn out the light. "We both need to get some sleep," he said, pulling the covers up over Catherine and then himself.

A monumental clap of thunder made them both jump. A cry from the children's room echoed down the hall. "I'll go see who it is," Trent insisted.

Catherine rolled to her side and stared out the window. The clouds finally relieved their gut-wrenching bowels of heavy rain, and the pounding on the roof made it impossible to hear anything. She turned over and fixed her eyes on the open door to the hallway watching for Trent and thinking back to the time of their first meeting.

X X X

She had graduated several years earlier from Galveston Medical School and decided to make a new beginning in Rosenberg, Texas, as the town's new doctor. After a difficult start, she decided that raising her children and being a doctor would be enough and she would never marry again. While she was still a young woman of twenty-five, her incredible beauty and English charm brought many suitors to her door.

Catherine's small medical practice provided her a decent living. The large Victorian five bedroom, two story home she bought was the perfect haven for her and her children. Three rooms downstairs were used for her medical practice. Located in the back was a separate carriage house, which included a large upstairs bedroom and small bathroom.

Love can sometimes hit you head on when you least expect it. Trent came into her life over a year ago. As a scout for a Houston oil company, his job took him all over the countryside. Often, he would have to make a temporary camp by a cluster of trees or a creek. Sleeping under the stars and moving from town to town made him vulnerable to wild life and robbers. He was shot as he slept by a creek bed outside of Rosenberg. The robbers took everything, including his horse and equipment, leaving him for dead. He was outnumbered three to one and faked his death. The next morning he managed to walk over a mile into town.

Finding his way to Catherine's clinic, Trent's gunshot wound was already infected. She gave him a place to recuperate in the room over her carriage house. They fell in love during the five days she nursed him back to health. His warm gentle mannerisms and incredible good looks were impossible to ignore. Neither wanted to admit their love at first, but over a period of several months Catherine discovered that her life was missing something. Trent won her heart and she finally said "yes" to his marriage proposal. His patience had also proven he was capable of being a father to her children, and they had taken a shining to him. Except for the nightmares that haunted her, Catherine felt that her life was in perfect harmony for the first time since coming to America.

2

The roaring of the constant rain propelled onto the roof ricocheted like rocks from a tin can. Catherine lay silent and waited for Trent to return. Moments later she saw the shadow of his towering muscular body fill the doorway. She smiled as he joined her on the bed.

"It was Adam," Trent said pulling up the covers. "He wet the bed and I put him in with Daniel. They are both asleep now. I checked on the girls and they're fast asleep."

Catherine felt his warm body snuggle close to her as he reached across her breasts and pulled her into his arms. Trent fell asleep almost as soon as his head touched the pillow. A small flutter inside her womb made Catherine smile. She touched the place on the outside of her abdomen and wondered if the baby was a boy or girl. She had no preference, but knew Trent would be pleased if it were a boy; a son that would carry on the family name. The thought of new life being formed inside her brought so much joy. *Thank you, Lord. Please let my baby be healthy.*

Waking up within minutes of each other the next morning, Trent rolled over and stared into Catherine's eyes. "I love you Catherine, and nothing you do or say will ever change that."

Catherine smiled at him and touched his lips with two of her fingers. She reached up and gave him a sweet tender kiss. "Promise?"

"Forever, I promise," he reassured her.

Catherine grabbed his hand and moved it to her belly. "Feel that?"

A smile lined his face and his eyes twinkled. "Our child," he said as he pulled her into his arms and kissed her forehead. "It's an honor to be your husband."

Moments later, Catherine sighed and looked at her timepiece. "Oh my word, it's eight o'clock. We've never slept this late." Jumping out of bed, she pulled her nigh gown over her head exposing her naked body. She noticed the look of desire on Trent's face.

"Not a chance." She flung her bathrobe around her and ran to the bathroom. It was Sunday and the last day they would be together for a while.

She hated that Trent's job was demanding more of his time at Humble Oil Company. The time passed too quickly when he was home on the weekends. It was unsettling and each time he left, it became harder to watch him leave. Now that she was pregnant, she wanted to be with him more and more. Eventually, she thought, this problem would have to be addressed. It was difficult for the children as well.

When Catherine came out of the bathroom she was wearing a half camisole and long slip. She gave him a sexy look and said, "Are you planning to spend the day in bed, Mr. Matthews?"

"Only if you are planning to join me."

She gave him a wicked look. "Hang on to that thought. The children will be up soon and I think the bed might get a bit crowded."

Trent chuckled. "I can hope, can't I?"

Catherine opened the large wardrobe and selected a dress she knew Trent was fond of and slipped it over her head, smiling at him. She walked over to a chair, pulled on her stockings and slipped her feet into her shoes. Placing her hands on her hips, she gazed at him.

"I'm going downstairs now, and I hope you will join me soon."

Trent sighed. Life with Catherine was never dull and he had to admit she had a way of keeping him on his toes. He jerked the covers off and got out of bed. Walking over to the wardrobe, he took out a pair of underwear and selected a clean pair of trousers and a blue and white checkered shirt. He slipped off his long linen nightshirt, finished dressing, and hopped around as he tried to pull on one of his boots. *Doggone it. I must be getting old. When I was younger, I could pull them on with just a little effort.* He finally sat down in a chair and pulled the other one on.

Mornings with the children were always crazy. Catherine felt guilty that her mind would be on them and not her husband. Even though she made it clear to Trent that the children would always be her first priority, she tried to include him in everything. She knew he loved her children, but still it had to be difficult for him. A teenage nanny and four children would take anyone some getting used to. Constant activity and attending to their needs was an everyday occurrence. Trent always tried to do his part.

Trent was Catherine's third husband. After returning to Galveston, she was briefly married to Alex Cooper and became pregnant with Emma. A tragic accident caused Alex's memory loss and he had no recollection of his marriage to her. She reluctantly consented to an annulment prior to Emma's birth. A year later, she discovered he had birthed another child with a Cherokee woman who died in childbirth. Unforeseen circumstances brought Isabelle to Catherine. Since Isabelle was Emma's half-sister, Catherine took her in to raise as her own.

The children, especially the boys, wanted to dominate Trent's time. He shared as much of the responsibility as he could when he was home. Catherine's patience and ability to always know how to handle the children amazed him. Trent was a patient man, but he left the discipline mostly up to Catherine. He had not earned the right to decide on their punishment. There were times when Adam needed a good spanking, but Trent never followed through. Trent's father was very strict and thought nothing of taking a belt or a switch to him when he was growing up. While he respected his father, he often resented the fact that he thought a good old-fashioned spanking was the answer to everything.

Everyone was seated when Trent entered the dining room. "Good morning everyone," he said, as he walked around the table and planted kisses on the children's foreheads.

"Good morning, Papa," the children chimed in.

Martin Boudreaux, their French cook and housekeeper, picked up the coffee pot and began filling Trent's cup.

"Thank you, Martin, and how is your day?" he asked.

"Very well, Mr. Matthews."

"How long have you and Emily worked for Catherine?"

"Less than a year. It was our good fortune that she needed a nanny for the children. We came to America and somehow ended up here. During our interview, I offered to take over the meals and housework. In exchange, she gave us the apartment over the carriage house and a weekly salary. Emily loves being a nanny."

"We all certainly enjoy the meals you prepare,"

After the food had been placed on the table, Martin and Emily joined the family at breakfast and enjoyed scones, scrambled eggs, ham, bacon, and fruit. It was customary for Trent to say grace and he looked around the table to make sure the children had bowed their heads before he began.

"Bless this bounty of food you have placed before us, Father. Your kindness is plentiful and you have graced us with much. We thank you for these blessings. Amen"

After breakfast Adam asked if they could go outside and play.

"I'm afraid not," Catherine replied. "There is mud in the streets and too many puddles of water in the backyard. We will have to find some activities to do inside."

Adam frowned and crossed his chest with his arms. His lower lip stuck out and before he could throw a tantrum, Trent stared down at him.

"Adam, it's not your mother's fault that the rain ruined your day outside in the sun. I want you to think long and hard about having one of your fits, because if you do, I will have to take the matter into my own hands." Trent had everyone's attention. It was the first time he had ever intervened in Adam's discipline. "Why don't we all finish breakfast and then I'll take Adam and Daniel outside on the back porch. We'll come up with some new games."

Catherine bit her lower lip so she wouldn't smile. Adam picked up his fork and began eating. The hum of breakfast conversation finally came back and they finished eating without interruption.

Daniel was five years old; one year older than Adam and he felt protective of his little brother. Until Trent married Catherine, it was Daniel's responsibility to look after his little brother.

Trent took their jackets from a hook and helped with the buttons after each boy slipped into it. He opened the door and looked at Adam and then Daniel. They held hands and walked out the door together. Trent looked at Catherine for approval and she nodded her head in admiration.

Trent pointed at the picnic table outside on the porch. He waited while Daniel crawled up on a bench. Trent picked up Adam and sat him on his knee after taking a seat on the bench across from Daniel. He noticed Daniel watching him closely.

"Your mother tells me how well you look after Adam and your sisters. She is very proud of you, Daniel."

"Yes sir. Thank you."

"Who has an idea of what games we could play on the porch?" Trent asked. Both boys searched the porch and then looked at each other. "I have an idea," Trent said. "When I was little, we used to play like we were going fishing after a huge rain. My mom wouldn't let me or my brother play in the mud either. We could make a fishing pole out of a long stick and tie some string onto it and add a hook. Then we could fish for leaves off the back porch." Both boys' eyes lit up. "Wait here and I'll go cut some small limbs off the tree."

The boys watched Trent's every move as he cut two long limbs from the small oak tree. As he walked back to the porch, he whittled off the small branches leaving long clean limbs. Trent placed the limbs on the table and walked over to a large covered wooden box used for toys and other outdoor items. "Ah, here it is," Trent said, taking out a ball of string and a small box of fishing hooks. He was delighted the boys seemed interested as he made the fishing poles.

Catherine anxiously looked out the back door window and smiled to herself when she saw what Trent was doing. She silently thanked God that he had answered her prayers and even given her more than she had asked for. Trent not only was an excellent, faithful, and loving husband, he was the most loving and attentive father she could have hoped for.

The boys eagerly caught on to gently swinging their lines out into the yard and snagging leaves. By the time they were getting bored with their playtime, Martin called them in for lunch.

The conversation around the dining table at lunch was filled with the boy's chatter and how much fun they'd had. "Mine was bigger than your fish," Adam said proudly.

"Uh-uh?" Daniel said. Laughter riddled the room and for now everyone was happy.

After lunch, Sadie took the children to their respective rooms for their afternoon naps.

Sadie was a young sixteen year old girl Catherine had known from the orphanage in

Galveston before the great storm. Sadie had run away from her abusive adoptive parents. By chance she'd ended up in Rosenberg and moved in with Catherine. She worked with Catherine in the clinic and loved the idea of becoming a nurse or a doctor someday. Catherine's love of books was also shared by Sadie, as well as sewing.

Catherine prepared lessons for Sadie and homeschooled her since she was needed at home to work. Sadie adored Catherine and she was made to feel like a member of their family.

3

The day had gone by much too quickly and it was soon time for Trent to leave on the afternoon train for Houston with connections to Humble, Texas. He picked up his duffle bag and unzipped it. Before he could open the drawer to get his socks, Catherine grabbed his hand and pulled him over to the bed.

"We don't have a lot of time before you go to the train station, but what little time we have I'd like to lie on the bed and just hold you."

Smiling, he picked her up and gently placed her in the middle of their bed. He took off his boots and lay beside her, folding his arm across her warm breast.

"I was impressed with the way you handled Adam this morning. He adores you and so do I," she whispered.

"And I adore you."

Taking their time, they undressed each other. Kissing, caressing, and enjoying their tender moments. Trent glided his hand to her abdomen and stroked it. He kissed her breast, continuing south below her navel. She arched her back so he could fondle her and continue their foreplay. Trent loved to tease her and her response to his touch encouraged him to mount her. Catherine gently pushed him to the side and said, "I think I'll get on top."

Taking in a deep breath, he waited for her as she gave him a wanting glance, and gently eased him inside her. It was only a matter of moments before Catherine came and Trent followed. A gratifying moan came from Catherine's mouth and Trent bit down hard on his lower lip to hush the growl that had whaled up inside him. Catherine fell gently on top of his chest and they held each other, not wanting to let go. Slowly, she slithered off and settled into the curve of his arm.

They both fell asleep and when Catherine woke up, Trent was sitting up on his elbow glaring down at her exposed breasts "You're so lovely. I can hardly take my mind off of you. I'm afraid I must leave you now and get dressed if I want to catch the five o'clock to Houston.

Catherine felt depressed as she silently waited for Trent to pack his bag with clean clothes. She watched him fold his pants and two shirts before he stopped and walked over to where she was sitting at her desk.

Taking her hand, he smiled at her. "Meet me in Houston next weekend. I can bring my work there and we'll have some time together alone. It's only a short hop on the train for me. I need to be close to Humble and I just can't stand the thought of not seeing you for two more weeks." His eyes gazed into Catherine's trying to read her face. She looked down at Trent's hand as he held hers.

Looking back up at his wanting gaze, Catherine smiled at him. She had not been to Houston in over two months. Previously they both decided it was important for Trent to spend more time with the children, especially the boys; so he was making the trips from Humble to Houston and then Rosenberg. "That sounds like a wonderful idea. I need to do some shopping and..." Catherine stood up and wrapped her arms around Trent's neck pulling his face down to hers and kissing him with a hunger that sent goose bumps up his neck.

Trent gave a throaty growl and pulled her closer to him. "You, my beautiful wife are addictive and you really bring out the beast in me," he said, kissing her back with the same passion. A knock interrupted them. "Yes?" Trent said.

"I've brought the wagon around so you won't have to walk in the mud," Martin said.

"Thank you," Trent answered. He took out his timepiece, looked at it, then at Catherine. "I need to go now. Martin can take me to the station. I don't want you to get mud on your dress walking in the streets."

Catherine followed Trent downstairs. The children were still taking their naps and after giving Trent a long kiss goodbye, she watched as the two men took off in the wagon. She sighed. As the wagon headed off into the distance, Trent turned and waved, grinning back at her. She blew him a kiss and he caught it with his hand and placed it on his heart as he always did. It was the little things that Trent did that made Catherine love him even more, if that were possible.

Her mind wandered to the next weekend and she began feeling excited about being alone with her husband in their rented apartment. The memories of the time they had spent in the tiny apartment would have to sustain her throughout the coming week.

X X X

Emily and Martin Boudreaux were devoted employees. Catherine had grown fond of them during the eight months they'd worked for her. They appeared to be the perfect couple, helping Catherine with her large Victorian home, and taking care of the children's needs. Catherine knew very little about them when they first arrived in town. She was impressed with their initial interview. Having lost her previous help, Catherine agreed to give them a chance to prove themselves. Emily's patience with the children was remarkable and they loved her. Martin took over the kitchen and his abilities as a chef couldn't be denied.

Sadie was skeptical of the couple, but kept her feelings to herself. As long as she could assist Catherine with the clinic and help Emily with the children, it was not a problem. Still for some reason she was uncomfortable around Martin.

One day Sadie overheard Martin and Emily talking in the kitchen. They usually spoke French when they were alone, but for some reason Martin spoke in English. "Be careful of what you say around Sadie. She does not belong to this family and her mother or father must have been black. She is very loyal to Catherine and will tell her everything you say. Keep quiet. The less they know about us, the better."

Sadie was stressed over the conversation for days. The earlier conversation was probably nothing. She decided to try and forget about it, but she couldn't help but be cautious around Martin. There was no need to upset Catherine now, unless they gave her another reason.

X X X

The Boudreauxs gained Catherine's trust after they moved into the carriage house. During their initial interview with Catherine, they told her they had been quarantined when they got off the ship in New Orleans because of a fever that had broken out in their quarters. Actually Martin was caught picking pockets at the dock. The authorities locked him in a small holding room at the shipyards while they decided whether or not to send him back to Liverpool. After two days, he learned they were putting him on a cargo ship leaving for Liverpool the next afternoon.

Martin formed an alliance with one of the guards and bribed him to aid in his escape. While visiting Martin early that morning, Emily slipped him some money to pay the guard. Everything went according to plan and Emily was waiting at the train station that afternoon with two tickets on the next train; destination, Rosenberg.

While they saved their meager wages from Catherine, it was never enough for Martin. He supplemented their income relying on his old bad habit of picking pockets. It was easy for him to mingle throughout the train station when visitors arrived on incoming trains and pick the easy pockets. He only did it when he had a reason to be at the station dropping off Trent, or picking him up in the buggy. After he returned to the carriage house, he would take the money out of the wallets or coin purses and save them to put in the burn barrel. He was usually home by the time the visitors realized they had lost their money.

Martin learned his trade early in life after he ran away from the Liverpool Seamon's Orphan Institute when he was fourteen. It was a way of life for the boys on the streets, and they learned from each other. He was very quick with his hands and his courteous mannerism gave no reason for anyone to suspect he might be a thief. He was French, tall with a slender build, and extremely handsome. He had the eyes of a hawk, dark, eerie, and piercing.

In the eight months the Boudreauxs had been working for Catherine, Martin had saved over two hundred and fifty dollars and had stolen four gold watches. He kept the money and watches hidden in a small tobacco can in the attic in the carriage house. Most of the time his take was usually a few ten and twenty dollar bills; but one day he managed to pick the pocket of a man that carried over a hundred dollars in his wallet. He rarely picked more than one or two at a time because anything more would be too obvious. At night when he and Emily were alone in the carriage house, he would talk about their good fortune. As long as no one suspected them and they kept a quiet countenance, they could stay with Catherine indefinitely. Martin never liked grass to grow under his feet, and when he found out Catherine was with child, he was already plotting a new plan to make even more money.

4

When Trent and Martin arrived at the train station, Martin insisted on getting off the wagon to carry Trent's satchel into the station.

"I don't expect you to carry my satchel for me."

"I need to take a little break from the housework and being gone fifteen minutes shouldn't be a problem. I've completed all of my chores for the day."

Trent didn't argue with him. He marvelled at all the things Martin was capable of doing; moreover his cooking was the best Trent had ever eaten. He turned to retrieve his bag from Martin when the train approached the station.

"Have a nice trip," Martin said. He watched as Trent took out his ticket from his vest pocket and handed it to the porter. Turning back to the station, Martin followed a small group of people, who had collected their bags, and were entering the station.

Martin was quick and managed to pick a gold watch and a lady's coin purse from her half-open handbag she had dangling from her arm. He didn't even stop walking as he continued through the station and out to the buggy. He pressed his lips together to prevent a big grin from appearing on his face. *Have to keep a poker face.*

Martin knew Emily was content living in the carriage house and playing nanny to a bunch of spoiled children. While she desired children of their own, Martin had no intention of fathering a child. Their constant moving around made it impossible to have any kind of normal family life. He also took special precautions so Emily would not get pregnant. He watched her monthly cycles closely and made no effort to try and please her.

After Martin drove the horse and wagon into the carriage house, he took his time removing the tack and settling the horse into its stall. He quickly picked up a pitchfork and hurled a small stack of hay into the pen. Checking the water supply in the barrel and seeing it half-empty, he decided it was enough until morning.

X X X

Five years earlier in a small church in Liverpool, Martin married Emily three weeks after they'd met. When he arrived on a train from London the week before, he decided he would find himself a French girl and marry her. He was afraid to have random sex again. It had taken him weeks to get over the crabs he had contacted with the last little lass he had taken to bed. Besides he was twenty-five now and if he could find a wife that had a steady job, the pressure wouldn't be so great for him, and he could be more selective with his victims. It would also mean he could bed her at his convenience.

Martin learned to cook from an older man at the orphanage. Working in the kitchen meant he could snitch food when no one was watching. At first he thought about becoming a chef, but soon realized he did not want to be confined to a kitchen. Pandering the streets and picking pockets was more fun. He was making a decent living while living in London until he was spotted by the police after he picked a customer's pocket. Running for his life, he escaped by ducking into an open doorway as a tenant came out of a building and shut the door. Worried they might recognize him, he decided to leave. When he arrived at the train station, he bought a ticket on the first train out. Its destination was Liverpool.

After arriving mid-day, Martin wandered the streets and managed to pick up some pocket change on the way. Later on he approached several pubs before finding his way to The Corner Pub and Emily. Her French accent was thick when she asked Martin for his order. "What would you like to drink?"

"Je voudrais une biere." (I would like a beer.) He answered in French bringing a big smile to Emily's face. They carried on a conversation for a few minutes until the owner interrupted her and told her to get back to work. Martin made his way to a chair in the corner and kept his gaze locked on Emily. He couldn't take his eyes off of her.

Her dark long hair was pulled back behind her shoulders and tied neatly in a yellow ribbon. Even with the oversized apron she wore, he could see her slim silhouette was nicely shaped and her breasts were enticing. Not too large, and he couldn't help but picture his lips locking around one of them.

When she brought him another beer, Martin decided she was the one.

"What time do you get off work?"

Shy and unsure of herself she took a step back. "I, I get off tonight at midnight."

"You are very beautiful and I would like the pleasure of walking you home."

Emily blushed and looked down as she knotted her hands in her apron. No one had ever paid attention to her. Especially a Frenchman that was as handsome as he. "Je suppose que ce serait bien." (I guess that would be all right.)

Emily continued working and carrying drinks to the patrons in the pub. Every once in a while, she would glance over and Martin would wink at her.

Noticing his empty glass, she returned to his table and asked if he would like a sandwich or another drink.

"A sandwich would be nice and I would like to have some ale, please," he said smiling at her.

When she returned and placed the drink in front of him, she whispered, "This one is on the house. Your sandwich will be ready shortly."

Again Martin smiled and winked at her causing her to blush and look down.

Before she left, Martin took her hand and kissed the top. She slowly moved it away and left, heart beating faster, and filled with a new excitement she had not experienced before.

At midnight Martin was still seated in the same spot and she nodded to him as she took off her apron.

Following her outside, Martin took her hand and asked, "Do you live close by?"

"Not too far, only a few blocks."

As they talked, he flirted with her and told her it was love at first sight. She was not beautiful but her plain ordinary face was pleasant to look at. Her teeth were a bit crooked and her long thick hair hugged her porcelain face. Being only twenty-one years old, Emily was no match for Martin. He'd swept her off her feet by the time they arrived at her one room apartment.

"C'mon, just one little kiss." Emily looked away, but Martin tilted her chin up and kissed her softly on the lips.

"I've never met a man quite like you. Do you treat all the other girls you meet the same as me?"

"Non, vous etes special." (No, you are special.) Martin squeezed her small hand. Martin wanted to bed her that evening but thought better of it. Emily was obviously a virgin and he would have to sweep her off her feet. *She might be worth my time.*

During the next week Martin was at the pub at eleven-thirty to walk Emily home every night. One evening when Emily finished her shift, he took her to supper and insisted she drink some ale. When they arrived back at her apartment he talked his way inside. After moments of kissing and petting, she suggested he leave. He teased her and told her he loved her and wanted to get married. She laughed, but he quieted her with his kisses. They were on the bed a few minutes later and after removing her pantalets, Martin mounted her and forced himself inside her. She cried out begging him to stop, but he continued until he was satisfied.

"You're mine now," he said in a low growl. Emily's tears remained unstoppable, and Martin finally began coddling her. "Shh," he said. "It always hurts the first time. You should have told me you were a virgin. It won't hurt as much next time." They fell asleep holding each other.

Emily awoke several hours later with Martin on top of her again. The pain was even greater, but she gritted her teeth and held her breath. She was afraid to cry out; afraid the landlord might hear them. Unable to hold it in, she began to cry softly.

"Detendez-vous ma douce jeune fille." (Relax my sweet maiden.) Martin whispered. It will be over soon." It seemed to take longer for Martin to complete his sexual act. He growled and forcefully plunged himself deeper inside her until he found his release.

When they woke the next morning Martin was still in bed with Emily. He rolled over and took her into his arms. He whispered sweet endearments in her ear in French and she giggled.

"I am very serious. I love you. I knew it from the first moment I saw you. I want to marry you."

"I, I need some time to think about it. We hardly know each other."

Martin adjusted his broad shoulders, moved his hand between her legs and teased her. He nuzzled his face in her neck and then began suckling her breasts.

She moaned, as his touch aroused her. The sensation coming from her abdomen was foreign, but she allowed him to continue. "Ahh. That feels really good."

Martin didn't really care for foreplay, but if he was going to win Emily's heart, he knew he had to get her hooked. Obviously, she had never experienced the pleasures of sex before. It was just a matter of time. He would not take "no" for an answer.

"That's it sweetheart. Just relax and do what your body tells you. Feels good, doesn't it?"

She moved closer into him and he told her to open her legs. As he kissed her passionately, she

29

kissed him back and willingly let him get on top of her. She was so tender, but after a while it began to feel better, and she was actually enjoying it.

He began whispering commands in her ear in French and she complied with his wishes. Martin was gentler this time as he whispered, "Je t'aime" (I love you) over and over.

"Je t'aime aussi," (I love you, too) she answered, surprised when she told him that. It was the first time she had climaxed and the sensation was overwhelming as she clung to him tightly, not wanting to let go.

"See baby," he said, as he lay beside her still breathing heavily. "I told you it would get better."

"Oui." She prayed he was not just taking advantage of her and that he really loved her. The next day was Emily's day off.

"Show me the city. I want to see your favorite places."

Martin hailed a carriage and asked the driver to take them on a ride around the city. They got off at the waterfront and strolled along the boardwalk. A mist of rain caused them to take shelter inside a pub. Hungry, they dined on venison pie, pastries and jelly. "Tell me, why is such a beautiful little lass like you unmarried?"

Blushing, and caught by surprise, Emily thought for a moment. "I've not met a man I want to be with the rest of my life. I was raised by my aunt and I helped her take care of her five children. They had little money and soon they asked me to leave. I saw a sign in the pub window wanting to hire a waitress. I applied and went to work that afternoon. I've not had much opportunity to meet anyone. Most of the men that come into the pub are married and are drunks."

"My sweet Emily, it is meant for us to be together."

5

Martin left early that evening. He had spent more money than he intended and there was a ship coming in from America at nine o'clock p.m. It was necessary for him to be there to take care of business. He bent down and kissed Emily on the cheek when he left her at her door. "I'll see you soon," he said as he turned and walked away.

Confused, Emily touched her cheek where he kissed her. She wondered if she had done something wrong. It was not like him to leave so abruptly. Sleep challenged her throughout the night as she tossed and turned. Morning did not come soon enough. She moved about her small one-room apartment doing her chores and laundry. Often she would peek around the curtains to see if Martin might be coming. *Will he come back? Of course he will. He said he loved me.* Doubt yawned in her head and she prayed for his return.

The next evening Martin came into the pub at eleven o'clock and sat at the counter. Emily's face brightened as a relieved smile irradiated her pink lips. *He was for real. He really loves me*

Over the next few weeks, Martin bought her small gifts and walked her home from work every night. One evening he stopped under a street lamp and turned to Emily. He took out a small gold wedding band and got down on one knee.

"Marry me. Marry me tomorrow."

Emily put her hands over her mouth in surprise. "You, you really want to marry me?"

"Yes, the sooner, the better. I don't want to wait any longer."

Emily had to work the next day but after telling her employer she needed to get off early so she could get married, he let her leave at two o'clock. They were married in the preacher's study at a small church Emily frequently attended on Sundays. The preacher's wife acted as the witness. When Martin placed the thin gold band on her ring finger, she felt happier than she had ever felt in her life.

Martin insisted they stop and eat in an inexpensive restaurant before going back to Emily's apartment. She asked if he wanted to go to his place and pick up his clothes. "I'll pick them up tomorrow while you are at work. Let's just go back to your place for now."

After they returned to Emily's apartment, Martin decided to lay down some strict rules for Emily. "I will handle all the finances now that we are married. How much money do you have?"

"Enough to pay the rent on Friday. My landlord comes to the pub to collect."

"Give it to me now. I'll handle the matter of the rent."

Emily walked over to her small wardrobe and opened the bottom drawer. Grasping one of her stockings, she took it over to the bed and poured out some coins.

"How much is the rent?" Martin demanded. "There is barely twenty shillings here."

"The rent is two pounds. I get paid on Friday and will have enough then."

"Good, I'll hang on to this," Martin said as he scooped up the coins.

"When do you get paid?" Emily asked hesitantly.

Martin roared with laughter. "You are so stupid."

Taken aback by his comment, Emily flinched and took a step back.

"You have no idea how I make a living, do you?"

"I, I just assumed you worked in the pottery factory because your clothes have that kind of smell."

"Well, I don't. That smell is the street. I work the streets."

"You mean. . ."

Martin broke in. "I steal for a living."

Unable to speak, she stood frozen as she watched a sheepish grin curl his lips upward.

He walked over and grabbed a fistful of her hair and pulled her to him. His grip was forceful and he covered her mouth with his, pinning her up against the wall. She cried out as he began to force himself on her. A few moments later, he ripped off her clothes and took her savagely.

When he was done with her, he stood up and buttoned up his pants.

"Now, my sweet inquisitive wife, you will never ask me any more questions. You will do as I say, and when I decide I want you, you will want me too. Understand?"

Emily moved herself into a sitting position and tried to pull her camisole together. Her fingers were shaking so badly she could hardly button it. She slowly looked up when Martin walked over and straddled her.

"Answer me," he demanded gazing down at her.

"I, I understand."

Martin reached down and pulled her to her feet. "You got any whiskey?"

"No," she whispered."

"Never mind," he said as he closed the door behind him and left.

Dazed, hurt and scared, Emily wondered what she had done wrong. When she was young, her father used to beat her mother and now she had married someone just like him. *I'll try harder to please him.*

Several hours later, Emily heard Martin bang on the door. She quickly got up and opened it. Smelling of whiskey, he lunged at her and pulled her to the bed. He flung her face down on the mattress and straddled her as he pulled up her nightgown. She lay still while he violated her from behind. She bit into her knuckles trying not to scream from the pain. Afterwards, he fell to the other side of the bed and went to sleep.

The next morning Martin left early and told her he would come by her work later. After he left, Emily tidied up the small apartment and began washing up in the small basin in the kitchen. She had just finished tying her apron around her grey flannel dress when Martin stormed through the door.

"Pack up your things. We're leaving."

Afraid to say anything, she grabbed her small carpetbag and began emptying her wardrobe. Martin stood by the window peeking out through a small hole in the corner. After a while he removed the pillow from its pillow case and began stuffing his few belongings into it.

Martin took one more look out the window and turned to Emily. "Keep your mouth shut. Do you understand? If anyone stops us, I'll do the talking."

Emily clutched her bag as Martin led her through the streets and down an alley. They were both breathing hard as they finally stopped at a way station.

A well-dressed older man with a rough beard and top hat was standing next to a horse-drawn covered carriage. He had one leg cocked up on the first step and he was smoking a cigar. "Need a ride?" he asked.

"Yes," Martin said pushing Emily into the carriage. "Take us to Manchester."

Manchester, England, was a small town east of Liverpool and a two hour ride. They could hide out there for a while. This had been a close call. Martin managed to escape from the police when they caught him stealing from a street vendor. He was quick on his feet and the streets were crowded with morning shoppers. He had outrun them before, but this time one of the policemen got a good look at his face. He knew it was time to move on.

They moved from town to town whenever Martin felt that the police might be catching on to him. They lived in London, Paris, and several railroad towns in England.

Throughout their journey they continually overheard travelers talking about America. The more Martin heard, the more he dreamed himself of going to America. No one would know him there. He finally made the decision to leave when he saw a drawing of his face hanging by a nail to a hitching post. He was now a wanted man.

It took over a week for his beard to grow enough stubble to change his looks. He pawned his gold watches, and changed his guineas and shillings into American dollars at the bank. They made arrangements to get the necessary papers for their travels and boarded a steamer in Liverpool. Its destination was New Orleans in the United States of America. They originally thought about going to New York, but heard the arrival was difficult and overcrowded and it sometimes took weeks to get through immigration lines. Too many authorities at the port and overcrowded quarters did not appeal to him.

X X X

Martin and Emily now lived in Rosenberg longer than they had lived in any other town. Emily was relieved their past was behind them, and she actually thought Martin had given up his thievery when they went to work for Catherine. That is, until she walked in on him one day when he was counting the money. She knew better than to say anything.

Martin let Emily know early on that her opinion was not important. He tried to teach her the trade, but she was too weak and nervous while Martin tried to give her lessons. She wanted no part of it. While Martin was nice and considerate to her around Catherine and her family, he continued to abuse her when they were alone in the carriage house. He made a conscious effort to curtail his drinking because they had free room and board. If he was caught drinking, he would lose his job. His plan was to move on after a couple of months, but when he discovered Catherine was pregnant, he began to devise another plan.

Before the daily *Houston Chronicle* was thrown away each day, Martin would take it to his room every night to read. Several articles about babies being kidnapped and sold caught his attention. One article said a boy with good breeding could fetch as much as five thousand dollars. Picking pockets was peanuts compared to this kind of money. Being patient was not easy for him, but in the end it would be worth the time he put in being someone else's slave. While Catherine and Trent were not rich, they lived well in Martin's eyes.

6

Catherine sat quietly in her office and found it difficult to concentrate on her record keeping. All she could think about was Trent. Their time together had passed so quickly. She always felt this way and found it bearable after reminding herself that he would only be working for a week this time.

Pondering her conversation with Trent, she decided to make an appointment with a doctor and have a full examination while she was in Houston. It had been months since she had spoken to Dr. Samuel Allen, a good friend from her past. They had been engaged at one time, but extenuating circumstances had pulled them apart.

Catherine picked up the receiver and waited for Lillie, the telephone operator at Cumings Drug Store, to place a call, person to person, to Dr. Allen at Houston General Hospital.

"I'm sorry, Dr. Allen no longer works here," the lady on the other end of the phone said.

"Did he leave a forwarding telephone number?" Lillie asked.

"No ma'am, but here is the number I have to his home, PR7-8861."

After disconnecting the call to the hospital, Lillie asked, "Want me to call that number for you?"

"Yes, I would appreciate that."

Samuel answered on the second ring. She could hear a baby crying in the background. "Samuel, this is Catherine." There was silence for a few seconds and Samuel finally acknowledged her.

"I hope you are well," she said. "I can hear a baby crying."

"That's my son, Samuel, Jr. How are you?"

"I'm wonderful. I've remarried and am several months pregnant. I was hoping you could give me the name of a doctor that I might see when I come to Houston this Friday."

"Dr. George Benton, a friend of mine, delivered Sammy and I think you would like him." Samuel gave Catherine Dr. Benton's office phone number. "Dorothy and I bought a house and I've recently opened up my own clinic with three other doctors."

"I'm so happy for you," she said.

"And you? Are you happy?" Samuel asked.

"I've married a wonderful man, but he travels a good deal. Except for his traveling and being gone a lot, I'm very happy."

"I have Friday off this week and I was going to my clinic that morning to get caught up on some paperwork. Perhaps after your appointment I could see you?"

"I would like that. I'll call you back after I make my appointment tomorrow with Dr. Benton." Samuel gave Catherine his new phone numbers and said goodbye.

She sat at her desk and thought how nice it would be to see Samuel again. He sounded happier than the last time they had spoken, and she hoped he had worked out his differences with his wife.

Catherine met Samuel at St. Mary's Hospital in Galveston in 1903 where she worked part-time while attending medical school. She was pregnant with Emma and Samuel delivered her. They became friends and later they became lovers. Catherine thought about their relationship and how very close they came to getting married. Feeling Samuel wasn't right for her, she called off the wedding. Thinking about it now reassured her that she had made the right decision.

The rest of the week went by quickly and soon Catherine was saying goodbye to the children and giving last minute instructions to Martin, Emily, and Sadie.

Martin carried her bag to Union Train Station and after she boarded the train and sat down, she watched out the window and saw Martin leaving. He was crowded up against a group of people trying to get through the door and she thought it peculiar when an altercation happened. Apparently, Martin had bumped up against the woman that was with an older man. Martin took off his hat and it looked like he was apologizing. The man was shaking his finger at Martin. Catherine thought about getting off to see what was taking place but decided against it when the conductor said, "All aboard." She sighed. *Martin is a grown man and surely he can calm the man down.* She forgot about the incident after the train pulled away from the station.

X X X

Once the crowd and Martin were inside, a woman screamed that her coin purse was missing from her handbag. The sheriff happened to be in the station when the man turned and accused Martin of being a pick-pocket. The sheriff asked Martin if he could frisk him and Martin said he had nothing to hide and agreed. After checking all of Martin's pockets, the sheriff turned to the gentleman and said, "Mr. Boudreaux does not appear to have your lady's coin purse and I happen to know the family he works for and can vouch for him. Perhaps your lady friend lost her coin purse on the train she just got off."

The sheriff told Martin he could go and Martin was relieved as he made the short walk back to the house. *That was really a close call. It was a good thing I tucked the coin purse inside the wide band in my hat or I would be in jail by now. I have to be more careful.*

X X X

Catherine adjusted herself on the bench beside the window and stared out as the train picked up speed. Splashes of spring gathering on the countryside reminded Catherine of how quickly her time in America had passed. Her mother's terrible death at the hands of a madman, her time spent at the orphanage, all seemed like bad dreams now. She was only fifteen when she was sent to St. Mary's orphanage. Her mother's friend, John Merit, visited her often and they fell in love. They were married on her sixteenth birthday and it was one of the happiest days of her life.

Abducted shortly after their marriage, she escaped, but not before she was brutally abused and disgraced by the same man, David Brooks, who murdered her mother. Then there was the great storm of 1900. She and her husband survived the storm, but over three thousand people had lost their lives. Tragedy seemed to follow her everywhere, but after the storm she regained her hope and passion to become a doctor. Not only had she survived the storm, but David Brooks also survived, escaping the chain gang he was working with in Sugar Land, Texas. After he made his way to Beaumont, he became an undertaker and kidnapped her again.

David Brooks forced Catherine to be become his muse and told everyone she was his deaf-mute, mail-order bride. She was pregnant with Daniel at the time. Her husband, John Merit, spent many hours and hundreds of dollars trying to find her and after a year, he had her declared dead and married another. After giving birth to Daniel and fearing David Brooks might harm him, she delivered Daniel to some nuns in Beaumont and asked that they take him to her friend, Father Jonathan in Galveston. Two months later she was pregnant again with David Brooks' child, Adam.

Prior to Adam's birth, some gamblers tracked down David and hung him from a tree on their property. She watched in horror as his body shook and then grew limp as he hung from the branch.

So much had happened. Now twenty-five, married to a wonderful man, and pregnant, she marvelled at how much everything had changed. She was so much like her mother, strong willed, determined and educated. *Yes, I couldn't be happier now.*

After arriving in Houston, she crossed the street and boarded a trolley. Catherine loved riding the trolleys in Houston. Even though they were open air, the sixty degree temperature didn't bother her. She breathed in the fresh air and looked up at the sun peeking through the white floating clouds. Excited about her appointment with Dr. Benton and being alone with Trent for two days, made her smile and feel giddy. She was daydreaming and almost missed her stop. Frantically, she grabbed her satchel and exited the trolley. Not paying attention, she waited at the corner to cross the street and then took a step forward.

Surprised by a man grabbing her arm and jerking her back to the curb, she narrowly missed being hit by an automobile turning the corner. A squawk from its horn blasted its warning as she dropped her satchel.

"Ma'am, are you all right?" the man asked as he picked up her satchel. "Those new motor cars are really hard to get used to."

"Yes, yes, I think so. It just frightened me."

"You should be more careful, especially in your condition."

Catherine smiled up at him. "Thank you. Thank you for saving me. I might have been killed."

Once in her apartment, Catherine collapsed onto the bed. Taking in a deep breath, she tried to control her breathing. *In and out, slowly, in and out.* She rested for a few minutes until her heartbeat began to slow. Still a bit shaken up, she placed her hand on her belly and gently patted it. *We're all right, my sweet child. Mummy needs to be more careful.*

Looking at the clock on the wall and noticing there was little time left before her appointment, she decided it would be wise to hail a carriage.

7

Dr. Benton's office was filled with patients and Catherine waited anxiously for her turn. She was surprised when her name was called before some of the other patients and relieved at the same time.

Dr. Benton was in his forties with salt and pepper hair, and wore glasses that fell down his nose. He was extremely professional and listened carefully as Catherine told him about the difficulties she'd endured after delivering her other children.

"Apparently, my blood does not clot very quickly. Probably nothing that a few stitches won't cure," she laughed, feeling silly.

"I will take every precaution after your child is born. I assure you I won't leave your side until that little problem is taken care of. Taking your history into consideration, I think it wise that you come to Houston at least a week before your delivery so that you will be close to the hospital when you deliver. After delivery, I will take the necessary precautions to make sure you are fit before you leave for home."

Catherine and Dr. Benton both agreed that the baby would arrive around the second week in May. "Everything looks fine otherwise and I see no reason why you won't have a normal delivery."

Relieved that everything seemed to be normal, Catherine made her way to Samuel's clinic. Catherine was supposed to meet him at his office which was two blocks away and she decided to walk. The sun was bright in the clear blue sky and there was a soft breeze blowing as she crossed the street. She stopped in front of several shops and admired some things in the windows since she had some extra time. Noticing a thrift store across the street, she crossed over to take a closer look. Her eyes focused on the children's mannequins that were dressed in soft linen dresses. She entered the shop and walked over looking more carefully at the way they were made. She recognized the name of a Paris designer and then looked at the price. They were very reasonable so Catherine asked the clerk if she could buy them. While the clerk removed the dresses off of the mannequins, Catherine continued to shop, finding two outfits for the boys.

"Would it be possible for me to return after lunch for my packages? I have an appointment and I must admit I'm getting a little tired."

"Certainly," the clerk said.

When she arrived at Samuel's office the waiting room was full of people. "I'm here to see Dr. Allen, I believe he is expecting me." After a few minutes the receptionist showed Catherine into an examination room.

Samuel walked in and apologized that one of the other doctors had a family emergency and called him to finish the day for him. He wanted to kiss her, but thought better of it, so he gently brushed her cheek with his lips.

"You look wonderful," he said, smiling. He showed her around his new offices and then he took her into his adjoining office. "I've been looking forward to seeing you all week. Marriage seems to agree with you."

"Trent is a wonderful husband and I can't imagine life without him. He loves my children and he is extraordinarily patient. What about you?" she asked.

"Dorothy and I have finally made peace with each other. I bought her an expensive house in an upscale neighborhood and she loves being a mother. Samuel, we call him Sammie, is really a good baby and we both want another child." He smiled at her and gave her a funny look.

"What?" She grinned. "Why are you looking at me like that?"

"I can't help but think that maybe in another lifetime, we'll be together."

Catherine blushed. "I'm flattered that you feel that way."

Samuel let out a loud sigh. "How are the children?"

"They are wonderful. I have help again, a French couple who have been with me for eight months now. I'm surprised I haven't gained more weight than just the baby's because Martin is a fabulous cook."

"Dorothy has help three days a week. It gives her some time to shop and have lunch with her girlfriends," Samuel remarked.

"You still have your boyish good looks," Catherine said. "Why is it that men age so much more gracefully than women?"

"You have no reason to be concerned, Catherine. Even six months pregnant you still look like you are a teenager." They both laughed. "One of my partners had to leave town unexpectedly and I'm afraid I have patients waiting in the front, so I'm sorry we can't spend a little more time getting caught up." He bent down and kissed her. "Promise you will let me know when you come back to have the baby. I'm glad you are going to let George deliver the baby. He's the best."

"I'll let you know. Thank you, Samuel. It's comforting to know I can always call on you." Catherine reached up to kiss Samuel on the cheek, but he took her in his arms and gave her a long slow kiss. She didn't pull away and knew she should have. Samuel opened the door for her to leave.

Afterwards, she returned to the store to collect her packages. Catherine was excited about seeing Trent later. He was constantly in her thoughts and she smiled just thinking of spending two nights alone with him. She took a trolley to their Houston apartment, hoping she would get there before Trent. She was fumbling in her purse for the key when Trent walked up behind her and said, "I'll get it." She was surprised he had come home so early. He often did not return until dark. When they entered the apartment Trent put down his satchel and pulled Catherine into his arms.

"My God, I've missed you so much, it hurts."

Catherine removed his tie and pulled his jacket off. "I have some good news," she giggled. "I saw a doctor earlier in the day and he assured me everything was fine and the baby will be here the second week of May."

"That's wonderful," Trent said pulling her towards the small bedroom. "I know I probably need to clean up a bit, but I want you now."

Taking in a deep breath, Catherine said, "You smell like my husband and I don't want to wait either. How about we get undressed and we'll take a bath together?"

Trent went to the bathroom and put the stopper in the tub. After turning on the water, he met Catherine at the door and they began shedding their clothes. Their exposed nakedness made it impossible for them to wait. Pulling Catherine into the bathroom, Trent stopped kissing her, bent over and turned off the water. After turning around, he pinned Catherine up against the door holding her arms over her head. Mouths wide open; their bodies ached with desire for each other. Trent passionately kissed her neck, her shoulders and then gently suckled on her breasts. They began to slide down to the floor, but Trent grabbed her, picked her up and carried her to their bed. Each touch, each kiss brought them closer and closer to the realm of satisfaction. They were both suffocated by their longing for each other. Moving as one, their desires brought them to complete satisfaction, coming together and reaching a climax at the same time.

Resting, they snuggled and whispered in a quiet language of love. Both contented and happy just being alone together. After a while when Catherine heard the slow deep breathing of her contented husband, she quietly got out of bed, dressed and wrote a note that she was going to the store.

Catherine loved Houston and decided to walk as she made her way three blocks to the corner market. There was still a chill in the air and she stopped abruptly when she heard an oncoming streetcar. She stepped back, remembering her near accident earlier in the afternoon. Wanting to prepare something special for Trent's dinner was foremost in her mind. He seemed to like all kinds of foods, but he was still a meat and potatoes man. Arriving at the market, she gathered up some pork chops, rolls, potatoes and corn. She also picked up some breakfast items and left with two full bags. The walk home took a while longer because she was constantly shifting the bags as she walked. It was beginning to get dark and she was relieved to finally get home as she unlocked the door and went in.

A small light glowed in the living room and she quietly placed the groceries on the kitchen table.

Stepping closer to the bedroom, she could hear his slow easy breathing and she gazed at his beautiful physique. It brought back memories of the first time she'd accidently viewed his naked body when he stayed in the carriage house after he was shot. The infection from his wound caused him to be a very sick man. She was the one to bathe him, clean his wounds, and doctor him. He had asked her to shave his week-old beard while staying there. She couldn't help but smile when she remembered his arousal under his robe. He had apologized at the time, but it was verification to her that he was getting well.

Catherine had fallen in love with him almost immediately. His soft gentle eyes and compassionate heart drew her to him during his stay. She shuddered at the thought that she almost lost him.

Trent opened his eyes and met her gaze. They both smiled at the same time. "I was just checking on you before I started supper," Catherine remarked.

"Come here, please," Trent summoned. "Just lie on the bed beside me. I want to smell your delicious scent." Catherine smiled and walked over to him and lay on top of the sheets. He pulled her into his arms and nuzzled his face between her neck and shoulders. "This is my favorite place to be."

"I have a favor to ask of you," Catherine said. "Do you think you could take off a couple of days when the baby is born?"

Trent released his hold on her and stretched. "I've already told my company I would be taking a week off when it was time. They weren't happy about it, but they'll make out," he replied. "How long until dinner? I'm really hungry."

Catherine grinned back at him. "Not long."

"How about we share that bathtub after we have dinner?"

"Love to," she answered.

8

The next morning they slept in. Catherine woke first and started breakfast. When Trent smelled the bacon frying, he woke, dressed and joined her in the kitchen. After breakfast they took a slow stroll to Trent's office where he was planning to work for several hours. Catherine spent the next few hours shopping for baby things and visited a few pharmacies she had accounts with. After she finished, she returned to her apartment to leave her packages. She did not tell Trent about her next appointment that afternoon.

Catherine had met Dr. Philip Seymour over two years before at Oakwood Sanatorium where her then husband, Alex Cooper, was recovering from a brain injury. She was very impressed with Dr. Seymour and knew he had an office in Houston. She set up an appointment for twelve-thirty and was looking forward to their visit.

Dr. Seymour did not normally see patients on Saturday, but agreed when Catherine mentioned she was suffering from recurring nightmares, which was why she sought his council.

Dr. Seymour invited Catherine into his office and offered her a chair rather than the couch he usually had his patients sit on. He sat in a chair opposite her so she didn't feel intimidated by his line of questioning.

"Tell me about your life now, Catherine. I see you are with child and I assume you are happy about that."

"Oh, yes. Very much so. My husband, Trent, is a wonderful husband and father to my children."

"I'm glad to hear that." Dr. Seymour smiled. They visited for a while about Catherine's annulment from Alex and her move to Rosenberg.

"It was difficult at first. I had no idea Alex lived in Rosenberg when I decided to make the move," Catherine began. "It was a bit awkward, but after a while it was decided we could be friends. It didn't take long for our secret to be exposed. His wife was very understanding and they have a son now."

"Yes, I still counsel with Alex and Meredith from time to time. I grew quite fond of both of them while Alex was recovering at Oakwood Plantation Sanatorium. I understand you are raising his daughter."

"Yes, Alex was still recovering at Oakwood when the mother of Isabelle died. She was barely a year old and Alex's old boss called me. Since Isabelle was my daughter's half-sister, I took her in until I could locate Alex. After finding him in Rosenberg, it was his desire that I raise Isabelle as my child. He agreed that since Emma and Isabelle were so close, it was not in either child's best interest to separate them. At that time Meredith had no knowledge of Alex's past with the Indian woman. He continues to visit both of his daughters."

"How do you and your husband feel about that now?"

"We're overjoyed. Emma and Isabelle are very close and we love them equally. We couldn't be happier. Our baby is due in three months"

"Tell me what brings you here. You mentioned you had some recurring nightmares?"

Catherine hesitated and tried to find a way to tell Dr. Seymour about her past life. Dr. Seymour listened with interest, finding her to be absolutely charming. She had been in his office for over an hour revealing the indignities of her past life, and the torture she had endured at the hands of David Brooks. She went on to tell him about her encounter with Joe Brady and how she had been forced to shoot him to save her own life. She finally broke down her wall and began shaking and crying uncontrollably. Dr. Seymour poured her a brandy from his liquor cabinet and handed it to her. After she dried her eyes with her handkerchief, she took a few sips and then inhaled a deep breath. "Thank you. I already feel better," she said.

Dr. Seymour nodded. "You have stored a lot of guilt and hate in your mind for a long time. I'm glad you came to see me. I've never met anyone that has suffered as much mental anguish as you have. Until you confided in me, I would have never guessed that you were having difficulties. Your husband was right when he suggested you see someone and it is my recommendation that you share some of these things with him. If he is the man you say he is, he will love you unconditionally. He is aware of your two previous marriages and already knows some of your history. I suspect that he will be more understanding than you think and by confiding in him, you will be more at peace. Tell him in short stories at first and see his reaction. It will probably bring you closer together."

Catherine noticed the marble clock sitting on top of some file cabinets and it finally registered with her that it was almost two-thirty. She jumped up and explained that she was to meet Trent at their apartment around this time. "May I use your phone?" she asked. "My husband will be worried."

"Of course," he answered. Catherine made the call letting it ring a dozen times, but there was no answer. "I must leave now. I'm sure Trent is on his way to our apartment," she said, getting out her checkbook. "How much do I owe you?" she asked. Dr. Seymour wrote out a quick bill and handed it to her.

While Catherine wrote the check, Dr. Seymour asked, "Would you like to make another appointment?"

"I'll have to call you. I'm not sure when I'll be back in Houston," she replied.

"I'm at Oakwood Sanatorium on Tuesdays and Thursdays. It's just a short ride from Rosenberg," he said. Catherine handed Dr. Seymour her check and quickly walked to the door. "You need more counseling, Catherine. These nightmares are not going away overnight."

"I know," she replied. "I just need to talk to Trent first. Perhaps we will both come to see you."

"That's an excellent idea," he answered and walked out the door with Catherine.

Catherine stood on the street corner waiting for the trolley, along with several other people. The trolley was ten minutes late and Catherine paced as she heard grumbling from some of the other waiting travelers. It was at least twenty blocks to her apartment and she decided to wait, knowing that it would probably come any minute. Finally ten more minutes and the crowd began lining up. A kind young man offered Catherine a seat and she gladly accepted.

Trent was pacing up and down the apartment at a half past three o'clock wondering where Catherine was when he heard a key in the door. He raced over and jerked it open to a surprised Catherine. All he wanted to do was hold her. "I was so worried about you. I've been waiting for over an hour," he said.

"I called, but didn't get an answer. The trolley ran late and the time just got away."

Trent interrupted her with a long kiss and then smiled at her. After taking a deep breath he finally asked. "What have you been doing?"

Catherine hesitated as they broke away from each other's embrace and walked over and put her purse and small package down. "I went to see a psychiatrist like you suggested," she finally said. She had Trent's full attention. "I was there for almost two hours."

"Do you want to share any of the details with me?" he asked.

"Not now. I'm really tired and I think I will lie down." Catherine turned and walked over to the bed and sat down, unlacing her shoes. Trent put his hands on his hips and watched her.

"I need a drink," he said as he turned and walked out the door.

Catherine curled into a fetal position resting her hand on her belly. The baby was restless and she felt terribly guilty that it was hard for her to tell Trent about her past. The look on his face when she put him off was devastating. Catherine finally drifted into a deep sleep.

9

Trent wasn't a heavy drinker, but he found it impossible to stay and see Catherine sink into a state of depression. He walked several blocks and heard the noise coming from a saloon at the end of the street. He looked in and decided that the Saturday afternoon crowd of men boasting about women and other business was just too much for him. Instead he strolled to the Roosevelt Hotel and walked inside to the bar. The quiet atmosphere was appealing and was an attraction for bankers and businessmen.

Trent sat on a stool at the bar and ordered a shot of whiskey, downing it quickly, and ordering another. He grimaced as the alcohol burned his throat. His patience was wearing thin and he had probably been too easy with Catherine. He should have made her tell him early on about her past. The longer it was put off, the more Catherine was building a wall between them and her nightmares were not helping the matter. He knew that being married to Catherine and the responsibilities that came with her would be a challenge, but it was harder than anything he had ever encountered. Trent pondered the situation a while longer weighing his options. After a third shot of whiskey he realized that if his marriage was going to work, he needed to be a full time husband, at least until after the baby came.

Trent walked the eight blocks to his office and unlocked the door. He was surprised that his boss, Clarence Henry, was there. The two men shook hands. "Glad you are here. I've made a decision about something," Trent said. They talked for over an hour and Clarence agreed to allow Trent a leave of absence without pay until after the baby came. "I'll be back in three, at the most, four months," Trent said. "My family needs me."

Trent felt relieved he had made the right decision. He should have recognized early on that Catherine needed him more than four or six days a month. His family needed him full time. His only worry was that he might get bored having little to keep his mind occupied, but he was willing to make the sacrifice. Money was not a problem and between his and Catherine's savings and the right investments, they could coast for a long time. He might even find some odd jobs to keep him busy in Rosenberg.

Catherine was still asleep when Trent entered the apartment. The dim light from the lamp embraced the room with just enough light for Trent to see his way over to a chair where he sat and removed his boots. After taking off his coat, he removed his vest and tie as he watched Catherine sleep. He smiled when he thought about being with her every day, and hoped that the closeness wouldn't be too smothering. *This life is different than my job which moves me from place to place. It's not mundane or boring. Catherine is anything but boring and the days always go by quickly having to tend to the children's needs.* He decided not to worry about it anymore. He had made the decision and it was done.

He pulled his suspenders down from his shoulders letting them dangle below his waist as he walked over and knelt beside Catherine. He gently took her hand and kissed it. Her eyes opened and she bent over and kissed the top of his head. Trent grinned at her. "I want you to get dressed because I am taking you out on the town tonight, that is, if you feel like it," he said in a soft husky voice.

Catherine smiled and put her hand over his shoulder, staring up into his gentle hazel eyes. "I think I'd rather just have a quiet evening here, alone with you. We have a lot to talk about," she said. "I will tell you everything."

Trent smiled and said, "Your favorite restaurant isn't far. I'll bring dinner home."

Catherine watched as Trent pulled the suspenders back over his shoulders and put on his coat.

After pulling on his boots and putting on his hat, he reached down and kissed her. "I told my boss today I was taking a leave of absence for three months. Looks like we'll have a lot of time to talk," he said as he turned to leave.

Catherine sat up abruptly in bed. "What did you say?"

He smiled at her. "I'm taking a leave of absence for three months starting now."

Catherine's mouth was wide open and she got out of bed and approached him. "I'm not sure what to say." She spoke almost in a whisper as she wrapped her arms around his neck and reached up and gave him a loving kiss. She stared into his eyes. "Why?"

"Because it's the right thing to do, Catherine. The baby will be here soon and I want you to stop worrying about the what-ifs. You're everything to me and I want to be there for you and the children. I can't promise that I won't eventually go back to work, but for now it's all about you and the baby, and of course, our children. I love you Catherine and I'll do anything for you."

She clung to him crying softly into his shirt. He knew she was overwhelmed and they stood holding each other for a while. Gently, he took her arms from around him and looked at her, giving her a reassuring smile.

"No one has ever given me so much. Oh, Trent, thank you."

After Trent came back with supper, they took their time eating and making plans. Knowing that they would be back in Houston before the baby arrived, they decided to leave a few things at the apartment and tidy up in the morning before they left. Catherine didn't bring up her past because she wanted the evening to be special since it was the last time they would be alone for a while. There would be plenty of time for them to talk.

Trent was sleeping soundly with his arms and body wrapped around Catherine. She was so excited about Trent coming home with her she couldn't sleep. It was as though he knew what she was thinking. She would have never asked him to take a leave of absence, but it was certainly what she wanted. Three whole months she thought smiling to herself.

The next morning, after cleaning up the small apartment, they packed and boarded a ten o'clock train leaving for Rosenberg.

Emily and Sadie were with the children when Catherine and Trent came home. Adam heard them first and screamed, "Mama."

The other children joined in the excitement and ran to the front room. Jumping up and down at first, then throwing their little bodies at Trent, they took turns kissing him. Catherine sat in a chair as the children, one by one kissed her, and squealed.

Martin stood in the hallway too, taking in the full account of Trent's announcement that he was taking a leave of absence from work. It would mean that Martin would have to be on his guard and he was not happy about that. Having a full-time man around would mean a lot more work for him, but he just had to be patient for a few more months. Then he would put his plan into action. Trent was just one more obstacle he would have to overcome, and he was going to do everything he could to stay on the good side of Trent.

10

After a week, Trent wondered how things managed to get done while he was away. It seemed there was always something to do. The entire fence surrounding the back of the house needed to be replaced. The children needed their own play area where they could run off some of their energy and be safe. Studying the size of the back-yard, he drew a design on a tablet and bought the material needed for each project. Martin agreed to spend several hours a day away from his regular duties to help.

"We'll get started on the children's play area first," he told Martin. "That way, they will be able to play outside while we work on the fence," Trent said.

Martin agreed. "That sounds like a good idea."

The two men dug a large twelve-foot square block under an old oak in the backyard, lining the perimeter with rocks and filling it with sand. They hung two swings from the old oak tree and then constructed a seesaw several feet away from the sand box. The boys had a great time digging with the grown-ups, and it was endless pleasure for all of them. Emma and Isabelle anxiously waited on the porch as Sadie and Emily tried to keep them entertained.

Trent looked up when he heard a family friend, Jason Brady, call out to him. After getting down from his horse, Jason took a closer look at what the two men were doing.

"Looks like you two could use some help," Jason said, smiling at them.

"Sure would be nice to have an extra hand, but I don't expect you came by to find a job," Trent teased.

"No, I heard you were home for a while and I'm all caught up with my chores. I have a couple hours free, so I'll give you a hand. It will give us a chance to catch up."

"Then grab that hammer by my tool box. Martin has to quit in an hour to go in and prepare supper."

Over the next few weeks, the men completed the fence, as well as several other repairs to the house and carriage house.

The two men had stopped to rest on the back steps when Jason turned to Trent. "I'm heading out early Monday morning for a trail ride. I've bought a herd of cows and will meet up with some friends in Seguin, Texas, to pick up the herd and head back. It will be a five to six day trip depending on the weather. Why don't you join me?"

"I'd really like to, but I better check with Catherine first. I'm sure she won't mind."

Later that evening when Trent and Catherine were getting ready for bed, Trent turned to her. "Jason has invited me to ride to Seguin, Texas, and move a herd of cattle back here to Rosenberg. I hated to say no since he's helped me with repairs around here. I feel like it would be the right thing to do."

"You really want to go, don't you?"

"I have to admit it's been an adjustment for me. I mean, it's been great being with you and the children, but I do miss riding my horse."

"I think you should go. The change will be good for you and I don't go back to the doctor for three more weeks." Trent smiled as he watched Catherine slowly take off her apron and then her blouse.

"Want me to help?" Grinning, Trent walked over to Catherine and unbuttoned the last button, taking her blouse off, and then pulling her camisole over her head. Her rounded breasts stood at attention as he cupped them in his hands and leaned over and kissed her ear. "I love you," he whispered softly, and led her to their bed.

He quickly removed his shoes and clothes, then helped her remove the rest of hers. They slid under the covers and with each kiss, their desire intensified as they explored and caressed each other. Trent slowly turned Catherine to her side and wrapped his large muscular body around hers as he teased and played with her most vulnerable spot. Her rapid breathing and moaning encouraged him. He resisted, not wanting to hurt her or the baby. His face was buried in her hair and he held her tightly not wanting the moment to end as he felt the tremors shiver through both their bodies. It was getting to close to the delivery date and he was uncertain about their intimacy.

"It will be all right," Catherine assured him. "Just let me take the lead."

He smiled as she adjusted her small body and moved into him. She spoke softly as he did what she suggested. The wait was worth the extra effort it took for both of them to give in to their physical desires.

Trent lay still as he listened to Catherine's slow easy breathing. She had fallen asleep with his arms wrapped around her and he eased away from her so she would be more comfortable. A slight breeze filtered through the open window and he could see the curtains moving. He thought about getting up and closing the window, knowing that the night would become cooler, but decided not to. He liked the crisp cool feeling of the approaching spring weather.

As he stared up at the dark ceiling, his mind wandered to what things would be like when their child arrived. Interrupted sleep, wet diapers, and Catherine nursing were all new to him and he smiled as he thought about it. He was happy and had no regrets, but it still concerned him that Catherine had not opened up about her past. She was sleeping better and had not had another bad dream since he'd left his job. Perhaps the visit with the doctor eased her guilt.

It wasn't important, he told himself, as he drifted off to sleep.

Trent was especially attentive to Catherine and the children throughout the weekend. In a way, he felt guilty about wanting to leave and get away with Jason, but he didn't say anything and Catherine seemed fine about his leaving.

That evening as they were getting ready for bed Catherine was sitting at her vanity brushing her hair and turned to Trent as he dressed in his night shirt. "I need to tell you something before you go off with Jason."

"Now?"

"I killed Jason's father over a year ago. I shot him in self-defense."

Trent's mouth shot open and he glared at her. He was absolutely stunned. A moment later he walked over, picked up a chair beside the bed and sat it down next to Catherine.

"I'm listening."

Catherine cleared her throat, took Trent's hand and placed it in her lap squeezing it tightly. "Jason was just a teenager when his mother died. He hated his father, so he went to live with her parents, his grandparents. Mr. Brady was a drunkard and somehow managed to get a young mail-order bride. She was barely nineteen when I met her, pregnant, undernourished, and scared. Mr. Brady abused her something awful and one day she came to the clinic for help. I begged her to go to the sheriff and tell him about the abuse, but she was terrified of her husband." Catherine wiped her eyes with her handkerchief and cleared her throat.

"One night Mr. Brady came to the house and fetched me. He said his wife was bleeding and in terrible shape, so I got my bag and we rode in his wagon to his house. It was too late. He had beaten her half to death. He was drunk and then tried to rape me. I managed to get away and run. It was dark and I fell. When he caught up with me, he stood over me with his gun and began opening his pants. I kicked him and he fell backwards dropping the gun. I was able to grab it first and begged him to leave me alone. He tried to take it away from me and it went off shooting him in the chest."

"Catherine, you were so brave. I can't imagine the pain you must have felt."

She sighed and continued, "Several weeks later Jason showed up on my doorstep. When he introduced himself, I was afraid he might want revenge, but he said he was glad I shot his old man and that he hated him. Jason thinks Mr. Brady killed his mother. That was why he left and went to his grandparents. Mr. Brady left the farm to Jason, so he moved back to Rosenberg. He fell in love with Shelby who was helping me in the clinic. They were married several months later. I just thought you needed to know that."

"Jason has never mentioned it to me. I had no idea."

"Jason is a very honorable man and it doesn't surprise me that he has said nothing."

"Yes, he and Shelby think very highly of you. I'm glad you told me, Catherine. Not that I plan to say anything to him about it, but getting it out on the table is good for you."

"What time do you plan to leave in the morning, with Jason?"

"I'm to be downstairs at four o'clock. Jason's bringing an extra horse for me. I'll try to be quiet when I leave."

"Please don't. I want to kiss you goodbye."

Trent smiled at her. "Are you sure?"

"Promise, if I'm not up that you will wake me."

Trent bent down and kissed her cheek. "I promise. Thank you for sharing that with me. I can only say that you never cease to amaze me and I love that about you."

11

Trent woke early and turned off his alarm. Having laid out his clothes the night before, he quickly found them and dressed. When he finished putting on his boots, he walked over to the bed and kissed Catherine on the cheek.

"Are you leaving now?" she asked sleepily.

"Yes, my love. Now go back to sleep."

Picking up his leather satchel, Trent quietly opened the door and looked back at the bed. Catherine had gone back to sleep and for some reason he regretted leaving. His saddlebags were waiting at the bottom of the stairs along with another pouch filled with homemade bread, beef jerky, and some apples Martin had prepared for him. There was also a canister of fresh brewed coffee. *God bless Martin.*

Jason anxiously waited in front of Trent's house. Resting on top of his new quarter horse, he was ready to go. Trent mounted the extra horse and turned, taking one last look at the upstairs window.

At the edge of town Jason asked, "Everything good at the Mathew's house?"

"Absolutely. I'm just feeling a little guilty about wanting to go on this trip with you. I see you bought that new quarter horse you're riding. She's a beauty."

"Yeah. I bought her at an auction in Richmond a few days ago, made a good buy."

"Want to sell the mare I'm riding?"

"She would never forgive me. She's been my companion for several years now and I'm too attached to her. You are welcome to ride her anytime you want."

The two men rode hard for over two hours and stopped on the bank of a small stream to water the horses and rest. The coffee was still warm and the two men shared biscuits stuffed with eggs and sausage Jason's grandmother had prepared for them. Rested and bellies full, they mounted their horses again and continued on the trail. They planned to arrive in Hallettsville around lunch time.

Neither of the two men had been to the county seat in Lavaca County, and both were surprised by the large stately courthouse in the middle of the square in Hallettsville. The town was bustling with people taking care of business and shopping. Jason and Trent found their way to the local stables at the end of the dusty street. They unsaddled their horses and gave them food and water. The blacksmith suggested they have lunch at Mabel's Kitchen across from the Hallettsville National Bank and the two men left. Both men left their rifles with their saddles for the blacksmith to watch and made their way to Mabel's Kitchen. Neither was prepared for what happened next. While walking in front of the Hallettsville National Bank, they heard several shots inside the bank. Running to the side of the bank and taking cover in an adjoining alley, they waited to see what was going to happen. Turning down the alley and coming toward them was an automobile driving so fast they had to jump out of its way. It stopped just as it got to the back entrance of the bank. The door opened. Two masked men carrying a bag jumped into the car and they sped away.

Trent and Jason, both on the ground, stared at each other. "What just happened? Are you all right?" Jason asked.

Rising to his feet and dusting off his pant leg, Trent said, "I think they just robbed the bank."

"Hold up you, two," a sheriff said, aiming his gun at them.

Jason and Trent looked at each other and raised their hands.

"Thought you could get away with it, didn't you. What happened? Did your friend drive off after you put the money in the car?"

Speechless, neither said anything. A deputy arrived on horseback and joined them with guns in hand.

"You've made a mistake," Trent tried to explain. "My friend and I were on our way to Mabel's Kitchen when we heard gunshots. We took cover in the alley just as an automobile car came up and opened the door. The two men that robbed the bank jumped in with their bag of money. We had nothing to do with it. They almost ran over us."

Trent and Jason were handcuffed and forced to walk in front of the sheriff and deputy who were mounted on their horses. The station was only a few blocks away. Jason looked scared, but Trent felt certain that someone who witnessed the robbery would be able to clear them soon and they would be on their way. The local sheriff interrogated them for over an hour before they were locked up together in a jail cell.

Jason was angry and lost his temper several times, but in the end he finally settled down, and lay on his bunk saying nothing. A few minutes later they were paraded in front of the bank president and two bank tellers. Masks were put over their noses and mouths to make them look like bank robbers and then they were led back to their jail cells. Neither man had any identification with them, having left everything in their saddlebags. Trent suggested to the sheriff that they could find his business card in his duffel bag at the stables and that the sheriff in Rosenberg knew both Jason and Trent.

An hour later, the sheriff unlocked their cell door and apologized for keeping them so long. Their story had checked out and they were free to go. The clock in the hallway showed three- fifteen.

Disgruntled and out of sorts, the two men headed to the diner. "That was certainly a turn of events," Jason remarked.

"Not very good timing on our part. I've never witnessed a robbery before," Trent said.

They sat at a table in the back hoping they wouldn't be interrupted by on-lookers. They both ordered steak, potatoes, and black-eyed peas. Ignoring the stares, they ate their lunch and headed for the stables. Now over two hours behind, they would have a hard ride ahead of them if they were to make it to Seguin before dark.

It was almost eight o'clock when the two men saw the light in the farmhouse window.

Jason's friend was anxiously waiting when his barking dog alerted him of their arrival. Sitting in a rocking chair on his front porch, Bert Reynolds stood up and walked out to meet them. "Thought you might have gotten lost," Bert said.

"No, but we got arrested," Jason replied. Laughing, he continued. "We'll tell you all about it once we get the horses settled in."

Bert laughed as Jason and Trent told their story over a bowl of beef stew.

"I didn't think it was that funny," Jason said, slapping Bert's shoulder. They all laughed as they ate, and talked about the plans for the next day. After rolling their sleeping bags out on the hardwood floor in the living room, the two men settled in and immediately fell asleep.

The next day, they left early and met up with three more of Jason's friends. After stopping for supplies in town, they traveled north another ten miles to the Yeager ranch just north of Seguin to round up the seventy-five head of cattle Jason had bought. The cattle were spread out over a twenty-five acre patch of land and each man rode off to round them up. Once the bellowing herd of cattle was gathered, the men began the slow tedious task of driving them back to Rosenberg.

It rained hard the first day, making their trip slow and treacherous. What was supposed to be a four-day turnaround ended up taking five and a half days. The men finally relaxed when they set eyes on familiar surroundings a couple of miles from Jason's ranch. It was almost sundown, and each man kicked their horse and whistled for the cows to speed up.

Watching from the window, Jason's grandfather hurried outside to open the main gate. Grinning from ear to ear, his grandfather waved and whistled, turning the cows into the large corral. "Good to see you made it back safely," his grandfather remarked.

"We're glad to be home, Grandpa." Jason shouted over the grunting moans of the herd.

It had been a long hard ride and all the men were glad it was over.

When the last cow was in the pen, Jason looked over at Trent. "Go on home, friend. I know Catherine's waiting for you. I'll drop by your house tomorrow to pick up my mare and give you your wages." Trent saluted him, turned his horse south, and gave her a swift kick.

12

It was late after dinner when Trent returned to the house. He settled the mare in the barn, fed, and watered her, and almost ran into Martin when he left the barn.

"How was the trail ride?"

"Tiring, but I enjoyed it." Trent could tell something was on Martin's mind. "How were things here?"

"The same as always," Martin answered.

"Well, I'll take that as good news. Everything all right with you?"

"I was wondering if you could spare me for a couple of days. I have some relatives who live in Houston and I thought I might look them up."

"I wasn't aware you had family here in the United States."

"I didn't know I did until I ran into an old acquaintance of mine in town one day. He told me my aunt and uncle were now living in Houston and he gave me their address."

"Well, of course, by all means. Will Emily be going with you?"

"Oh no. She doesn't think she should leave the children."

"Nonsense, take her with you and make it a little vacation. We'll pay your train fare. I'll talk to Catherine. I'm sure she will agree. When would you like to go?"

"Day after tomorrow, if that is agreeable with Dr. Merit, I mean Dr. Matthews."

Trent chuckled. "She'll be fine with it."

Martin watched as Trent left to talk to Catherine. The last thing Martin wanted to do was take Emily with him. *This is a business trip. She'll just have to plead sick at the last minute. Having her under foot would be a problem and I don't want to put up with her whining. Besides, I need some time alone.*

Catherine was undressing when Trent knocked lightly on the door and opened it. "You're still up?" She flung herself into his arms.

"Oh how I've missed you."

"And I, you. I've not bathed in a few days so I need to wash up."

"You always smell just fine to me."

Thank you, but I've been sleeping with cows for five days now, and I don't want to sleep with that smell for another night." They both laughed.

X X X

The next morning Martin was in the kitchen when Trent joined him. "It's all set. Catherine insists Emily go with you. She and Sadie will do just fine with the children. If we run out of something to eat, I'll take them to the cafe. Go, and enjoy yourselves." Trent poured himself a cup of coffee and poured a cup of tea for Catherine. "I'll take this upstairs and we'll be down shortly."

As Martin prepared the breakfast, Emily came in. Martin motioned for her to follow him outside. "I need to talk with you about something." Emily listened as Martin told her of his plans.

"Will you take me with you?" she asked.

"I'm going alone and that's final. We'll just tell them you weren't feeling well and didn't want to go. You can stay in our room for the day. You can sew or read. I don't want to discuss this anymore. Do as you are told." He saw her eyes fill with tears, but ignored her.

Martin grabbed both of her arms and moved closer, speaking French, so not to be overheard. "Vous devez me obeir." (You must obey me.) "Ce sont les affaires." (This is business.)

Emily nodded her head and dabbed her eyes with her apron. Taking a deep breath, she finally answered. "Oui."

The next evening after dinner Catherine noticed Emily seemed withdrawn. "Are you feeling all right, Emily?"

"Uh, I'm just a little tired."

"Well, you and Martin have a big day ahead of you tomorrow, so I'll help Sadie with the children. Go up to your room and get a good night's sleep. If I don't see you in the morning, have a safe trip."

"Thank you."

Martin was in the kitchen finishing up the evening dishes when Emily walked through. "What are you doing?"

"I told Miss Catherine I didn't feel well."

Martin smiled. "Good." He watched as Emily went out the back door.

Before Martin left the kitchen, Trent came in and gave him a twenty dollar bill. "This should cover some of your expenses."

"Thank you, Mr. Matthews. That's very generous of you."

The next morning Martin rose early and prepared biscuits, ham, and an egg casserole to leave warming on the stove for the family. He made a small tray of cheeses, fruit and bread and took it up to Emily so she would not have to leave the carriage house.

Martin quickly changed into a white shirt and used a suit he'd purchased at the local thrift shop. He and Emily had a terrible argument the night before and he walked over to the bed and looked down at her. After forcing Emily to write a note informing Catherine it was her time of the month and she was not going to Houston, he'd struck her. It was too dark to see if there were any bruises on her jaw. He'd purposely hit her under her chin so it wouldn't be noticed. He wasn't concerned. Emily was clumsy and it wouldn't be the first time she fell on the steps in the carriage house and struck her chin. He laughed to himself.

Martin turned and stopped suddenly.

"Martin," Emily called.

"Oui?"

"You will come back, won't you?"

"Oui." His reply was cold and harsh.

Martin went inside the main house and placed the note on the kitchen table. Smiling, he checked the time on his gold watch. He would be in Houston soon and he couldn't wait.

After buying his ticket, he put the rest of his change in his pocket and placed his hat on his head. The train was on time and Martin felt the thrill of freedom spread throughout his whole body. He took in a deep breath and waited for the passengers to exit the train.

Careful not to call attention to himself, he weaved quickly through the small crowd of early morning travelers and boarded the train. He slid a man's wallet inside his vest and fingered a coin purse he had taken from a woman's purse. Smiling, he found a seat in the back and stared out the window. He would wait until the train was halfway to Houston before he stepped into the men's room and counted his bounty.

Martin leaned his head back. He felt free and marvelled at how easy it was to convince Trent he had family in Houston. Closing his eyes, his mind wandered, and he began developing his plan to make new contacts and arrangements for the future. It wouldn't be too long now before he would be free of everything keeping him in Rosenberg. He had been patient long enough and when the timing was right, he would be able to begin a whole new life. His plans were still being formulated in his mind, but he was certain the details would fall into place.

Martin opened his eyes when he felt the steady rhythm of the engine picking up its pace. The majestic scenery rolled by as the morning daylight painted a beautiful landscape of colors over the meadows. Getting up from his seat, he strolled to the next car in search of the men's room. The porter motioned to him that the room was clear. Upon entering, he locked the door and took out the wallet he had stolen at the train station. Several dollar bills generously filled the pouch; one five, a ten, two twenties, and several ones. Not bad, he told himself. It was enough to pay for a hotel, a few drinks, and a lady for the evening. The coin purse added little to the till, two dollars, a few dimes, and quarters. He tossed both the wallet and coin purse out the partially open window.

By the time he settled back in his seat, the porter was announcing their arrival into Houston. Feeling his heart race with anxiety, Martin fidgeted in his seat for a moment to allow other passengers to get off first, and then followed. After he exited the train, he noticed two police officers watching the arriving passengers. He tucked his head down and walked through the crowd. He couldn't risk getting caught, not this early, so he kept his hands in his pocket. *No need taking a chance.* He walked over to a bench and sat down for a while.

Martin removed his hat and took out his handkerchief. Beads of sweat accumulated on his receding hairline and he dabbed at it with the cotton cloth. His eyes locked on a well-dressed man wearing a gentleman's hat and suit. He looked to be in his late thirties and had a distinguished look. For some reason the man seemed familiar. It happened so fast no one noticed, no one except Martin. The man continued working the crowd and then he looked over to see if the policemen were watching. An attractive woman, probably in her late twenties, occupied their time. They were deep in conversation with the pretty lady. *Well, what do you know? The distinguished man has a female partner.*

Martin's eyes remained fixed on the pair. The woman glanced in the direction of the distinguished man. The man nodded and the woman excused herself and made her way through the train station. Martin followed her out to the street. She met up with the gentleman who approached from the side of the station. The woman took the man's arm, and continued walking. Martin followed.

13

Several blocks later, the man escorted the woman into the Baxter Hotel. Following, Martin entered the hotel and looked around. The woman sat on a settee off the main lobby. Martin scanned the elegant surroundings and noticing she was alone, approached her.

After he took off his hat, he introduced himself. "Good morning, my name is Martin Boudreaux."

"The lady is already taken," the distinguished man said, coming up from behind. "What is your business? You've been following us since we left the train station."

"My name is Martin, Martin Boudreaux. I thought we might do some business together."

"What kind of business?"

"I think you have an idea. I watched both of you at the train station. You are very good at your trade."

The man smiled and looked past Martin. "I have no idea what you are talking about."

"Your friend did a splendid job of keeping the police occupied."

The man looked around the room and said through gritted teeth, "What do you want?"

"My name is Martin Boudreaux and I'm looking for information; why don't you buy me a drink and we can talk?"

"Not here. There is a place around the corner. My name is Ira Gentry and this is Gilda Perkins."

"My pleasure to meet both of you."

They selected a dark booth at the back of an old run-down hotel two blocks away. Ira and Gilda slid into the booth and Martin sat across from them.

Ira stared at Martin and then said, "You're not American."

"No, I'm French. I've been in America about nine months. My wife and I live in Rosenberg, 'bout an hour's train ride. She cares for a family and I maintain the house there. I wanted to get settled first, understand the American ways, and make a little money."

Ira was shaking his head as he listened. "I was fifteen when my family came from Russia. Gilda and I met a year ago and have been working together ever since. What are your plans and how do we fit in?"

A stout older woman approached the table and took their drink orders.

After she left, Martin leaned over the table, and in a low voice said, "I'm looking to make contacts in the baby selling business. The woman I work for is with child. I'm ready to leave Rosenberg and head out. Figured I could make a good purse off the baby."

"Interesting." Ira looked at Gilda as if to ask her permission. Her nod was slight and Martin almost missed it.

Clearing his throat, Martin said, "I was wondering if you might know of someone and could pass the information on to me. I'll pay you a small fee for the information."

"If we were able to help you, when would this take place?"

"The baby's expected date of delivery is early May. If the child is healthy and able to suck milk from a bottle, I figure no more than three months. The family is wealthy and well-educated. The infant should bring a nice bounty. I've heard families will pay up to five thousand dollars for a premium specimen."

"Perhaps I might know of someone. If I could arrange this, there will be a fee for the man arranging the adoption. What will you pay me for this information?"

Martin chewed on his bottom lip and looked up. The waitress set two beers and a cup of hot tea on the table. The two men took several swallows of their beer while Gilda swirled her tea bag in the hot water. Martin scratched the side of his scrubby face. "I don't have much cash with me. I would prefer to pay a stipend of two hundred dollars when the deal is done."

Ira laughed and winked at Gilda. "You have much to learn about Americans."

"Perhaps I do. But I am the one with the goods. I will have all the liability and you will have none, unless you want to purchase the child yourself and pay me off for the delivered goods."

Ira's interest piqued and he gave a slow nod to Gilda.

"If you can deliver the baby in good health and it's a boy, I'll take him off your hands for five hundred dollars. For a girl, two hundred."

Martin picked up his beer and chugalugged the remainder. He placed it back on the edge of the table and slid out taking a quarter from his pocket and putting it on the table. "I have more important appointments."

Ira reached over and wrapped his fingers around Martin's boney wrist. "Sit."

Martin gazed at his hand for a minute before removing it and took a seat.

"My apologies if I have offended you," Ira said.

"I'm listening."

"Let's just suppose I've done this before. Understand, I would have to pay a solicitor a tidy sum. They would expect fifty percent. If we split, say, three thousand dollars three ways, I could pay you one thousand dollars for a male child; five hundred for a girl. Cash on delivery."

N.E. Brown

Martin knew the reason why a male child fetched more. A male could begin working at a young age if he were sold to a rancher or farmer. If he went to a more affluent home, his family would send him to college and he would be able to take care of them in their old age. He pondered the deal for a moment. His resources were limited and a thousand dollars would set him up nicely in a more legitimate business. At least he could give the appearance of having money and be able to rub shoulders with the more high-class criminals. "It's a deal."

Martin reached over and shook hands with Ira. Another round of drinks was ordered and this time Gilda ordered Sherry. When the drinks arrived, the glasses were held up. Gilda proposed a toast. "May he be strong and healthy."

The two men talked about the arrangement. Martin wasn't surprised when he found out this was not Ira's and Gilda's first baby transaction.

As Ira began to feel more comfortable around Martin, he shared some interesting details. "I met the solicitor several months ago. He has helped us with a number of adoptions. This will be our last one in Houston. Gilda doesn't want to leave Houston, but it's time to move on. After this one, we will head north." Gilda glared at Ira, but said nothing. "You say the baby will come in early May?"

"Yes. The mother is also a doctor and has four other children."

"I will be in touch with you sometime in late July after the baby comes. There will not be a return address on the envelope. Instructions and arrangements will be inside. It's important you destroy it after you read it."

"I can do that."

"Good, give me a phone number and I will call you." Ira handed Martin a piece of paper and a pencil. "Write it down."

Martin did as he was told.

Afterwards the two men shook hands.

"There is one more thing," Martin said. "I'd like to get a room somewhere this evening, preferably one that comes with a woman, if you know what I mean."

"That's her department," Ira said looking at Gilda.

Gilda sighed. "You have money?"

Martin nodded his head.

"Very well, then." Ira handed her a piece of paper and a pencil.

After writing down an address and room number, she slid it over to Martin. "Be there at nine o'clock tonight."

Martin stood up, turned and left without paying his part of the bill. *He can afford it better than me.*

Martin could barely contain his excitement, and whistled as he strolled down the street. Life in America was getting better by the day. Martin stopped at what looked to be an expensive restaurant and decided to treat himself to a good meal. Before going inside, he went back to a fruit stand on the corner, stopped, and examined the produce. He picked up several before he found what he was looking for. Carefully he picked up a fruit fly and gently smashed it between his fingers. He took out the paper Gilda had given him and placed it inside, folding it so the fly would not fall out.

He passed several restaurants and soon stopped at a Restaurant called "Latiffs." The sign boasted European cuisine. Once inside the maître d' showed him to a small table by the window.

After ordering a five-course dinner and a bottle of fine wine, Martin rolled and then lit a cigarette while watching people stroll by. The soup, appetizer, and bread were all excellent. He waited until he was nearly through his meal when he looked around the room. Keeping his hands under the table, he removed the fly from the paper and held it while he took a sip of wine. When he was sure no one was looking, he placed the fruit fly on his plate. He picked up his fork and took one last bit of his meal before moving the fly around in the juices. "Waiter," he yelled. Everyone stopped eating and stared.

The waiter immediately came to his table. "Look at this, how disgusting." The maître d' followed. "I am so sorry, sir. Please let me bring you a new dinner."

"No, I've lost my appetite." Martin got up and stalked out while everyone watched. *That was easy and so much fun.*

14

When Martin returned to Rosenberg, he kept up his charade of being a dutiful servant, much to his dislike. Inside he was aching to leave and counting the days until he would have money and be free of his laboring over the Mathew's family.

With Trent around most of the time, there were few opportunities for Martin to go into town. When he did, the town was mostly filled with laborers who had little money. Occasionally, his bad habit would overtake him and he would slide a woman's coin purse from her bag. He would be halfway down the street before she realized it was gone. He always made sure there were other people in the store so he wouldn't be accused.

On one occasion, Martin watched a man at the drug store try to slip his wallet into his back pocket. He missed and the wallet fell to the floor. Martin was behind him and quickly kicked it away causing it to slide behind a book display. Martin got out of line and walked over to the book display and waited for the man to leave. When no one was looking, he quickly picked up the wallet and slid it into his waistband under his coat. When Martin returned home, he quickly went to the barn and looked in the wallet;

three twenties and eight one dollar bills; not bad for a day's work.

There were many opportunities to steal money from the Matthews. Trent never carried his wallet and always left it on the nightstand beside the bed. It was tempting, but Martin knew if he took any money, it would jeopardize his future plans. *No, I can resist the temptation.*

X X X

The summer heat was gruelling in the small community of Rosenberg, but it didn't stop its population growth to over one thousand people. Many immigrants coming through the Union Depot often stayed overnight looking for jobs and a place to settle. A new company, the Brazos Brick & Drain Tile Works was now underway and their business was thriving. Trent was offered a supervisor's position by its owner, but he had to decline because of his commitment to Humble Oil Co. He often helped Jason when he needed an extra hand on his farm, but Trent refused payment. Catherine and the children were his primary concern and he didn't want any distractions.

With Trent home and working odd jobs, Catherine stopped seeing patients. She only attended to emergencies; but as she grew tired, Trent insisted she place a closed sign on the front door.

"You need to relax and just take care of yourself, Catherine," Trent finally said.

"You are right. I just hate to say no to someone in need of help."

"Everyone knows the baby is due soon. They will understand."

Catherine never found the right time to tell Trent about her past after he took time from his job, and he didn't ask her. Her nightmares had faded since her appointment with Dr. Benton and she didn't want to spoil their time together by dragging up memories. *Soon. I'll tell him when the time is right.*

As the smell of spring filled the air, the family spent more time outdoors enjoying the nice weather. On weekends they would often picnic in their favorite spot along the Brazos River. Trent tied a rope on a large tree limb that hung over the river. He would wade in the water as each child grabbed the rope and flew out into the water dropping into his arms. It was how the children learned to swim and it gave the children motivation to be good during the week.

Catherine made sure they studied their numbers and alphabet, educating each child so they would be prepared when they began first grade at the elementary school across town. Daniel's eagerness to learn made him excited to attend school in the fall.

As Catherine's due date approached, she sewed and made preparations for the baby. Sadie and Emily helped by mending the other children's clothing during their free time while the children napped.

Catherine and Trent made one more trip to Houston for her last check-up, and after a good report from Dr. Benton, they shopped and dined at a new restaurant not far from the apartment. Before going back home, they shopped for a bassinet and arranged for it to be delivered the next week. Catherine was feeling tired and they decided to cut their weekend trip short and go back to Rosenberg.

"I think I've taken care of everything on my list and I miss the children," Catherine told Trent.

"This is your trip and I'm just along for the ride," he teased. "I miss the children, too."

X X X

The days and weeks passed quickly and it was soon time for Trent and Catherine to go back to Houston and wait for the baby's arrival.

After their bags were packed, Trent carried them down to the carriage. Catherine gave last minute instructions to the Boudreauxs and Sadie. "We're only an hour away by train and if something comes up you can't handle, Trent can come back. You have the phone number for our Houston apartment and I will call you frequently."

The children lined up to say goodbye to their mother and father, waving furiously as the carriage took them to the train station. Catherine looked back, tearfully, and waved. Soon they would bring back a new brother or sister to her growing family, and she was overwhelmed.

They had been in Houston for three days, shopping, eating at wonderful restaurants, and enjoying their time alone. After breakfast one morning, Catherine decided she needed to tell Trent about the hardships and trauma she had encountered when she arrived in America. She left nothing out when she explained the indignities she'd suffered after she arrived in Galveston. "At first, we were so happy. Mum had a difficult time finding employment and that's when we met a widower, John Merit, who was my mother's banker; the man I married. He told my mother about a job at the Grand Opera House. She loved working there, but the maintenance man, David Brooks. . ." Catherine stopped short of finishing her sentence and took a deep breath. "We believe he was responsible for my mother's death. It was very painful. I was sent to St. Mary's Orphanage and John Merit would visit me often. I believe he felt guilty because he'd referred my mum to that job. Anyway, we fell in love and he made a request to Father Jonathan that we marry when I turned sixteen. After we married, everything was good again and my plans after I graduated from high school were to go to medical school."

Trent reached across the table and took Catherine's hand. "I know this is difficult for you and you can stop at any time."

"I want to finish and be done with it." Trent shook his head and leaned into her as she dried a tear.

"The same man that murdered mum later kidnapped me and raped me. I managed to escape and he was sent to a prison farm in Sugar Land. John was a very patient husband and a month later I discovered I was pregnant. I had no idea if the baby was John's or David Brooks.'" Catherine closed her eyes tightly willing her tears to cease. "I miscarried after seven weeks. Everything began to get better and then the day of the terrible storm, I was working at St. Mary's and John was home putting up shutters when he became stranded. God was looking out for us again, and John was one of the few that made it out alive. St. Mary's Hospital had some terrible damage, but those that took shelter there survived."

Trent got up, took Catherine's hand and led her over to the small sofa. He pulled her close to him as they sat down and he wrapped his arms around her. He kissed her on the cheek. "I am so in love with you and I wish I could make it better."

"You already have. You are so strong and I take comfort in that."

"Do you want to stop?"

"No. I need to get it out. I was attending medical school and working part time at the hospital while rebuilding our home. We were told David Brooks had died when a tornado struck Sugar Land right after the storm. But somehow he managed to get away and become an undertaker in Beaumont. Oil was discovered there at Spindle Top and the city's population grew substantially.

"One night after I got off work at St. Mary's, David overtook me and put me in a casket inside a hearse and drove me all the way back to Beaumont. I was drugged and groggy. When we got to his small farm, he locked me up for days in the house, abusing me and. . . ."

"Oh, Catherine, I can't imagine."

With patience, Trent continued to listen as Catherine poured out her soul recounting the abuses she suffered. The tragic tale brought tears to Trent's eyes on numerous occasions; even though David Brooks was now dead, Trent was sorry he had not been the one to kill him.

The thought of her being put in a casket and taken away in a hearse made him fist his hands and curse under his breath. Trent held her and stroked her back as she sobbed. "That's enough. Shh. It's behind you and nothing and no one will ever hurt you again. I promise that. Breathe in slowly and let it out. You have to calm yourself."

Catherine sucked in a deep breath and sat up. Clutching her abdomen, she looked up at Trent, "Oh my, the baby. I think it's time for the baby." She looked at the clock on the table.

"What do you want me to do?" Trent asked, still trying to console her.

"Nothing, but wait. We'll watch the time and keep track of the contractions." Catherine ran quickly into the bathroom as her water broke.

While waiting for her contractions to get closer, Trent called the hospital and asked them to alert the doctor.

They boarded a trolley to Houston General Hospital. Catherine was calm and unconcerned, but Trent was nervous and worried.

"I'll be fine. Dr. Benton is a wonderful doctor and will take great care. Please, don't worry."

Trent paced the halls as he waited, getting periodic updates from a nurse. Catherine previously told him about the difficulties she had with the other deliveries, and he couldn't help but be nervous. Two hours later, the doctor came out.

"Congratulations, Mr. Matthews, you have a healthy boy, six pounds-four ounces. Your wife is doing just fine."

Trent looked at the doctor and his concern turned into a wide grin. "A boy, I have a son." The two men shook hands.

"She is back in her room and you may go see her now."

Grinning from ear to ear, Trent joined Catherine in her private room and bent over, kissing her on the cheek. He stared at the beautiful creature swaddled in a plaid pink and blue blanket beside her. "Are you feeling all right? Were there any problems?"

"No, we are both fine."

"I want to show you something."

Carefully, she pulled the blanket away from the baby's neck." See the birthmark."

Trent took a closer look. Three inches below and to the left of the baby's Adam's apple was a perfectly shaped birthmark in the shape of a fish. He stared in fascination. "'I've seen birthmarks before, but none shaped like this."

"I know. The other children have small birthmarks, but this one is so unusual."

After the nurse took the baby back to the nursery, Trent took Catherine's hand and kissed it. "I don't know when I have ever felt so proud, a son, you gave us a son."

"I'd like to name him after your grandfather, Jacob, if you approve."

"Of course, my grandfather would be so proud. When do you think we can take him home?"

"Dr. Benton said we could leave in a couple of days, but he wants me to stay in Houston for a few more days to rest. He wants to be sure there are no complications."

Their excitement grew daily and after two days, Dr. Benton finally signed the release papers. Trent had a carriage and driver waiting outside the hospital to take them back to their apartment.

While the apartment was small and cramped, Trent did his best to keep things tidy, and even cooked some of their meals. At first he was nervous holding such a small infant, but as his confidence grew, so did the bond between him and his son. He had never experienced this before and it gave him a whole new purpose. He marvelled at Catherine's patience. There was no question that Jacob had brought both him and Catherine closer together.

Jacob slept in a large basket on the floor by their bed and even though Catherine tried not to disturb Trent, he always woke and sat up with her, watching in fascination. "I know this is nothing new to you, but I want to enjoy these next few days and get to know my son," Trent said.

"These are special moments to me no matter how many times I've done this."

"Tomorrow I'm going to buy that new washing machine we looked at a few weeks ago, but I really think we need to buy the larger model. I had no idea babies used so many diapers." They both laughed and Trent leaned over and kissed her. "You've made me a very happy man, Catherine."

15

The children were lined up outside the train station as the trained pulled into Rosenberg. Jumping for joy and screaming, they all gathered around young Jacob and stared. "He's so little," Adam said. Everyone laughed.

The children were in awe of the tiny bundle. "He looks just like you, Mr. Matthews," Sadie said. "May I hold him when we get to the house?"

"Yes. You'll be holding him a lot as we get settled in."

After returning home, Catherine noticed Emily was quiet as she watched everyone make a fuss over Jacob. "Emily, I think Jacob's diaper might need changing. Why don't you take him upstairs and change him while I rest downstairs?"

Emily smiled, "I'd be happy to, ma'am." She bent down, picked up Jacob and walked carefully towards the staircase.

"May we go with her and watch?" Emma asked.

"Of course," Emily answered.

Trent put his arms around Catherine and watched as the four children followed Emily and

Jacob upstairs. He reached over and kissed her on her cheek. "I think the children really like their little brother."

While Emily was changing Jacob's diaper, she couldn't help but notice a dark smudge on Jacob's chest. Pulling his undershirt down the distinct picture of a fish astounded her. She licked her finger and began rubbing at the fish. The children watched and asked what it was. "I think it is a birthmark."

"I have one of those on the side of my butt," Adam said. "I keep washing and washing, but it won't come off. Mama says almost everyone has one someplace on their body."

A while later Emily returned with Jacob and the four children in tow. "He is beginning to fuss a bit. Is it time for him to nurse?" Catherine was sitting on the sofa and Emily placed Jacob in Catherine's lap. "Did you notice the birthmark on his chest?

Swaddled in his blue blanket, Catherine carefully slid the blanket down from around his face and held him while she unbuttoned her blouse with her right hand. "Yes, isn't it remarkable? There's no question about it looking like a fish right now. Some birthmarks fade as the child grows older so it will probably change."

Jacob's small delicate mouth opened and he searched for Catherine's nipple. "Look," Isabelle said. Their mouths wide open and their eyes glued to Catherine's breast, each child stood over her, speechless.

"Did I do that when I was a baby?" Adam asked.

Smiling, Catherine looked at her four curious children. "Yes." For a moment she looked at Isabelle, but said nothing. In time she would tell Isabelle when she was older that she had not birthed her. Perhaps one day they would go to the reservation where Isabelle was born. *But not now. None of the children would understand. They were too young.* To this day she was unsure of her legal right to be Isabelle's mother. There had been no legal adoption. Alex had verbally given her permission to raise Isabelle, but still it remained in the back of her mind.

When Catherine finished nursing, she gave Jacob back to Emily and the children followed her upstairs to change Jacob's diaper. A knock on the front door diverted Catherine's and Trent's attention. "I'll go see who it is," Trent responded.

"I hope I'm not interrupting anything, but I have some business to discuss with you and your wife," Sheriff Raymond Boise said.

Catherine finished buttoning her blouse and looked up when the men entered the room. Sheriff Boise looked around the room to see if they were alone.

"What is it?" Trent asked.

"I have been hearing rumors around town and I am a bit concerned."

"What kind of rumors?" Catherine asked.

"We have no proof as yet, but apparently there is someone that has been stealing and picking people's pockets in town. Mostly people arriving at the train station and recently someone at the general store had some things taken from their pockets."

"What does that have to do with us?" Trent asked.

"Well, like I said, I have no proof, but people are saying it is Martin Boudreaux. He has been identified as a bystander each time these incidents occurred. Once, I was at the train station when someone accused Martin of stealing something and I asked if I could check his pockets. He was very gracious and I frisked him."

"Did you find anything?" Catherine asked.

"No, and that's why I said I have no proof. I just wanted to make you aware of the rumors. Have you noticed any money or jewelry that has disappeared from your home?"

"Absolutely not," Catherine remarked. "He and his wife have been loyal and dedicated employees and I have no reason to be suspicious of them."

"I'm not trying to upset you. Like I said, I just want you to be aware of the rumors. I'll let myself out. And, congratulations on your new son."

After Sheriff Boise left, Catherine and Trent sat on the living room sofa, and were momentarily stunned. "I can't believe this happened," Catherine remarked.

"How often does Martin go into town?" Trent asked.

"Every other day or so he walks to the grocery store for fresh eggs and milk. Sometimes more often if the need arises. He does walk to the post office every day to collect the mail, but he is never gone very long."

"Maybe I should take over that duty. I'll let Martin know that he needs to give me a list of the items he needs and I'll go into town and get them. If he isn't seen, maybe they will find whoever is doing the stealing. The town is filled with new laborers every day looking for work. I wonder why they think it might be Martin. It could be anyone."

"Won't that make him suspicious?" Catherine asked.

"I'll just tell him I need something to do. We'll do it for a few weeks or until I return to work." Trent saw concern in Catherine's eyes. "I think Martin is being accused of something he hasn't done," he replied.

"When do you plan to go back to work?"

"Catherine, you knew I was only taking three months off. Before we left Houston, I called my boss and told him I'd be gone another couple of weeks and then be back at work. You know our money will run out if I don't continue to work. You've not had the clinic open in a couple of months and I really think you shouldn't reopen it. The children need you."

Tears swelled in Catherine's eyes and she looked away. Taking in a deep breath she finally looked into Trent's eyes. "I've just become so used to your being here. That's all. I can't bear the thought of only seeing you every two or three weeks."

"I don't like this arrangement either. The only way we can solve that problem is for us to sell the house and move to Humble or North Houston. We could buy something closer to my work."

"You're an oil scout and they require you to travel all over the countryside. If we sold the house and bought something closer to your work, what would we do if they moved you somewhere else? I don't want to live like a bunch of gypsies."

"I'm not trying to hurt you, Catherine. I can't tell you that my company won't move me someplace else in the next couple of years. You knew that when we married. You said you had no problem with me being gone. I know having Jacob changes some things."

"I'm sorry. I guess I'm a little bit overwhelmed. I think I'll go upstairs and rest."

Trent watched as Catherine climbed the staircase until she disappeared into the shadows. Grabbing his hat from the hall-tree, he quickly opened the front door and hurried down the steps. Marriage was still new to Trent and he needed to take a walk to clear his head.

Trent was approaching thirty years old and he had lived alone most of his life. He had lived with another woman for a while, but always kept an apartment, so it never seemed permanent. He went from being totally independent to being responsible for a wife and five children plus three employees that now depended on him.

Not wanting to stop and talk to people on the street, he turned down an alley and headed the back way to the stables. There was a black mare that belonged to the blacksmith and Trent would often take the mare for a run. He had considered buying it, but adding another mouth to feed wasn't practical, so he offered the blacksmith a few dollars to ride it. When Trent got to the stables the mare was gone.

"Sold him yesterday. Got a good price for him. I'm talking to your friend, Jason, about buying one of his."

"No problem. Thanks."

Walking back home, he heard voices coming from the local saloon and decided to go in. "Whiskey," he said to the bartender. Trent drank the liquid down quickly and grimaced as he felt the strong liquid slide down his throat.

"Want another?"

Trent nodded his head and the bartender filled his glass. He drank it slowly, put fifty cents on the counter and left.

16

Martin was listening outside the door when Sheriff Boise informed the Matthews of Martin's possible involvement in the crimes. He was only three months away from his freedom and he couldn't afford to lose his job and a roof over his head. *I can do it. I've saved over three hundred fifty dollars and with another thousand from the baby deal, my future would be secure. Later, I'll write a letter to Ira confirming the male child.*

X X X

Catherine was pacing the front porch when she saw Trent walking home from town. Running to meet him, she grabbed him around the neck and kissed him. "Please forgive me for being so weak. I understand our needs and you have so many responsibilities that weigh heavy on your heart. I don't want to burden you with my unreasonable demands. I know my condition is somewhat fragile, and you have given so much of yourself. I don't deserve you."

"My darling, you don't need to apologize and you deserve everything. I want to be there for you and the children. It's hard on me, too." They stood in the street clinging to each other until they felt small drops of rainwater on their faces. They ran hand in hand toward the house and made it to the front porch just as a gray dark cloud exploded, followed by thunder, and a minute later, lightning blazed across the sky.

Daniel was watching through the screen door and ran to the kitchen for a towel. "Here Papa. You can dry Mama off." Trent opened the door and picked up Daniel.

"I'll let you dry Mama." Trent leaned Daniel into Catherine and watched as Daniel carefully dried Catherine's face.

After entering the house, Trent placed Daniel on the floor and watched him run to the playroom in the back. "With Daniel here to keep an eye on you, I won't need to worry. He hardly lets you out of his sight." They both laughed. "I guess I need to find Martin and have a talk with him." He noticed a concerned look on Catherine's face. "Don't worry, I'm not going to accuse him of anything and I'm not going to fire them." He gave her a gentle hug and left the room.

Martin was sweeping off the back porch and Trent was glad they were outside where he could have a private conversation. The rhythmical pounding of rain on the tin roof made it difficult to hear.

"Follow me to the stables." Both men ran at lightning speed and made it inside with wet shirts hanging on their bodies.

"The sheriff was by here earlier and told me several citizens had complained that there was a pickpocket in our midst. Since you aren't a local, some people have complained that you might be behind the disappearance of some of their personal belongings. Now I know you are a man of high moral standards and Catherine and I are sure they have jumped to conclusions."

Martin stood motionless and stared blankly at Trent, saying nothing.

Trent continued. "Catherine and I think it would best for me to collect the mail and do the shopping until I go back to work in a few weeks. It will give the rumors a rest." He waited, but Martin stood silent. "I'm sorry and I can't imagine how you must feel." Martin continued glaring at him.

Trent slapped Martin on the shoulder. "Don't worry; your job has not changed. Keep up the good work."

After Trent left the stables, Martin walked over and picked up a pitchfork. Rearing back, he began hacking at a hay bale. His thrusts were violent, each hit ripping and tearing apart the hay from the twine that bound it together. When he was finished, he threw the pitchfork so hard into the wall, it impaled into the wood, leaving it fixed and parallel to the dirt floor. Anger and contempt riddled his body and he was panting. Martin pushed back the long strands of black hair that had fallen into his face. *Three more months of this shit. Just three more months.*

Upon returning to the house, Trent met Catherine at the back door. "How did it go?" she asked nervously wringing her hands.

"Surprisingly well, I guess. He never said anything; just stared at me in disbelief. I'm sure he's not involved. We just need to give it some time."

Catherine felt uneasy and wanted to believe that Martin was innocent. Still, it bothered her that the sheriff was accusing Martin. She became more anxious as the days passed. Soon Trent would leave and she would be back in charge of everything.

Catherine was also concerned because she and Trent had not been intimate because of the risk of infection. The bleeding had lasted for several weeks and finally stopped, but Dr. Benton warned her to wait for at least six weeks until her periods were normal again. It meant Trent would be leaving before it was safe, causing her more anxiety and stress.

Friday evening before going to bed, Trent turned to Catherine. "I spoke with Clarence earlier in the day, and he told me unless I could begin work on Monday, they would have to hire a replacement." He watched as she slowly brushed her long golden hair. Approaching her, he placed his hands on her shoulders and watched her reflection in the vanity mirror. "I'll be back before you know it. I've given instructions to Martin, and Sadie will be running all the errands."

Placing her hand on his she turned and gave him a slight smile. "I know we must both be strong.

Don't worry about me. I haven't been quite myself lately, but that's normal after child- birth."

"Perhaps you can join me at the apartment in Houston when you feel up to it. I know traveling with a baby is difficult and you need to nurse." He bent down and kissed her.

Catherine stood up and put her arms around him holding him tightly.

"I love you so much. Yes, I'll come to Houston when I'm better."

The children hovered around Trent most of Saturday morning. They begged him not to leave and promised they would be good if he stayed.

"I'm afraid that's not possible. "Papa has to work to make money. I'll be back soon." He was also finding it difficult to leave. They had all grown so close over the summer.

Later that afternoon, there was an abundance of tears as he bent down kissing each one on the cheek. "Daniel, I expect you to be man of the house. Look after your brothers and sisters."

"Yes, Papa, I will," he answered proudly.

Catherine insisted on walking Trent to the station. "I'll take care of the errands while I'm there and it will occupy my thoughts after you leave." They held each other tightly and Trent finally pulled away when the train began moving.

"See you in two weeks," he yelled, grabbing hold of the iron handle and hopping on the moving train.

Catherine watched until the train disappeared. There was a hollow feeling in her chest and she sucked in a deep breath. He'll be back soon, she reassured herself.

The small post office was her first stop. The attendant handed her a small bundle. She walked over and sat on a bench to go through it. There were a couple of medical journals, an advertisement flyer, several bills, and the last was a letter addressed to Mr. Martin Boudreaux, c/o of Dr. Catherine Merit. There was no return address on it and the postmark was from Houston, Texas. *A letter from his uncle, perhaps.*

Catherine put the journals, bills, and Martin's letter in her large straw shopping bag. She made the rounds of her favorite shops, finishing up at the grocery market. She reached up to get a bag of flour and felt a wet spot on the front of her breasts. Looking down, she realized that it was time to nurse Jacob and he was probably screaming by now. Grabbing her last few items, she paid the attendant, picked up her bagged items and rushed back to the house.

Jacob was sucking on Emily's finger when she found them in the playroom. "I'm sorry it took me so long."

Catherine sat in the rocker, unbuttoned the front of her dress, and adjusted Jacob in her lap. His anxious mouth latched onto Catherine's wet nipple immediately and relief came to both of them.

"Have you considered weaning Jacob from your breasts? Perhaps he could be supplemented with the cow's milk." Emily said as Catherine glared at her.

"I just thought it would give you more freedom to travel to Houston and leave Jacob here if he were able to take the cow's milk," Emily continued.

"Yes, Emily, I have thought about it and I have decided to wait another month. I've noticed I am not making as much milk as when he was first born."

Emily left the room and went to the kitchen where Martin was preparing dinner. "She just told me she was going to introduce cow's milk to Jacob in a month," Emily told him. Martin's smile showed his approval.

Later that evening after Martin finished cleaning the kitchen, Catherine came in and handed him a letter. "I believe this might be from your uncle." Martin took the letter, hiding his annoyance that she'd waited several hours to give it to him.

"If you don't need anything else, I've finished my chores and will retire for the evening."

"Of course, supper was spectacular, as usual. Thank you."

When Catherine left the kitchen, Martin removed his apron and hung it on a nail by the door. Emily would not join him until she finished bathing the children and putting them to bed. He was relieved that he had over an hour to read Ira's letter and contemplate his future before Emily joined him.

17

Martin opened the letter as he took the stairs two at a time to his apartment. He wadded up the envelope and threw it into the trash. Sitting by the window in his chair, he read and then re-read Ira's letter.

Congratulations. I'm delighted it's a boy. Moving forward; will mail you within the month to make further arrangements. Ira, Date: July 14, 1907.

Irritated that it was not more specific, Martin opened the drawer in the makeshift kitchen and pulled out a box of matches. He struck the match and held the flame close to the letter. It burned quickly and he released it, letting it fall into the sink still burning. He turned and stared at the sparsely decorated room that was his home. He had been nagging Emily to coerce Catherine into letting her wean the baby from her milk. Today she found an opportunity and took it. *Emily, poor sweet Emily. She is so naive. Once the transfer of the child takes place, I'll get rid of her. She knows too much and there is no way she could make her own way.*

Martin cleaned up the mess in the sink and found a tablet he had hidden away deep under the mattress. He drew a timeline, sketching notes of towns and places he might explore once the deal was done. Walking over to a shelf, he retrieved a large book that said, <u>Large Cities in the United States</u>. He opened it to a map of the country and used his finger to move from Houston to Dallas and then northeast to Chicago. He had read about Chicago in the newspapers Catherine subscribed to. The city was large and one could fade into the fabric of the city.

Hearing footsteps, he quickly put the tablet back under the bed and replaced the book. "You're back early."

"Yes, Sadie offered to bathe the children and put them to bed so I could spend time with you. Who was the letter from?"

Martin eyed her carefully. "No one you know. It's business."

"Please tell me what you are thinking. Why is it so important for the baby to be taken away from his mother's breast? You aren't still thinking. . ." She stopped talking when Martin grabbed a hand full of her hair and pulled her close to him.

"Stop it. Just stop it," he said through gritted teeth. He bent down and kissed her hard on the mouth and began tearing at her clothes.

Emily knew better than to resist, so she allowed him to take her on the floor. He slapped her hard several times, careful not to hit her hard enough to cause any bruising on her face. The rest of her body took the brunt of his brutality. He punched her in places where bruising would not be noticed and she forced herself not to scream. He was a madman and she prayed one day he would not kill her.

"Get up," he demanded.

Emily uncurled herself from the ball she lay in. Pain ravaged her body and she groaned with each move.

Martin sat in his chair and watched her. When she got up, he reached for her, pulled her into his lap, and held her. "Now if you wouldn't ask so many questions and do as you are told, I wouldn't have to hit you. It's your own fault. Let's go to bed."

X X X

Catherine had not felt well for the past few days and she thought it was just fatigue. She took her pulse and her temperature -101 degrees. Worried that she might have an infection, she placed a call to Dr. Benton. He returned her call two hours later.

After telling him of her symptoms, he said he would have his nurse deliver some medication to the train station and asked if someone could meet the six o'clock train from Houston.

"Yes," she replied, "I can do that."

"I suggest you stop nursing Jacob immediately. He's old enough to drink regular milk if you warm it. Not too hot. I'm afraid you will have to manually squeeze the milk from your breasts to eliminate the pain from the build-up of milk."

After giving her some more instructions, Catherine hung up the phone and left the room. Sadie met her at the door.

"What did the doctor say?" Sadie asked.

Hesitating and trying to hold back her tears, she finally answered. "He said I must quarantine myself from everyone. You will need to meet the seven o'clock train to pick up a package for me. Dr. Benton is sending medication. Tell Emily that I won't be able to nurse. I have some baby bottles above the glasses in the kitchen. She will need to boil and sterilize them, then warm the milk." Tirelessly, she climbed the staircase, closed the door to her room, and fell into her bed sobbing.

It was after eight o'clock when Sadie tapped lightly on Catherine's door. She put the tray on the floor and slowly opened the door. She could barely see the outline of Catherine's body on the bed. Picking up the tray, she walked over and sat it on the night table. She turned on the lamp and shook Catherine awake. "I have the package of medicine and some water for you." She helped Catherine sit up and handed her the package to open. After pouring a glass of water, she helped her open the bottle and take two pills. "Do you feel like eating something, Miss Catherine?"

"No, dear, I feel nauseated and I don't think I could keep anything down. You need to leave in case I'm contagious."

Sadie went into the bathroom and wet a washcloth. She picked up a small child's chamber pot and carried it to the side of the bed. "I'm putting this on the floor in case you get sick and here is a cool wash cloth to put on your forehead. I'll come back in an hour and check on you."

"How are the children? Are they well?"

"Yes, ma'am. They seem to be fine. Is there anything else I can do?"

Catherine groaned. "My milk has come in and I'm beginning to leak. Please raise me up and hand me the chamber bowl." Sadie complied. Catherine grimaced as she squeezed milk from her breasts into the bowl. Sadie ran for a towel and helped Catherine relieve the pressure. Thirty minutes later Sadie poured the milk down the basin drain. Catherine lay back on her pillow and closed her eyes. Sadie stayed until she was sure Catherine was asleep.

After helping Emily put the children to bed, Sadie checked on Catherine once more and then made a pallet on the hall floor. She usually slept in the girls' room, but she wanted to be able to hear Catherine if she needed her and be close to Jacob and the children at the same time.

Catherine woke when she heard Jacob's cry. Sadie and Emily had moved Jacob's bassinet earlier that evening into the girls' room. Sadie immediately went to fetch him and carry him downstairs to prepare a bottle of milk for him.

"I'm here," Emily said. "I slept on the divan last night so I could help with Jacob's feeding."

After handing Jacob over to Emily, Sadie went back upstairs to check on Catherine. The light was on in her room. "How are you feeling?"

"I'm afraid whatever is wrong with me isn't going to run its course for a while. Dr. Benton said if I wasn't better in a day or two, I might have to come to Houston." Catherine picked up the pill bottle and read the instructions-take two pills every six to eight hours. She unscrewed the cap and took out two more pills, downing them with a glass of water."

"Would you like some hot tea?"

"Not right now. Where is Jacob?"

"Emily slept on the divan. She is up now and tending to him."

"Go back to sleep. We'll see what the morning brings," Catherine said closing her eyes.

18

The medication sent by Dr. Benton seemed to ease the pain from the infection Catherine had developed in her uterus. She had promised that as soon as she was able to travel, she would come to Houston for a check-up.

Trent called the night before and Sadie informed him of Catherine's condition. He was furious that no one had called him. "I'll be there tomorrow. Don't tell Catherine I'm coming. I want to surprise her."

Catherine was asleep when Trent entered the room. He pulled up a chair close to her bed and stared at her pale gray face. He wiped a tear from his eye when he realized she seemed to have aged several years. He took her hand in his and kissed it. Her eyes fluttered and then opened. A smile appeared on her lips and she grabbed his hand in both of hers.

"You didn't need to leave your job. I'm not as sick as I look. Just tired."

Trent bent down and kissed her cheek. "Wild horses couldn't keep me away. You need to rest now. I'm taking you to Houston tomorrow morning. And I'm not taking no for an answer."

"Have you seen Jacob?"

"Yes, and I swear he's grown three inches in the two weeks I've been gone. The children really do miss you and are worried about you. I've assured them that you will be over your tummy-ache soon." They both laughed. "Promise me you'll call my office the next time you get sick. Sadie said you thought it might be an infection in your uterus. I spoke to Dr. Benton and he is expecting us tomorrow at ten o'clock. We'll have to leave early. Will you be up to it?"

"I'm feeling much better and should be able to travel." Catherine sat up and turned to get out of bed.

"No, you are staying put. I'll see to things here. You rest." He bent down and kissed her on top of her head, turned and left the room.

Trent joined the children in their playroom and sat in a chair next to Emily to watch her feed Jacob from a bottle. "He seems to be happy with the new bottle," Trent said. Adam crawled up on Trent's lap and put his small hands on each of Trent's cheeks.

"Is mommy going to be all right? Is her tummy ache better?" he asked.

"Yes. She is better, but just to be sure, we are going to Houston tomorrow to see the doctor."

"Will you bring mommy back?"

"We're coming back the same day if she is better. I promise I'll call if we spend the night. Mommy might be too tired to come home tomorrow."

"Mommy will be well soon, Adam," Daniel assured him. "I'll take care of you while they are gone."

"What about us?" Emma asked.

"I'll take care of all of us. Papa said I could."

"What about Sadie and Emily?" Adam continued.

"Papa said I was in charge so that includes everyone, including Martin."

Trent couldn't help but laugh.

Martin came in and told Trent he had prepared Catherine's dinner and did Trent want to take it up to her.

"Yes, by all means," Trent answered.

"Dinner will be ready shortly," Martin said.

"Don't wait on me. I'll be down after Catherine finishes."

Catherine was sitting up in bed when Trent came in with the tray. "Hmm, that smells wonderful."

"I understand you haven't been eating much," Trent said. "I'm not leaving until you finish everything on your plate."

Watching Catherine eat made Trent smile. "You are eating like a farm hand. I guess you are feeling better."

"Yes, Martin makes the best chicken and dumplings."

"I can see I won't have to stand over you. Do you mind if I join the children downstairs?"

"Of course not. Go."

The children were seated at the table when Trent joined them. Everyone bowed their heads as Daniel said the prayer. "Dear Lord. Make mama well and thank you for this food. Amen."

"Papa?" Adam asked.

"What is it son?"

"Can we go into mama's room tonight and kiss her goodnight or will we still catch her tummy-ache?"

"Mama would like that very much and she is feeling much better. You will not get sick from kissing her, I promise."

X X X

Later that evening Martin was pacing up and down his room. He was angry that he missed an opportunity to execute his plan. He had no way of getting in touch with Ira. They were still several weeks away and he was expecting a letter or a phone call any day now, telling him where they would meet up. The plan was to wait until Catherine returned to Houston for a weekend with her husband and he and Emily would take Jacob from his home to a small town south of Houston. He had been anticipating a letter from Ira giving him the arrangements and a phone number to call when the Matthews' trip to Houston was firmed up. *Patience, I have to be patient.*

The next morning Martin had the horse and wagon waiting before dawn when Trent and Catherine came out of the house. "Thanks for getting up so early, Martin. Don't want to miss the seven o'clock train."

Catherine slept with her head on Trent's shoulder most of the way to Houston. They arrived early at Dr. Benton's office and were escorted into a small examination room by the nurse. "The doctor will be right with you. Mr. Matthews, you will need to have a seat in the waiting room just down the hall. I'll come get you when the examination is finished."

Trent gave Catherine a kiss and smiled at her. "I won't be far away."

Thirty minutes later Trent was escorted into an office and took a seat next to Catherine. "I believe the worst is over," Dr. Benton said. "You responded very well to the new medication I prescribed. I'll give you some additional medication when you leave that should stop the infection from coming back. I suggest you stay in bed for a few more days, but its fine for you to walk to the dinner table and such. Just don't overdo it. Lastly, it's not a good idea to participate in any kind of intimacy. Wait a month or so or until after you have another period."

"My periods aren't always regular."

"Then it will be fine after thirty days or so; when you are back to your old self. Do you have any other concerns?"

"No, I don't think so. I appreciate your time and working me into your schedule today. Thank you."

"Would you rather go back to the apartment and rest for a while before we go back to Rosenberg?" Trent asked.

"No. Let's just go home. When are you due back at work?"

"I left a lot of things unfinished so I'll see you home and then head back up to Conroe. I'll try to come back for the weekend unless you want me to stay."

"No, why don't you see me to the train and then get the next train to Conroe? I'm sure we can use a phone somewhere in the hospital and call home and have Martin pick me up in the wagon."

"Are you sure? I don't mind the extra travel."

"I'm sure," she said with a faint smile. "I'm just going to sleep anyway."

Trent waited for Catherine to find a comfortable seat on the train before he leaned over and kissed her. "I love you," he whispered.

Before he left, he tipped the porter two dollars. "My wife has been ill and someone will meet her in

Rosenberg. Please see that she is kept comfortable and gets off in Rosenberg. She might be asleep."

"Yes sir. I will make sure she is awake before we reach Rosenberg," he replied.

19

Martin waited anxiously outside the train station. It was not in his nature to sit and wait, but he did. It would be too risky for him to attempt anything. His departure was only a few weeks away and getting caught stealing at this point would not be in his best interest.

The letter from Ira had come the day before. He was to go by buggy to Sugar Land, Texas. A hand-drawn map was on a separate sheet of paper with directions from Rosenberg to Sugar Land which was several miles southwest of Houston. There was a note that said it was about an hour by wagon. The address of a small hotel was also marked on the map along with instructions to check in under the name of Martin Harris.

Martin stood up when he heard the train whistle about a half mile out. He waited until he saw a porter helping Catherine step down from the Pullman car. He walked closer and took her small bag and then her arm.

"Thank you, sir," she said to the porter.

"How are you feeling, Mrs. Catherine?"

"Better, but a bit tired from my travels. I'm ready to go home."

Martin aided Catherine in her efforts to get up the long staircase in her house.

Sadie was waiting for her at the top of the stairs and helped Catherine change into a cotton day dress.

"I don't want to be in a nightgown all day and night. Perhaps if I dress I'll feel more like getting up from the bed," Catherine said as she changed.

Over the next few days, Catherine grew stronger. She was waiting downstairs for Trent to come home for the weekend when she heard the train whistle. The children came running into the living room screaming their excitement. "Can we wait on the porch?" Daniel asked.

"Yes, we will all wait on the porch." It was a scorching hot August morning and Catherine fanned herself during the wait.

"Here he comes," Adam screamed. They all stared up at their mother.

"Go on, just be careful of the potholes."

Sadie joined her on the porch carrying Jacob.

"I'll take him from you," Catherine insisted. She watched in anticipation as Trent picked up each child individually and kissed each one. Heart pounding, she patiently waited for Trent to join her on the stairs. "Welcome home."

Trent leaned down, kissed her and then kissed Jacob. "It's good to be home. You look like you are feeling better."

"I am, but you look very tired."

"I am. I'll spend an hour or so with the kids and then I'll have to get some sleep. I've been working round the clock on a new well that's come in outside of Conroe. I'm really beat."

After an early lunch Trent retired upstairs while Catherine helped put the children down for their naps. Afterward, she stopped in the kitchen where Martin was finishing the dishes.

"I couldn't help but notice you've been somewhat withdrawn lately. You aren't worried about what you and Trent talked about, are you?"

"Oh no, ma'am. It's just the heat. Emily and I aren't accustomed to this hot weather."

"Are you comfortable in your room? I know with the windows open there is fresh air coming in, but we could let you use the large fan in the examination room until I start seeing patients again."

"That would be very nice."

"You are welcome to take it up to you room now. It will cool the room down some before you retire for the evening.

"Yes, ma'am. That's very kind of you."

"And Martin, please don't hesitate to ask me if you need something. I should have thought about the fan before now. I'm very sorry."

Nodding, he thanked her again and went to collect the fan.

Catherine crept slowly into their room and joined Trent on their bed. There was a large fan in their room and Trent had it blowing directly on him. The long hot summers were dreadful and for some reason Rosenberg was much hotter than Galveston, she thought. *Galveston. I do hope someday we will all move back there.*

The weekend seemed to fly by. Jason and his family came Saturday afternoon and joined them for supper. They attended the small country church Sunday morning and then it was time for Trent to leave again. Martin made it a point to be on the porch when Trent left. "I'll see you in two weeks. Houston, right? You'll come to Houston?"

"Yes, I can't wait."

After Trent left, Martin turned to Catherine. "Will you be taking little Jacob with you on your trip to Houston?"

"No, I don't think so. He's taken well to the baby bottle and I owe my husband a little vacation away from home. I know that will mean extra work for you and I hope you don't mind."

"Oh, no ma'am. You deserve a vacation, too."

"Perhaps the next time Trent comes home you and Emily could go to Houston and see you uncle over a weekend."

"That would be very nice. She has not seen my uncle in several years," he lied.

Later that evening Martin wondered how Emily was going to react when he told her they would be leaving. Uncertain of her reaction, he decided to wait until the night before to tell her of his plan. Only he wasn't going to tell her everything. He would just say that he knew she longed for them to have a child and this was their opportunity. *We'll have our own son and make a new life in a different city. Yes, that is what I will tell her. She will never agree if I tell her I am selling the baby. I'll deal with the true facts once we are on our way to Sugar Land.*

After Emily went to sleep that night, Martin made a list of things he would do. On wash day Martin always carried the laundry upstairs after it was folded. Before taking it upstairs, he would slip a few diapers, baby night shirt, and two blankets out of the stack and hide them. He had begun boiling the baby bottles, filling them with milk, and storing them in the ice box. He would make sure to have at least three or four bottles ready. They could buy more milk if it took longer than a day to hand off the child.

After completing his list, he took a book from the top shelf of the bookcase and retrieved his hand-drawn map. He wanted to commit it to memory. The first town they would go through would be Richmond, then on to Sugar Land. Martin opened the book and found a larger map of South Texas. Carefully, he used his pocketknife to cut the map from its page. Next, he turned to another page and cut out both sides of the pages. Martin figured out when the two pages are put back-to-back, it becomes a large map of the United

States. Carefully he folded it and placed everything inside the large book. It was necessary that they travel light. A large book was too cumbersome. He would allow Emily one small satchel of clothing, and assure her they would buy what they needed. He would throw the few items he needed into her bag.

Everything was set now, and Martin stared up at the dark ceiling from his bed. His excitement caused him to be aroused and he woke Emily insisting she succumb to his wishes.

The next morning after breakfast, Martin asked permission to take a letter to the mailbox. "I wrote my uncle to tell him that we will be visiting him next month and I need to mail it."

"Sadie is going into town for supplies and she will be happy to mail it," Catherine said.

Martin hesitated and then said, "I'll see she gets it before she leaves."

"You can just leave it on the buffet up front. I have letters to be mailed also and you can put it with them."

"Yes ma'am."

Martin went to the front room and saw three letters sitting on the corner of the buffet. He looked at his before putting it under the stack. It was addressed to: *G. Perkins, General Delivery, Central Station P.O., Houston, Texas.* Martin smiled. *Sadie probably wouldn't remember the name if questioned later on.*

The letter provided the date-Saturday, August 16, 1906. *If complications arise, I will send a telegram to the same general delivery at Central Station post office.*

There could be all kinds of reasons for the date to change: Trent's work, Catherine's and the children's health, Emily's refusal to leave. *I'll be glad when I am done with this family.*

Two more weeks and Martin would be able to move on with his life. He had come to detest Rosenberg and the Matthews family. He hated the never-ending cooking and cleaning. He was not born to be a servant and he sure as hell hated the Texas heat. Chicago was further north and the temperature would be similar to England. *Two more weeks, just two more weeks.*

Thursday before Trent and Catherine were to meet in Houston, the phone rang and Martin answered. "Matthews's residence."

"Martin, I only have a few minutes, so could you get Catherine to the phone right away?"

Catherine was in the playroom with the children when Martin told her Trent needed to speak with her on the phone as soon as possible. Catherine rushed in and picked up the receiver.

"Hello darling," she answered.

"I'm afraid I will have to delay our trip for a week. We are having difficulty with a well and I can't leave. I'm so sorry my love. Perhaps you could come early Friday morning the next weekend."

"Of course. I do miss you terribly."

"I miss you, too. I have to go, my darling. I love you."

"I love you." Catherine placed the phone on the receiver.

"Is everything all right? Martin asked.

"Yes, but Mr. Matthews won't be able to take time from his work until the next weekend." Catherine turned and went back to the playroom.

Martin looked at the grandfather clock in the living room. It was 10:20 in the morning. Slipping out the back door, Martin ran quickly to the railroad station.

He dictated his message to the railroad clerk: "G. Perkins, General Delivery, Central Station P.O., Houston, Texas. Dear uncle. Package will be delayed one week. Pick up August 23. M.B."

"That will be forty-two cents, please." Martin took the coins from his pocket and handed the exact change to the clerk.

"Thank you." Martin looked at the large clock over the clerk's window. 10:34. He would be able to make it home before anyone would know he'd left.

Walking in the back door, Martin was greeted by Catherine. His brow was full with sweat. "Oh Martin, you shouldn't be working outside in this heat.

I've been looking all over for you. The children are getting hungry and we would like to have an early lunch. I hope that doesn't interfere with your schedule."

"No ma'am. I'll get started on it right away."

"Thank you, Martin."

Martin took a deep breath, relieved that he was not caught going into town. One more week. He just had to get through one more week. He was slowly losing his patience, but he forced himself to stay busy. All he could think about was Chicago. He had seen some pictures in the book of Chicago - *tall buildings, a large lake and cool weather. Ahh, yes, cool, cool weather.*

Friday came soon enough and Catherine was packed and ready to go. She kissed each child and reminded them about being good and minding Emily and Sadie. Martin was waiting in the wagon feeling the heat penetrate through his straw hat. He was relieved when she finished with her goodbyes. He helped her up onto the back bench.

Back at the house after lunch, Martin pulled Emily aside and told her to come back to the kitchen after she put the children down for their naps.

She did as she was told. "What is it you want?"

"Is Sadie lying down with the children?"

"Yes, why?"

"Come with me." Martin grabbed her arm and pulled her out to the stable. "What time will the baby wake up for a feeding tonight?"

"He's sleeping through the night now, and wakes between five and six. Why?"

"You do want a child of our own, don't you?"

"Yes, you know I do."

"I do too. We'll be leaving tonight after everyone is asleep and taking Jacob with us."

"You mean we are going to kidnap him?

"Call it what you want. You can't bear me a son, and you love him. I can see that."

"But…"

"No. You will not argue with me. Keep your mouth shut. I've already taken diapers and the other things he might need and have packed them away. Think about a few things you want to take with us. We will put everything into one bag and buy what we need along the way. At midnight, I will prepare the horse and wagon. You will quietly go into Catherine's room and get Jacob. You'll bring him to the stables and we will leave. Everything has been arranged. Do you understand?"

"I, I guess I do," she said meekly. "What if we get caught?"

"That is not going to happen. Stop over-thinking everything. I'm in control and you will do as

I say. Don't make me angry. You know what happens when I get mad."

Emily turned and left. She stopped short of the door when she heard Martin call her back.

"Don't you dare say a word nor do anything that would give our plan away. Do you understand me?"

"Oui." Emily had to force the word from her mouth.

20

Anxious to see Trent, Catherine boarded the nine o'clock train to Houston. It was hard to leave the children, but she was looking forward to some alone-time with Trent. Her milk had finally dried up and she was beginning to feel like her old self. She had brought along her last medical magazine and began thumbing through it. The advertisements were interesting, boasting a new skin cream to reduce rope burns, bee stings and other skin irritations. Another was an automobile ad with an advertised price of seven hundred fifty dollars. She studied it for a moment and wondered if some day they might own one. She closed the magazine and stared out the window. The thought of seeing Trent made her feel anxious. Their anniversary was a week ago and somehow the date had been overlooked by both of them. She would make it up to him.

Catherine was surprised when Trent met her at the train station that morning. She was not expecting him until suppertime.

Her heart melted when she saw him standing at the station with flowers. She almost jumped into his arms when she stepped onto the platform. "I've missed you so much," she shouted over the roaring of the steam engine.

"These are for my special girl."

"You have more than one?" she teased.

"One is more than enough for me."

"The flowers are beautiful. Thank you."

They walked inside the train station, hand in hand. Trent led her to a waiting area and motioned for her to take a seat. 'Are we waiting for someone?"

"Not exactly, we are waiting for another train."

Catherine gave him a questioning look.

She turned and looked up at the blackboard of incoming trains and outgoing destinations.

The next departure was in thirty minutes, destination, Galveston.

She studied the board and then looked at Trent. He was grinning from ear to ear. He took two train tickets from inside his vest pocket and handed her two round trip tickets to Galveston.

"Happy belated anniversary."

"Oh, Trent. You know how much I love Galveston."

"I certainly do. You talk about it all the time."

She leaned over and kissed him on the cheek.

"How are our children?" he asked.

"They miss you and they each drew a picture for you. I'll show them to you later."

"I didn't know Jacob could draw."

"Don't be silly. He's blowing bubbles now and he laughs all the time. He's beginning to develop his own little personality."

They both laughed. "You are beautiful when you laugh, Catherine. I want this to be a second honeymoon for us. I never really gave you an anniversary present."

After Trent retrieved his bag from the baggage area of the station, they waited on the outside platform for its arrival. Once seated, they held hands and watched through the window with excitement as the engine began to pick up speed.

When the train crossed over the bayou, Catherine's eyes were glued looking out at the vast inlet of water. "I can't wait to show you some of my favorite places. If the tenants are home, I'll show you the house we built after the great storm. I thought it might be our retirement home one day."

"I wouldn't mind living in Galveston after I retire. By the way, we're staying at the Tremont Hotel. Should we hire a horse and buggy?"

"The train station is only a few blocks from the Tremont. Let's walk."

Trent had never been to Galveston and he was in awe of the city. "I haven't even seen the gulf and I'm in love with this place."

"I know. It's so romantic."

After they checked into their hotel, Trent hailed a carriage. They rode the full length of Broadway and then looped around to Seawall Boulevard. The name was changed from Beach Road when the seawall was completed earlier in the year. The day was clear and you could see several ships in the gulf.

"It's taken the city years to recover from the storm in 1900. They have made significant improvements, including building this seawall. The grade-razing project and excavation for the seawall required a large influx of laborers. I'm still in awe of the progress. I believe the first section of the seawall was finished two years ago."

Catherine showed Trent where the orphanage had been and then they rode to the cemetery. As soon as the buggy stopped, Catherine was on the ground and standing over two graves.

"They replaced the marker on my mother's grave. It was lost in the terrible storm." Trent stayed close to Catherine who was staring at Anne Eastman's grave. The other marker beside it was John Merit. "I loved them both very much," she said wiping a tear from her eye. She knelt and Trent did the same, waiting while she prayed. When Catherine got up, she walked several tombstones over and knelt again. Trent waited this time. When she finished she returned to Trent's side.

"A friend?"

"Yes, she was our landlady, Minnie Wyman. She was one of the first people we met when we came to America and she was very kind to my mother and me. John and I stayed with her for a while after the storm while we built our new home. When she died she left the boarding house to me in her will. I've used some of the funds to renovate our home in Rosenberg and put the remainder in savings. Yes, she was a wonderful friend."

Catherine gave the address of her house to the driver. Twenty minutes later, they stopped in front of the address Catherine had given him. Piles of sand were piled up around the new piers and the landscaping was bare. "Oh my! I've not seen our street since the city razed the elevation of the houses. Everything looks so different," Catherine said.

Trent got down and helped Catherine. "We'll only be a few minutes." Trent said to the driver. They walked up the steps to the front door and knocked. An older woman finally came to the door, and they introduced themselves.

"My name is Catherine and this is my husband, Trent Matthews. We are the owners of this house. I know I should have asked Mark Graham, our real estate agent, to call first, but this was an unexpected trip. We were wondering if we might take a look inside the house." We won't stay long."

Hesitating, the woman at the door wiped her hands on her apron and said: "I'm in the midst of cleaning, but I guess it's all right. Please overlook the mess. Like I said, it's cleaning day."

"I greatly appreciate your willingness to let us come in and I'm very sorry for the interruption," Catherine apologized." Catherine took Trent's hand as they made their way through the house. The rooms were sparsely furnished and all the curtains were closed. The tenant finally turned on an overhead light.

"It gets too hot if I leave the curtains open and the lights on. I usually clean in the dark," she said and then chuckled. "I understand," Catherine said, feeling the warmth. The lady walked over and turned on a fan.

They picked up their pace and quickly walked through the remainder of the downstairs and the upstairs. Once they were back outside, Catherine turned to Trent. "I guess we should have called first. The house looks nothing like it used to. It's rather depressing."

"It looked great to me. The rooms are large and I think it would suit our needs perfectly," Trent commented. "Don't fret. You can add your special touch if we decide to make this our home."

They had practically ridden around the whole island, stopping for hot dogs from a street vendor who was selling them by the beach. They ate them in the carriage on their way back to the hotel.

"Thank you for this wonderful surprise, Trent. It's been a lovely day" They rested for a while, changed into different clothes and took a carriage to St. Mary's Catholic Church for confession and five o'clock Mass.

Father Jonathan was surprised when Catherine said, "Bless me Father Jonathan, for I have sinned.

My last confession was about a year ago when I married my new husband."

"My sweet little Catherine. Please come see me after Mass."

"My husband is Catholic and will come into confession after me. We would be delighted to visit with you."

Father Jonathan continued with Catherine's confession and then Trent's. After Mass Father Jonathan invited them into his study.

"It is my pleasure to meet you, Trent. You have made an excellent choice having Catherine as your wife. She is a real treasure."

"I certainly can't argue that."

They chatted for a while longer and invited Father Jonathan to dinner, but he had to decline because he was already engaged for the evening.

"Will you both be coming back to church on Sunday morning?"

"I'm afraid not," Trent said. "I have some paperwork at my office that I need to work on tomorrow when we return to Houston. We'll be going back to Rosenberg on Sunday. The children will be anxiously awaiting our arrival."

Father Jonathan chuckled. "Yes, I can only imagine. I enjoy getting your letters, Catherine, and I am so happy for both of you. I think you are well suited for each other."

After saying their goodbyes, they stopped at a seafood restaurant their hotel concierge recommended that was located on the Strand. They sipped wine and dined on sea bass, scallops, Cajun rice, and peas.

"Oh my, I don't think I can eat another bite. Do you mind if we walk for a while before we go back to our room?" Catherine asked.

"That's an excellent idea."

Walking hand in hand down the Strand, they stopped and purchased some gifts for the children." I can understand why you love Galveston. I've only been here one day and I'm in love with it, too."

"Then you really wouldn't mind moving here someday?"

"If I could quit my job tomorrow, I would. Maybe we should consider selling the Rosenberg property and moving here. It would only add about fifteen minutes to the trip we already make and there would be a lot for the children to do here. I think they would love it."

"Do you really mean it? The lease on my house is up in February next year and after the tenants move out, we could move in. Alex Cooper has expressed an interest in purchasing our Rosenberg property."

"I know. He made me promise if we were to sell, he would have first choice."

"The house is only four bedrooms. Sadie could share a room with the girls, but we wouldn't have a place for Martin and Emily."

"Martin and Emily won't have a problem finding another family to take care of. He could easily get a good-paying job in one of Houston's finer restaurants."

"Could we really do this, or are we just dreaming?" Catherine asked.

"You want to, don't you?"

"Yes. I shouldn't have any problem finding additional help once we get settled. I might even be able to work part-time at St. Mary's or even teach at the medical school. Oh Trent, I'm so excited."

21

Earlier Friday evening Emily joined Martin in the carriage house. She noticed a few things piled beside the door including a new leather briefcase with a handle. "I don't know if I can go through with this. I'm so scared."

"Did you say something to Sadie?"

"Of course not. But stealing another woman's baby is against God's will. He will punish us."

Martin snarled back at her. "You and your crazy religion. There is no God and the sooner you get that through your head, the happier you will be. Now go pack what will fit in your satchel."

Emily's shoulders slumped, and she fought back her tears as she walked to the wardrobe and removed her work clothes. She pulled a simple dress over her head and then a skirt over that. She put a long-sleeve blouse over her short-sleeve dress and tucked it into her skirt.

"Are you crazy woman? You'll die from the heat." Martin shook his head in disgust.

"There is barely enough room for my underclothes and wearing two layers will give me a change."

"I have a sack with a blanket and diapers for the baby. I'll collect the bottles when you go upstairs and get Jacob."

Emily was a bundle of nerves. She reached up and rubbed the back of her neck. Feeling as if she would explode, she said, "This is not easy for me."

"I just want you to be happy," he said, putting his arms around her. "No one will know us. I already have new names picked out for us. You will be Mrs. Elaine Carter, Jacob will be Josh Carter and I'll be John Carter. Nice American names. When we get to Chicago, we'll apply to the government for new papers." He bent down and kissed her sweetly on the mouth. She tensed and wanted to back away, but she did not want to antagonize him.

"Where is this Chicago?" she finally asked.

"Many miles north where it is cooler. It's a large city. Probably a three-days ride by train." Martin tilted her head up. "Smile for me. I promise you will be happy."

Emily tried to smile, but her heart was not in it.

"You need to sleep for a while. I'll wake you up when it is time," Martin said, picking up her satchel and heading for the door.

"Where are you going?"

"I'm taking these things downstairs to the wagon. I need to tend to the horse and make sure she eats well and has plenty of water. I'll be running her hard."

Emily sat in a chair and chewed on her fingernails. She really wanted no part of this. There were too many things that could go wrong. Still, she loved Martin and did not want to go against him. Perhaps, later when they got to Chicago, she could send a letter and explain everything to Catherine. She knew Catherine would be terribly upset about losing her child. Trent would probably kill Martin if they were found.

Emily moved about the apartment rubbing her arms and feeling trapped. Nothing made sense to her anymore. She knew she would not be able to sleep. Heavy footsteps on the stairs alerted her to Martin's return. She moved to the bed and lay down on top of the covers. The door opened and Martin grabbed the remainder of the items sitting by the door. He left again. There was a gnawing pain in the back of her throat and she swallowed hard. Bile rose from her stomach and she became nauseated. "Oh Lord." She raced to the bathroom and leaned over the toilet vomiting when Martin came back in.

Martin watched Emily from his chair as she grabbed a towel and wiped her face. He glared at her. He was too disgusted to say anything so he leaned back and crossed his arms, his cold dark eyes shooting daggers at her.

Martin paced the floor as Emily closed her eyes and tried to sleep. He retrieved the map from his back pocket, sat down in his chair, and studied it. It was after one o'clock in the morning when Martin woke Emily from a deep sleep. "Get up, use the toilet, and wash your face." Emily did as she was told. Afterwards, he motioned for her to follow him into the main house. "I'll wait at the bottom of the stairs for you to go up and get the baby. Whatever you do, don't wake him." He spoke in a hushed whisper.

As they entered the main house, Martin turned on a small oil lamp at the foot of the stairs so Emily could make her way up the staircase. A three-quarter moon filtered enough light through the windows for Emily see her way into Catherine's room. Staring into the room, she saw the outline of Sadie's body on the bed. She listened and could tell Sadie was asleep from her deep breathing.

Emily's hands were shaking. She shook her hands and flexed her fingers to relieve her stress. Looking down into Jacob's crib, the urge to run brought a cold chill. *I can do this. My little innocent angel is asleep. I have to do this*. Carefully she reached in and picked him up. Clutching him and his blanket to her body, she crept slowly out of the room and down the stairs where Martin was waiting.

Martin took her arm and led her roughly out the back door. When they got to the stables, the horse and wagon were ready and waiting. Martin helped her up to the back bench.

"Sit on the floorboard and wedge yourself between the seats. There's a blanket and pillow you can lean against. Once we are out of town we will be traveling fast and I don't want you to fall off."

Emily plopped down on the floor of the wagon and adjusted herself and Jacob up against a pillow. She looked down at the sleeping child and willed herself not to cry. *This is wrong, this is so wrong.*

"The baby bottles are in a bag under the bench. Make sure you can get your hands on them before we leave. We won't be stopping."

Martin took the reins under the mare's jaw and led her outside the barn and onto the road. Making sure there was no one around, he climbed onto the bench and clicked his tongue. The mare moved forward in a smooth trot. A half mile later, Martin picked up the whip and cracked it causing the mare to leap forward in a steady trot.

A slow smile crept across Martin's face, he was proud that he had executed the first part of his plan without any problems. He pulled back on the reins to slow the mare's pace when he arrived at a sign pointing to the town of Richmond. The map indicated there was a road that bypassed the town and picked up on the main road on the opposite side of town. He watched carefully for the cut-off and took the turn.

Back on the main road again, Martin saw automobile headlights coming toward him. They appeared to be far away, but he did not want to be seen. He pulled off the road and hid the wagon behind a cluster of trees. He took a deep breath and decided to get down and relieve himself. Afterward, he searched for the lights. The car had passed. When he climbed back onto the wagon, Emily looked up and asked, "What's going on?"

"Nothing, just needed to take a break, that's all. Go back to sleep. We'll be there soon."

Emily's mouth was dry and her back was hurting. Her arm had fallen asleep, and she carefully adjusted Jacob so he would lay in her other arm. It was extremely uncomfortable, but she knew she could not say anything. She silently prayed God would have mercy on them. Wiping a tear from her eye, she looked down at the sleeping child. The realization that they had a child of their own began to sink in. *Perhaps Martin will change now that we have a son.*

The wagon bounced continually as they hit every pot hole in the road. Martin's thoughts turned to Ira and Gilda and he wondered if he could trust them. He needed a plan in case they didn't show. Several ideas raced through his head. He could feel the anxiety creep up his back- side. Biting his lower lip, he glanced back at Emily. She had expressed to him on many occasions she did not approve of his bad habits. *I'm too old to change now. I would never be happy just being a family man. No. If Ira doesn't show up, I'll just check them into a hotel and leave. I'll go to Chicago myself.*

"Click, Click," he said through gritted teeth after he was back on the main road. He whipped the reins and the mare lunged forward into a steady trot. A sharp cry from behind him brought him out of his thoughts. He jerked his head around. Emily was struggling to reach the bag with the bottles. *I'm not stopping to help her*. The continued cry of the baby only infuriated him more. A second look showed Emily with the bottle trying to coax the baby to drink the cold milk. The baby continued to cry. Angry, Martin stopped the wagon.

"Can't you shut that kid up?"

"He's all wet and I'm wet too. I need to change him."

Martin paced outside the wagon while Emily changed Jacob's diaper and put a dry clean baby blanket around him. His cries died down to whimpers. Emily settled down between the seats and the infant began taking the bottle.

"Do we have to go so fast?"

Martin didn't answer. "Yaah!"

It was close to three o'clock in the morning when the Sugar Land sign indicated they were getting close to town. Martin tried to bring the map up in his mind, but for some reason he kept drawing a blank. He remembered the name of the hotel was the Wayward Inn. It was just off Main Street. Twinkling lights appeared on the horizon and a few minutes later, he saw a small wooden sign with an arrow pointing to the Wayward Inn. He stopped the wagon in front of it and looked back at Emily who was staring at him. "Stay down. I'll be back"

He jumped down from the wagon, stretched his sore muscles, then strolled toward the Inn. A dim yellow glow shimmered from a lamp in the corridor. He pulled the screen door open and turned the knob. The battered wooden door creaked open. He stepped inside. An old gray- haired man sat in an overstuffed chair with his feet propped up on an ottoman. His mouth was slack, eyes closed, and he was snoring a tune of contentment. Martin walked over and kicked the ottoman out from under his feet.

"What the...who are you?"

"You got a room?"

The man got up. "Sorry, I didn't hear you come in." He turned and looked at the clock on the wall. 3:22 AM. You're up mighty early. Where you from?"

"Houston. How much for one night?"

"That'll be two dollars. Are you alone?"

"My wife and baby are in the wagon outside."

"Good. I don't like no whores in my establishment."

Martin removed two dollars from his pocket and handed them to the man.

Nodding his head, he said, "3-A, down this hall and to the left."

"Do you have any mail for Martin Harris?"

"Yes, I believe I do." The man handed a letter to Martin, who stuffed it in his pocket.

"Can I leave my horse and wagon outside 'til morning?"

"I think it will be ok, but I'm not responsible if anyone decides to take it."

Martin went outside and saw Emily standing beside the wagon with the baby. He grabbed the bag of bottles and their satchel. "C'mon." Emily followed him inside.

The room was dank and musty. One window was open and after Martin switched the light on, he walked over and opened the other two windows to create some ventilation. Taking the envelope from his pocket, he ripped it open and read: *Second floor, 2-B.*

Martin turned to leave.

Worried and standing in the middle of the room, Emily asked, "You're not leaving us alone, are you?"

"I have business to take care of." He quickly left the room wanting to slam the door, but stopped and quietly closed it.

Jacob was awake and drooling. "It's gonna be fine. Your daddy will take care of us, I promise." Emily swayed while holding Jacob and began singing a song in French. His hand went to her face as he longingly stared up at her and smiled. She continued singing and began to feel more relaxed.

Martin went back to the front corridor and started up the side staircase, taking them two at a time. He tapped lightly on the door of 2-B. It opened immediately.

Ira was in an undershirt, pants with suspenders dangling from the side, and barefoot.

"'Bout time you got here. You got the goods?"

22

A hint of daylight was peeking through the shade when Sadie rolled over in her bed, and saw Emma staring down at her. "Emma, what are you doing up?"

"Where's Jacob?"

"What do you mean? He's in his crib." Sadie sat up and stared, trying to focus on the crib. Even though the moonlight was casting shadows in the room, it was difficult to see into the crib from Catherine's bed. Sadie jumped up and ran to the crib almost knocking Emma down. Emma started crying. Sadie snatched her up in her arms and stared down at the empty crib. She turned and ran into the boys' bedroom. *Daniel was six years old and small for his age, but maybe Jacob cried and Daniel took him out of the crib while she slept.* The boys were asleep and Jacob was not in either bed.

Carrying Emma, Sadie ran into the girl's bedroom where Isabelle was sitting up in bed rubbing her eyes. Sadie put Emma in her bed. "Stay in your room until I come back and get you, do you understand?" The girls looked at her blankly as Sadie left the room.

Sadie searched the entire downstairs and then ran out the kitchen door and up the stairs of the carriage house. There was no need to knock on the door as it was standing wide open. Sadie's heart felt like it had stopped beating. She turned on the light and saw a half-empty closet and an unmade empty bed. The small bathroom left no clues either. Hyperventilating, she desperately tried to breathe. Backing up against the wall, she shut her eyes tightly and bit down on her lower lip. She began gasping for breath and crying.

"No, no," she screamed out loud. Finally her breathing returned. Panting, she rushed back down the stairs and opened the door to the stable.

The mare and wagon were gone. Reality presented a whole new picture to her. *They're gone and they took Jacob.*

She stood motionless in disbelief trying to hold back a flood of tears. *No. I can't cry, the children. I can't upset them.* Sadie rushed back into the house and ran through every room finding all of them empty. She stopped at the table and picked up the note Catherine had left for her. She looked at the list of numbers: *Houston apartment: HO2-4762. Pick up the phone and the operator will answer. Ask her to call the number for you.* Sadie did just that.

Lillie, the phone operator placed the call and let it ring ten times. "No one is answering, Sadie. Is there another number you want me to call?"

"Yes, could you please ring Jason Brady for me?"

A sleepy gruff voice answered. "Hello."

"Jason?"

"Yeah. Who's this?"

"It's Sadie. Catherine and Trent went to Houston for the weekend. I think Martin and Sadie have taken off with Jacob. I can't find them anywhere and the horse and wagon are gone."

"Are you sure? Maybe Jacob got sick during the night and they took him to Houston."

"No, I slept in Catherine's bed last night. I would have heard Jacob if he got sick."

"I'll be right there. Have you called Catherine?"

"Yes, but they don't answer."

"Stay with the children. I'll call the sheriff and be there soon."

Sadie heard Jason hang up the phone and then she heard Lillie's voice. "Sadie, do you want me to call anyone else?"

She wasn't surprised that Lillie had listened in on the conversation. Everyone in town knew there were no secrets. "No, I'll wait for Jason and the sheriff."

"Well now, how 'bout I call the Mathew's number in Houston every fifteen minutes. If they've gone out to an early breakfast, I'll catch them when they get in."

"Yes, I would appreciate that."

Sadie turned around and saw all four children standing at the bottom of the stairs. Daniel was the first to speak. "Why would Miss Emily and Mr. Martin take Jacob?"

Sadie took a deep breath. "I'm not sure, but Jason and the sheriff will be here soon and we have to get dressed. Let's go up and get your clothes on. Daniel, dress yourself and then help your brother."

"Yes, ma'am."

Sadie ran to the wardrobe and pulled out two play dresses for the girls and a housedress for herself. She dressed herself first and then the girls. She heard banging on the front door. "Here take your socks and shoes into the boys' room and ask Daniel to help you put them on." Racing down the stairs she quickly reached the front door and opened it.

Jason was standing at the door with his gun in his holster. Sheriff Boise was half-way up the street coming toward the house on his horse. Jason waited until the sheriff got off his horse and joined him.

"Shelby will join us shortly to help you with the children."

"Will she bring your son?"

"No, my grandparents are in town and he will stay with them."

"Now start from the beginning. When did you first notice Jacob was gone?"

"I was still asleep when Emma came in to Catherine's room and woke me. She asked where Jacob was. I went to his crib and when he wasn't there, I checked the boys' and the girls' rooms first. I thought that maybe Emily had taken him to her room so I went to the carriage house. Their room was empty and then I checked the stable. The wagon and the mare are gone. I came back in the house, checked the downstairs and then called the Matthews in Houston. They were not there, so I called you, Jason."

"How long ago was that?" the sheriff asked.

"Not long, maybe thirty, forty minutes ago."

"We'll take it from here, Sadie. You take care of the children," Jason said.

Sadie sighed in relief. She was glad to have two adults making the decisions. She turned and went back upstairs and found the children standing at the top of the stairs. They had done a decent job of getting their shoes and socks on. Adam's shoes were on the wrong feet and his shoelaces were untied. "Adam wants you to help with his shoes," Daniel said. Sadie sat on the top step and put Adam's shoes on the right feet and tied his shoelaces.

"There now, who's hungry?"

Sadie led the children into the kitchen and told them to sit at the table while she collected bowls for cereal. When she opened the refrigerator, she noticed

Jacob's bottles were gone. She saw Jason and the sheriff through the window coming from the carriage house, and she opened the back door for them. "All of Jacob's milk bottles are gone," Sadie said. Jason and the sheriff looked at each other.

"How many do you think were in there?" Jason asked.

"Maybe three or four, I'm not sure."

"When did you last feed him?"

"I gave him his last bottle around nine o'clock last night and he usually wakes up around five in the morning for his next bottle, but...." She stopped.

Sadie looked up at the clock on the kitchen wall. It was six forty-five. They must have taken him during the night since I slept through his five o'clock feeding."

Jason and the sheriff went back to the carriage house and gave it a more thorough search, hoping to find some clues as to where they might have gone. Other than clothing and normal household items, they found nothing. As they started out the door, Jason looked up and saw a large book on the top shelf of the almost empty bookcase. He reached up and grabbed it. He held it up and shook it. A small piece of paper fell to the floor.

Sheriff Boise stooped down and picked it up. It was a plain piece of paper torn from a tablet with some kind of list written in a foreign language. The only thing in English was the date - Friday, August

23, 1907. "This is yesterday's date," Jason said looking over his shoulder.

"What do you think it means?"

"I bet Catherine will know what it says. She knows several foreign languages," Jason said.

"Let's go back and search the main house and see if we turn up anything," the sheriff said. He refolded the paper and put it in his shirt pocket.

23

Catherine and Trent spent a lazy morning in their hotel, ordering room service and enjoying each other's company. The closeness they felt from their intimacy the night before still radiated a glow from Catherine's cheeks. "This has been the most wonderful surprise," Catherine said. "We need to do this more often."

"I'm all for that. Maybe we could bring the children here before school starts?"

"That sounds like fun."

"I wish we could stay another day, but I need to take care of some business in Houston this afternoon."

"It's fine. I need to shop for some things. Daniel's birthday is in a couple of weeks and he wants a new truck."

After breakfast, Catherine and Trent gathered their things and Trent went to check out. "Do you mind calling home and checking on things? I told Sadie we would be in Houston and I neglected to call her with the change in plans."

Trent bent down and kissed her. "Good idea. I'll be back in fifteen."

After finalizing his checkout, Trent asked where he could find a phone to make a collect call. "Write down the number and I will have our operator place the call. There is a phone on the table by that chair." The clerk pointed. "When it rings pick it up and the operator will give you instructions." Trent waited patiently and picked up the phone when it rang. He heard the operator ask the person on the other end of the line if they would accept a collect call from Trent Matthews.

"Yes ma'am," a male voice said.

"Jason? What are you doing at my house this early in the morning?"

"I'm afraid I have some bad news." Jason proceeded to tell Trent about the events that had taken place. "Unfortunately, we don't know much more and we have no clue where they went. We did find a note, written in French, I think, with yesterday's date on it. Catherine reads French, doesn't she?"

"Yes. Thank you for being there, Jason. Catherine and I will be on the next train out. We may have to shuttle through Houston first and make a connection to Rosenberg, so it will be a couple of hours. We'll get there as fast as we can."

"The sheriff has gone to the train station to send telegrams out to surrounding cities, giving Martin and Emma's description to the authorities."

"Thank you Jason."

Trent hung up the phone as his face turned grim. He ran his hand through his hair and dreaded giving Catherine the bad news. He sat for a few minutes filtering the information and thought of how he might break the news to Catherine. He stood up and walked the two flights of stairs to their room.

Catherine noticed a strange look on Trent's face when he entered the room. His shoulders were slumped, and she immediately knew something was wrong. She went to him. "What is it?" she said almost in a whisper.

"Martin and Emily have taken off. They took Jacob with them."

"Oh, oh no. It's my fault. I trusted them too much," she whimpered and then fell in the chair.

"It's nobody's fault. We can't sit here blaming ourselves. Jason and the sheriff are at the house. They found a handwritten note in French that was left behind. We need to get home as soon as possible." Trent grabbed both bags and started for the door.

"Catherine!" He raised his voice.

She stood and followed him.

X X X

There was only one train scheduled out of Galveston to Rosenberg and it wasn't leaving until late in the afternoon. A train leaving for Houston was about to depart, so Trent and Catherine boarded just in time. He gave the porter his portion of their round-trip tickets. Finding their seats, Catherine found it next to impossible to stop her tears. Trent put his arm around her and pulled her close to him. "We'll get him back. I won't stop looking until I find him. I promise you that."

They barely made it on the twelve o'clock train leaving Houston for Rosenberg. It was one-fifteen in the afternoon when the train pulled into Union Station. They walked the quarter mile to their home. It was unusually quiet when they entered. Shelby met them at the door and hugged Catherine.

"Thank you for helping Sadie with the children. Has there been any more news?" Catherine asked. Shelby shook her head.

Trent sat their bags on the floor by the stairs and the adults went into the living room.

Sheriff Boise had returned to the house after he sent off the telegrams and he took the piece of paper from his pocket and handed it to Catherine.

"It's Martin's writing," she said looking at. "It's some kind of a list of things to do. 'Get diapers, Jacob's milk, blanket.' His writing is difficult to read, but I think it says, 'Tell Emily to pack light and that we will keep Jacob for ourselves.' There is another mention of getting the maps from the book, I think. That's all. It's dated yesterday." Catherine put her hand to her head and rubbed it, closing her eyes. "How could anyone do this?"

"I have an idea," Jason said. "My hound dog, Butcher, is a pretty good tracker. They are probably fourteen hours ahead of us, but if he could pick up the trail, at least we would have an idea of the direction they went." Catherine looked up with hope in her eyes.

Trent stared at him. "How soon could you be ready?"

"Give me thirty minutes."

Trent looked at Jason's wife.

"By all means," Shelby said giving her approval. "You would do that for us."

"I'll repack my satchel and be ready when you get here."

While Trent went upstairs to get his saddlebags, fresh clothes and his gun, Catherine and Shelby went to the kitchen to prepare some beef jerky, rolls, and cheese for the men's trip. She filled a large canteen with water and waited for Trent to come back downstairs.

Sadie walked into the kitchen and hugged Catherine. "Do the children all know?" Catherine asked.

"Yes ma'am. They overheard me talking to the sheriff. They are taking their naps right now. I've tried to reassure them that Jacob will be home soon. I'm so sorry. I slept in your room last night to be close to Jacob and I didn't hear them when they took him."

Sadie started crying softly. Catherine walked over and put her arms around her.

"We'll find him. Trent and Jason are going to hunt them down and bring him back," Catherine said, reassuring herself as well as Sadie.

Catherine and Shelby watched as their husbands headed southeast on horseback. Butcher had picked up the scent immediately from one of the mare's old blankets. Trent also had one of Jacob's dirty blankets to let Butcher sniff if they lost the trail of the horse and wagon.

"They will find him, Catherine. Butcher is a great hunter," Shelby reassured.

"There's no need for you to stay, Shelby. Go home to your son. It could be days before we hear anything."

After Shelby left in her buggy, Catherine sat in her office with her head in her hands. She tried to think if there had been any signs. Something she should have seen. Then she remembered Sheriff Boise's visit about Martin being a thief. *Why didn't I pay more attention? How could I have not seen the signs? I should have heeded the sheriff's warnings.* Still in shock, Catherine felt the only thing she could do was pray.

Sadie knocked on her door and opened it. "The children are up from their naps and are in the playroom, if you feel like joining us."

"I'll be right there," Catherine said. Trying to put a smile on her face, Catherine went to the playroom. The children were overjoyed to see her and began asking questions about Jacob.

24

Gilda woke and sat up in bed as the two men began bickering.

"My wife has the baby in our room. Do you have the money?"

"Yes. The solicitor could only get three thousand dollars. We have to split it three ways. It's a thousand or nothing," Ira said, bluffing.

Martin thought for a few minutes. "How do I know you are telling me the truth?"

"You don't. But you have two choices. Keep the boy or take the grand."

"I want to see the money," Martin demanded.

Ira walked over and took a wallet from inside a briefcase. He counted out ten One Hundred dollar bills. "We're losing time here. I want to see the baby."

Martin left the room and went downstairs. Emily was lying on the bed with Jacob beside her. Martin picked up the bag with the baby items and milk bottles in it. "I'm taking the baby."

"Why?" Concerned, Emily quickly got up from the bed. "I'm trying to get him back to sleep. Where will you take him?"

Martin took a step toward the baby and Emily moved between them.

Tears began filling her eyes. "You never intended for us to keep him, did you?"

"Get out of my way."

"I'm not going to let you take him." Emily grabbed the bag from Martin and began backing away.

His fierce eyes turned purple and then black. A slow grizzly growl pursed from his lips.

Without a second thought, Martin struck Emily under her jaw with his fist. The blow hit her with a force that picked her off the floor and into the air. She dropped the bag and collided with a wooden chair, breaking it as she hit the floor.

Martin picked up the bag, replacing the two baby bottles that had rolled out, and scooped Jacob into his arms. He never looked back, as he pulled open the door and left.

He raced back up the stairs and knocked on the half-open door. Ira was close by and pulled the door open.

"Here's the kid and a couple of bottles." Gilda got up and took the baby as Jacob began to cry. She laid him on the bed and examined all of his parts.

"He appears to be a healthy baby," Gilda said, getting a bottle of milk from the bag.

Ira picked up the money he had laid out on the dresser and handed it to Martin. Martin counted the money to himself and said, "Nice doing business with you."

When Martin returned to his room, Emily was awkwardly sprawled out on the floor with her eyes closed. He walked over and used his boot to give her a push. "Get up," he said gruffly. Emily didn't move. He stared at her for a while unsure what to do. Finally, he knelt beside her and felt for a pulse. There was none. Noticing her head was at an odd angle he opened one of her eyes and saw no movement. Blood had begun seeping from her mouth.

Martin moved over to the wall and sat on the floor with his knees up in the air, arms dangling on top of them. His breathing was ragged. Looking up at the ceiling, a lone tear fell down his cheek. He reached over and picked up her hand and attempted to remove her wedding ring. He wanted something to remember her by. The extra pounds she'd put on made the removal impossible. After several attempts, he got to his feet. He paced the floor, ran his fingers through his hair, and began mumbling under his breath. *Damn it, damn it, damn it. It wasn't my intention to kill her.*

Martin walked over to the bed, pulled the covers back, and returned to Emily. Kneeling down beside her, he removed the blood from her lips and mouth with his handkerchief, and undressed her. Lifting her from the floor took some effort. She had allowed herself to gain at least twenty-five pounds over the past year, and he struggled as he lifted her onto the bed. After pulling the covers up under her chin, he gathered his things, turned and gazed at her one last time. He had killed the one person in his life that actually loved him.

After closing the door he locked it and put the key into his pocket. He would throw it away later. He could hear the old man snoring and he quickly passed by him and out the front door. Martin climbed onto the wagon and clicked his tongue. The mare took off in a steady trot.

The heat radiated from the morning sun as dawn began to appear. Wanting to dump the horse and wagon, he saw a sign pointing to a livery stable. The blacksmith was hard at it, shoeing a horse. "You the owner?" Martin asked, still sitting on the wagon.

"That be me. I'm Sam, Sam Wilcox."

"I'm looking to sell or trade my wagon for some tack and saddle. Don't need the wagon anymore."

Sam put his mallet down and circled the wagon. "That mare looks pretty worn out."

"She's fine."

"Follow me and I'll show you what I got." Martin followed him into the stable. "This here is a three year old stud. I'll trade him, tack and saddle for say another fifteen bucks. He can run a hell of a lot faster than your mare." Martin looked the horse over.

"Can you walk him a bit? I don't want a limper."

Sam put a bridle on the horse and walked him out in the yard.

"Deal." Martin paid the man fifteen dollars and waited for Sam to put the blanket, tack and saddle on the horse.

"Where you headed?" Sam asked.

"South," Martin said as he climbed into the saddle and rode off towards Houston.

Sam watched him for a while shaking his head.

Stupid foreigner, he doesn't know north from south.

X X X

Jason and Trent followed Butcher watching his pace carefully as the dog alternated between running and walking. The men were an hour and a half into their ride when the hound left the road and went to some trees. He was excited and barking. Jason got off his horse, walked over and bent down. Trent followed him." It's a wet diaper," he said. "I think Butcher's on the right track."

A short while later they arrived on the outskirts of Richmond. Butcher seemed confused as he sniffed the road turning around in circles. Finally, he began trotting on a dirt road that went around the town.

Jason and Trent looked at each other, but followed Butcher. The trail was picked back up again on the main road. It was getting hot and Butcher was panting heavily. "We better stop by those trees and give him some water and let him rest a few minutes. He's not traveled at this pace before and especially in this heat." They waited while Butcher lapped up water Jason poured from his canteen into a tin pan. Both men drank water from their canteens and wiped sweat from their brows with their handkerchiefs.

"I'll never be able to repay you for this," Trent said. "You're a good friend."

"You would do the same for me."

They made frequent stops to allow Butcher to get his wind and drink water. It was five o'clock in the afternoon when Butcher stopped in front of the steps of the Wayward Inn. The two men got off their horses and walked into the hotel. They were greeted by the old man behind the counter. "Need a room?" he asked.

"No," Trent said, "just information. We are looking for a man and woman with a baby. The man has a French accent. Did they stay here?"

"What's it worth to you?"

"They kidnapped my son," Trent said as he reached over the counter, took the man by his shirt, and pulled him forward.

Jason grabbed Trent and he released his grip. "Easy now," Jason said.

The old man stared at him. "I figured that foreigner was up to no good."

"Then they were here," Trent said.

"She still is, but the man ain't nowhere around."

"What about the baby?"

"Cleaning lady went to the room about two o'clock to make the bed and said the lady was sound asleep. Figured they might be staying another night, so she locked the door and left."

"We need to talk to her."

Grabbing a set of keys from the wall behind him, the man took off down the hall and began banging on the door of room 3-B. "I never saw her leave. Maybe she and her husband had a fight and she thinks he is coming back. Don't blame her for not opening the door."

Trent pushed the man out of the way and began pounding on the door again. "Emily, Emily, open the door. I know you are in there," Trent said. They waited a few more minutes. Trent grabbed the keys from the old man and unlocked the door. The three men stood over Emily staring down at her. Her face was stone cold white and the smell of death had already begun to emanate from her body. "Go get the sheriff," Trent said.

Trent and Jason searched the room and found a wet cloth along with a soiled diaper. They looked up when they saw the sheriff come in the door.

"What's going on?" the sheriff growled.

Trent told the sheriff about the kidnapping and that the deceased woman was the wife of the man that kidnapped his son.

"I got a wire this morning about that. Any idea where the man might have taken him?"

"No, but we need to talk to the innkeeper some more. I don't think he could have done this by himself," Trent said turning to the innkeeper.

"Who else stayed here last night?"

"Follow me," the innkeeper said.

Looking down at the registry, he said, "A Michel Kelley from Galveston, an older man wearing a clergy collar; then there was a man and a woman; Tom Perkins from San Antonio. He looked like a professional gambler. She was a real looker. Heard him call her 'Gilda.' Then there was the man and woman in "4-B." He signed his name as Martin Harris."

"Can you think of anything else?"

The man thought for a minute. "Why yes. Martin Harris asked if he had any mail. That Perkins man left a letter for Harris before going to his room. I gave the letter to Harris."

"What room was Perkins in?"

"He was upstairs in 2-B. They left about the time the rooster crowed. Just got a glimpse of them heading out. I was asleep in my chair over there and I saw them leave. Come to think of it, she was carrying something in her arms. Could have been a baby."

"Could we see the room?"

"Ain't nothing in there. Cleaning lady already did her job and some other people are in there now."

The sheriff had been listening as Trent talked to the innkeeper. He decided to interrupt. "You will need to give me descriptions of the couple that took off with the baby," the sheriff said to the innkeeper. After getting the information, he turned to Trent. "Sorry about your son. There's not much I can do. They are probably in the next county by now. What should I do with the lady's body?"

"Bury her in a pauper's grave," Trent said and walked outside. Butcher sat up and started barking. Jason joined Trent and they left.

"Do you think Butcher's found another scent?" Trent asked Jason.

"I don't know."

Butcher continued barking and ran out into the street. Trent and Jason got up on the horses and followed him. Butcher led them to a blacksmith's stable. Butcher ran up to the wagon and started barking. The blacksmith came out of the barn.

"Where did you get this wagon?" Trent asked.

"Traded a three year old stud for a mare and the wagon. Ain't stolen, is it?"

"Was the man alone?"

"Yes."

"Did he say where he was going?"

"Said he was heading south, but he took off towards Houston. It was an honest trade. I didn't know it was stolen."

"Keep it. The man took my three month old son, too."

Jason looked at Trent. "Let's take Butcher back to the hotel. If Jacob left with another couple, maybe he can pick up the scent again."

Back at the hotel, Trent handed Jacob's small blanket to Jason. "C'mere boy; take a good sniff." Butcher pushed his nose into the blanket and barked. He ran to the side of the hotel and began sniffing at some tire tracks. He sat down.

Trent and Jason went back inside the hotel. "How did the couple arrive here?"

"Drove up in one of those new motor cars. Everyone came over to inspect it once the couple went to their rooms. Don't see many like that around here. Had the name Oldsmobile printed over the gears. Whatever that means."

Trent and Jason walked back around the hotel and looked to see if there were any tracks. A slight wind had blown in earlier and created a small dust storm. If there were tracks from the automobile, they had vanished. As they walked into the street, the dust began to kick up again.

"How fast you think those automobiles go?"

"Faster than our horses, I'm afraid," Trent replied.

"Maybe it's time for a short break," Jason said. The two men stood in front of the steps of the hotel. Jason looked up and down the street and noticed a small wooden building that said cafe. "We haven't eaten all day; let's go across the street and get some food. We can talk about our strategy while we eat."

They found a table by the window and stared across the street at the hotel. "What's going on over there? I saw you two talking to the sheriff," the waitress said.

"What else did you see?" Trent asked.

"Uh uh. I ain't getting involved in somebody else's business."

Jason studied her. "This man's son was kidnapped sometime Friday night and his trail led us here. If you saw something, you need to tell us."

"I have to be at work at five o'clock every morning and I live a half mile out of town. 'Bout a quarter mile before I got to town, a lone man on a horse was riding lickety-split towards Houston. Damn nearly ran over me."

"What else?" Trent asked.

"Y'all want something to drink while we talk?"

"In a minute. Tell us what you saw," Trent said.

"Well, we don't see too many of them new automobiles around here. None that stay long, I mean. But there was one parked outside that hotel when I was walking in. They didn't see me, but I saw them. A man and woman carrying a baby got in the automobile and took off in the direction of Houston. Now, what can I bring you two to eat?"

They gave the waitress their order and continued talking. "That's two witnesses that say they were headed to Houston. Think that's our best option?" Jason said.

Trent sighed, thinking for a while. "The Texas Rangers have offices in Houston and they have more resources there. You and Butcher have done a good job getting us this far. It's too late for you to head back home this evening. I'll put you up in the hotel for a night. I'm heading to Houston. That way I can go to the Ranger's offices as soon as they open up in the morning."

"Are you sure about that?"

"Yes."

"Why do you think he killed Emily?"

"I haven't spent much time around the two of them together except at the dinner table. I did pick up on his dominance over her and she never talked back to him. I figured it was part of their French upbringing. Maybe she just got in his way. I'm sure the Rangers will look into their past."

25

Trent left on the nine o'clock train that evening after spending another hour with the sheriff and Jason. Looking out the window, his thoughts were on his son and Catherine. There was little to see as he stared out the window. The lights inside the train flickered and he looked up as a man and woman with three children and a baby walked past him. He stared at them hoping to get a better look. They did not fit the description of the man and woman the innkeeper described and they had three children in tow. He tried to look closer at the small child, but they passed by too quickly. He fidgeted in his seat and finally got up. As he walked past them, he took a closer look at the infant. A pink blanket partially covered its face and the sprigs of baby hair showing were a different color than Jacob's. Trent continued into the next car. *It wouldn't hurt to go through all of the passenger cars and look. I can certainly hope.*

Trent stopped a porter in the next car and asked if there were any more families with babies on board. "Not tonight," he answered.

His shoulders slumped and he returned to his seat. It was like trying to find a needle in a hay stack. Trent's eyes filled with tears. *Is my son gone forever? Why was I so selfish? Had we stayed in Houston instead of going to Galveston we might have gotten to him sooner. I should have listened to Sheriff Boise when I was warned that Martin was not the man we thought he was.* Martin was a thief and he had taken the most valuable of treasures- his son.

When Trent arrived at the apartment, he stood outside the door holding the key. He knew as soon as he entered the apartment he would not be able to hold it in any longer. Once inside, a waterfall of emotion poured from his body. He fell to the floor pounding his fists and bellowing. This day would be a day he would never forget.

He didn't know how long he lay on the floor looking up at the ceiling, but he knew he had to pull himself together and call Catherine. Looking over at the clock on the mantel and noticing the time of 11:22 PM, he knew Catherine was probably sleeping on the downstairs divan waiting to hear from him. He pulled himself up, picked up the phone, and asked the operator to place the collect call.

Catherine answered on the third ring. "Yes, I'll accept the charges."

Trent found it difficult to speak.

"Trent, are you all right?" she asked.

"We were too late. Butcher tracked them to a fleabag hotel in Sugar Land, but we missed them. I'm not sure what happened, but we found Emily dead in their room. We found out that Martin traded the wagon and mare for another horse and took off alone toward Houston."

"And Jacob? What happened to Jacob?" she asked almost out of breath.

"The innkeeper said there was another man and woman there who checked into a different room and when they left, they had a baby with them. They did not have a baby when they checked in. They left the hotel before dawn this morning in an automobile."

"Oh no!"

"Jason spent the night there last night and he's coming back to Rosenberg with Butcher and the extra horse tomorrow morning. He promised to stop by and fill you in on all the details. I took the nine o'clock train to Houston this evening so I can be at the Texas Rangers' offices when they open in the morning."

"The Texas Rangers?"

"They have the resources to hunt this couple down. If Jacob can be found, they will know what to do."

"If..." Catherine put her hand to her mouth to hush her scream.

"I'm sorry, Catherine, I don't know what else to do."

It took her a moment to answer. "You've done everything you could. Will you call me after you've spoken to the Rangers?"

"Of course, darling."

"We need to pray," she said almost in a whisper.

"Yes, of course. I love you Catherine. We have to be strong for Jacob."

"I love you too, my darling." She could barely get the words out. Hanging up the phone, Catherine fell on the divan in tears.

26

After leaving the hotel in Sugar Land, Gilda and Ira drove northwest in Ira's newly- acquired Oldsmobile. It was now his prized possession, one that could make his business more profitable. Transportation of the children using the rails was too risky now and the law was not equipped with automobiles yet, at least not in Texas.

Gilda held Jacob up on her shoulder patting his back as he continued to squirm and cry. "What's the matter? Can't you shut him up?"

"He needs to be fed. There's no more milk. We need to stop and get some."

Ira cursed under his breath. "We're about ten miles south of Brenham, can't he wait?"

"He'll just keep crying."

Several miles later Ira noticed a herd of Jerseys and Holstein cattle being led out of a corral. Turning off the road, Ira headed for the barn.

An older man with a beard, wearing coveralls and checkered shirt, looked up and noticed the strange piece of machinery. The noise from the engine caused the cattle to scatter into the open pasture as the man scrambled to get out of the way.

Once he got closer, the farmer said, "Ain't never seen one of them before. Heard about um. You ain't from around here. What do you want?"

"My wife and I are traveling to visit some friends in Brenham and our baby needs milk. I'll be happy to pay you if we could fill up a couple of his bottles with some of that fresh milk of yours."

The farmer walked around to the other side of the vehicle and stared down at Jacob. Gilda moved the blanket down to give him a better look exposing his birthmark. The farmer looked up when he saw his fifteen year old son approaching from inside the barn.

"Wow, Pops, it's one of those new-fangled automobiles everyone is talking about. Can I go for a ride in it?"

"Not today, son. These people need some milk. Go fill up a bottle with this morning's milk and bring it out."

The farmer's eyes went back to Jacob, who was now looking at him with curiosity. "That's a mighty pretty baby. Must be three or four months old."

Ira and Gilda did not answer the man. "How much do I owe you for the milk?" Ira asked.

"Twenty cents ought to do it."

Ira reached into his pocket and took out some coins and handed them to the farmer. The young boy returned with a quart bottle of milk and handed it to his dad. "That ought to take care of him for a while," the farmer said, handing the milk over to Ira.

"Much obliged. As soon as we fill his bottles, we'll be on our way."

The farmer and his son went back to the barn, stopping to look one more time. "You think he's somebody famous?" the boy asked.

"Don't think so, Buddy. Probably a business man."

"She sure is a pretty lady. Don't see many like her in these parts," Buddy remarked.

The farmer stooped down, picked up a straw of hay, stuck it in his mouth, and began chewing on it. "City folks," was all he said as he walked back inside the barn.

Buddy continued to watch as the vehicle and its passengers drove away, leaving a cloud of dust and debris circling the air.

X X X

The train from Austin, Texas, was fifteen minutes late. Ira paced keeping his eyes on two police officers working the area. The first whistle caused him to look up and he was relieved the train would soon be there. Ira stood beside a bench, leg propped up, and finished his cigarette. He threw it down and stomped on it. As the people got off, Ira carefully scanned the boardwalk of people approaching the depot. The solicitor had given him a description of the couple.

After the crowd moved inside the station, a distinguished man and smartly-dressed woman stood looking up and down the boarding area. Ira approached, "Mr. and Mrs. Armstrong?"

Ira tipped his hat to the lady and shook hands with Nathan Armstrong.

"This is my wife, Trudy Armstrong."

"It's a pleasure to meet you. Do you have any luggage?" Ira asked looking at the attaché case Nathan was holding.

"No, we only plan to stay long enough to get the child and take the four o'clock train back to Austin."

"Well, my hotel is only a short walk if you will follow me."

The couple followed behind Ira and they were at the hotel in less than fifteen minutes. Ira tapped on the door of his hotel room. "It's me, Gilda."

Gilda opened the door and stepped back shielding the Armstrongs' view of Jacob who was asleep in the middle of the bed. "I assume you have the remainder of the payment in your case," Ira said.

Nathan nodded. "We'd like to see the boy before I hand it over." Gilda stepped away and the Armstrongs walked closer to the bed.

"Oh my," Trudy said, almost in a whisper. "He's so beautiful. May I?" she asked leaning over and removing part of the blanket away from his body.

"What is that mark on his chest?" Nathan asked.

"It's a birthmark. The doctors said it would fade over time. He's perfectly healthy," Ira said.

"He eats right good, too," Gilda added.

"Mr. Tyson said the mother and father were killed shortly after the baby's birth. Were there any other relatives?"

"Not really. The mother was from an affluent family and the young man she was to marry had no living relatives. You can understand the scandal it would have caused the family if they were to keep the boy. No, he's from good stock. As you can see, he's going to be extremely handsome someday."

"May I pick him up?" Trudy Armstrong asked.

"By all means."

All eyes were on Trudy as she carefully lifted Jacob and cradled him in her arms. "Does he have a name?"

"You may call him whatever pleases you. He's three and a half months old and will have no memories of where he came from."

Jacob opened his eyes and then yawned. Eyes fluttering, he slowly stretched his arms, looked at Mrs. Armstrong and farted. Everyone laughed. Beautiful brown eyes bulging, Jacob turned red, grunted, and dirtied his pants. The men stepped away from the smell. Mrs. Armstrong returned him to the bed and said, "I do hope you have some clean diapers."

While Gilda went to the bathroom to get a pan of warm water and wash cloth, Trudy began removing Jacob's diaper. Nathan watched as the diaper was removed and his bottom cleaned.

"I must say, he's a fine specimen of a boy," Nathan remarked opening his attaché case. He counted out twenty-five hundred dollars in one hundred dollar bills and handed it to Ira. We have a change of clothes for the boy and three empty bottles. If you have any leftover milk, we would appreciate getting it. We plan to purchase some milk from the dining car on our trip back."

Jacob cooed as Trudy dressed him, kicking his feet, and sucking on his fist. When they got ready to leave, Gilda handed her two diapers. "These are the only clean ones he has."

"Thank you," Trudy said. "I packed a few myself just in case.

Once the Armstrongs left with Jacob, Ira and Gilda sat on the bed and re-counted the money.

"What do you say we both get cleaned up and find ourselves a nice restaurant where we can celebrate?"

Gilda grinned and threw herself back on the bed grabbing the money and throwing it up in the air.

"My dear," Ira said, joining her as he took a fist full of hundreds and threw them up in the air. "Have you ever made love on top of twenty-five hundred dollars?"

27

Trent sat stone-faced on a bench as he waited to speak to a ranger. "Sorry to keep you waiting, Mr. Matthews. I'm Steven Morris, Texas Ranger."

"It's a pleasure to meet you."

Once they were settled in Morris' small office, Trent began pouring out all the details, careful not to leave out anything. Morris listened carefully and said nothing. After Trent finished his story, he stared at Morris who had been taking notes.

"Our job as Texas Rangers is to handle cases that are too big for local agencies to handle. We cover all of Texas, but we don't usually leave the state. That's where the U. S. Marshals come in. They are a governmental agency and when we have a case such as this, we work together. I hate to tell you this, but your case is not unique. We have five to ten baby abductions a month come through this office. It's a big business."

"So what are you saying?" Trent asked.

"We'll do everything we can to hunt down and find who did this, but sometimes the babies are passed on many times. Each time the baby is sold, the purse gets larger. We investigated a case several months ago and traced the baby through several solicitors before it ended up with a family out of state."

"Did you get the child back?"

"Unfortunately, no. These criminals rarely leave anything behind. We track them through witnesses and snitches we have out in the field. Because you acted so quickly and followed the trail before it got cold, we might be able to pick it up from there, but I don't want to give you false hope."

"Tell me, where do these babies end up? Who goes out and buys a child?"

"You'd be surprised. There are many barren families that are willing to pay up to three to five thousand dollars for a baby. The solicitors tell them the child came from an unwed mother whose family has forced her to get rid of it. The adoptive families choose to believe them and pay the bounty. I've had cases where the child has been ripped from the mother's arms while they weren't paying attention. One time a mother was distracted while another criminal replaced her baby with a doll in her carriage. It's becoming a big business."

Trent stared in disbelief.

"Do you think if I sent a sketch artist to this innkeeper that he will be able to provide us enough details to come up with a drawing?"

"Yes, I believe the waitress at the cafe will, too."

"Are there any distinctive marks such as a birthmark on your son?"

"Yes, yes, he has birthmark a couple inches down and left of his Adam's apple about a half inch in diameter. It looks like a fish."

"That's very important," Morris said.

"What can I do?"

"Go back home to your wife and kids. Every minute we waste talking takes time away from our investigation. I have a form here I need you to complete. We'll do a thorough background on this Martin Boudreaux. If he came through the port of New Orleans and caused any trouble there, they'll have a record. I'll contact the New Orleans Port Authorities. Meanwhile, answer every question. It will take you a few minutes so I'll check back with you."

When Ranger Morris came back to his office, Trent had finished filling out the form. Looking over the form, Morris said, "I know it will be difficult for you to heed my advice, but you need to go back home and continue with your normal life. You have four other children and a wife that need you there. I see you work away from home and have an apartment here in Houston."

"Yes, Catherine and I were married over a year ago. Jacob is my blood. I kept my apartment in Houston since I work in Conroe. Apparently Martin planned this kidnapping when he found out Catherine and I were going to spend the weekend away."

"I thought you said you were in Galveston when this happened."

"Catherine loves Galveston and I surprised her with a side trip for our anniversary. We didn't call home until the next morning. That's when we found out about Jacob."

"I'm going to be frank with you Mr. Matthews."

"I want you to be."

"We might never find your son."

"Is there at least a fifty-fifty chance?"

"I'm afraid not. Of all the cases we've handled, I'd say maybe one out of every hundred."

Trent stared at him in disbelief.

"I'm not saying we aren't going to do everything we can. I have a five year old boy and a three year old girl. I don't know what I would do if I were in your shoes."

Trent's brow furrowed and he tried desperately to hold back the tears. "I just want my son back. If we offered a reward and plastered it in all the newspapers, would that help?"

"Let me consider that. Meanwhile, I'm putting you in another room so you can work with our sketch artist. We need a good clear picture of him. From what you have said, Jacob's been passed on to another criminal or a solicitor, but we need to put a stop to Martin's escapades. Get him off our streets."

Trent nodded his head.

"The *Houston Chronicle* newspaper is two streets over. Your story would make front page news. There's a reporter there by the name of Agnes Sweeney. Tell her I sent you. Your son's birthmark may be the key to finding your son. If she takes an interest in your story, she could become your new best friend."

A few minutes later, Morris introduced another ranger to Trent. "This is Ranger Terry Andrews. He was with the rangers for over a year before we discovered his artistic talents. He will ask you some questions, so answer them as best you can."

Trent looked first at a blank sheet of paper in front of Ranger Andrews and then up at the ranger.

"Describe this man's face. Does he have a round jaw?"

"No, it's more square. He's French and about twenty-eight, maybe thirty years old. French.

"What about his eyes and nose?"

Trent thought for a minute. "His nose is slim at the top but fills out towards his nostrils. Bushy eyebrows and dark eyes." He watched as the Ranger began filling in the man's face. "He has thick, kind of puffy lips. Yeah, that's it."

"What about his hair line?"

"He combs his hair almost straight across and he has long sideburns. His ears stick out a bit, too.

Make his hair a bit fuller." The artist continued shading in around the eyes.

"The man's Adam's apple is more pronounced." The artist continued making changes as Trent spoke. fifteen more minutes and he was through.

"Wow, that's incredible. It looks just like him."

After finishing the sketch, Trent left and made his way to the newspaper's offices. "I'd like to see Agnes Sweeney, please," he told the receptionist.

"Did you have an appointment?"

"No, but Texas Ranger Steven Morris told me she needed a good story."

The secretary left her desk and went down the hall and through an open door. She returned, followed by an older stout woman with wiry red hair. She looked to be in her late forties or early fifties, and about twenty pounds overweight .She was well-dressed and had an intimidating look about her. Her dress was adorned with pins; a cross, some kind of shield of honor, and another for twenty years of service at the *Houston Chronicle*.

"Hello, I'm Agnes Sweeney, and you are?"

"Trent, Trent Matthews." Agnes grabbed Trent's hand and gave it a firm handshake.

"I only have about fifteen minutes, so you'll need to talk fast." Agnes turned and walked toward the open door she came out of, expecting Trent to follow.

"She says that to everyone," the receptionist whispered and smiled.

"Thanks," Trent answered.

Trent settled into a chair across from Agnes. Files, magazines, newspapers, and books adorned her desk. A lone black Underwood typewriter sat in the middle of her desk with a fresh, clean sheet of paper in the roller.

"You don't mind if I type while you talk? Do you?"

"Uh, no, of course not."

"Go ahead."

Trent cleared his throat. "Like I told the receptionist, Steven Morris at the Texas Rangers office told me to get in touch with you."

"Why don't you tell me something I don't already know," she said.

A bit intimidated, Trent adjusted himself in his seat. "My son, Jacob, has apparently been kidnapped by some criminals and I'm trying to find him." Trent waited while Agnes tapped keys on the Underwood."

"Is that it?"

"Uh no, I thought you might need some time to write that down."

"You let me worry about that. Just speak in your normal voice. I'll take care of the rest."

Trent started at the beginning, stopping occasionally to compose himself. He stopped when Agnes jerked the white paper from her typewriter and quickly replaced it with another clean sheet of paper. "Go on," she said. Trent continued, fascinated with her agility and ability to type so fast. Six pages later, Trent stopped. Agnes kept typing.

When she finished, she removed her last sheet and picked up the other papers, reversing the sheets until the first page was on top. She stared at him for a while and adjusted her glasses on her nose.

"I'm so sorry. These people have to be stopped. I'll need you to sign a consent form and give me the correct spelling of this sinister man's name. Did you get with their sketch artist at the Rangers offices?"

"Yes, he asked me to come by before I left to approve the final drawing, so I'm on my way back there."

"Ask him to call me when he finishes and I'll send a runner to pick up a copy. It'll be in tomorrow's paper if I get the picture before three o'clock today. Here are a couple of my cards with phone numbers. If you will update me on any progress, I'll see it gets in the paper."

"Thank you, you've been very kind."

Trent stopped at the Ranger's office and approved the sketch. "Heard you talked to Agnes?" the artist said. "She's really good at her job."

"I hope she's good enough to find my son."

"The Sunday newspaper has a huge distribution. The *Houston Chronicle* is the only newspaper that's sent to all the main cities in Texas via the railroad. Even gets mailed up- state."

"Good to know."

"Hey, if I were you, I'd buy up several dozen of those newspapers and send them to all the sheriffs in some of those little towns. You never know."

"How soon will that sketch be ready? Trent asked.

The main one is done. I've sent it downstairs to one of our older smaller printing presses. They are running off copies as we speak."

"Mind if I wait around and get a few of those copies. I want to take one to the newspaper."

"Sure thing. I'll go check on it."

A short while later the artist returned with a stack of pictures. Trent stared into the face of Martin Boudreaux. He was amazed how much the picture favored Martin. After dropping off a picture at the newspaper, Trent decided it was time to go home.

28

The mid-day sun was beating down on the dry brown cotton fields as the train made its way to Rosenberg. Trent replayed his conversation with the Texas Ranger over and over in his head as he stared out the window from the train. He looked up when he saw another family take a seat in front of him. An older woman was with them and she was holding a baby. When they settled, Trent leaned forward to take a closer look at the child she was holding. It was a boy, probably four or five months old, and larger than Jacob. Trent wondered if he was going to spend his lifetime staring at babies. He was sorry he didn't stay at home more than a couple of weeks after Jacob's birth. His own selfishness took him back to his job, leaving his son and the other children vulnerable to a madman.

Deep in his heart he knew that he probably would never get Jacob back. *Please dear God, if you don't bring him back home, let him be given to a good family.*

He dreaded walking the short trip home from the train station. He had no idea how he was going to tell Catherine what Steven Morris told him. She would be devastated. The children would be waking from their naps about now and it would be difficult to talk. They would want all of his attention.

When he got to the front door, he unlocked it with his key and went in. He could hear the children in the back room playing a game and he quietly went up the stairs. Sighing, he sat on the bed and took off his shoes and slipped into his house shoes. He was hot and tired from the long exhausting day, but he forced himself to make an appearance.

"It's Papa," Isabelle said when she looked up. All of the children screamed and ran to him.

Trent sat on the floor while the children circled around him. "Papa, did you find Jacob?" Daniel asked.

"No, son, not yet, but we will." The room went silent.

Noticing Trent's exhaustion, Catherine said. "Children, your father and I have things we need to discuss. Continue your game with Sadie. We'll be back shortly." Catherine took Trent's hand when he got up and they went upstairs.

"I'm afraid there is no good news. There is going to be a write-up in the *Houston Chronicle* tomorrow."

Catherine just looked at him unable to say anything. Finally she said, "Jason gave me some more details. I don't quite understand why Martin killed Emily. It's unthinkable."

"She might not have wanted to go along with his plan, but I'm afraid we'll never know. The Texas Ranger said baby-stealing is a new way criminals are making money. They are selling the babies." Catherine stared in disbelief.

"Selling the babies?"

"Yes, to families where the women are unable to conceive. They are bringing thousands of dollars."

Tears filled Catherine's eyes. "We have to find him."

Trent put his arms around Catherine. "The Ranger said our chances were one in one hundred. He said we needed to get on with our lives."

"Get on with our lives," she almost shouted. "How can we get on with our lives?"

"We have four other children to raise. What do you suggest I do? He's probably in another state by now."

"I don't want to argue about this. They'll find him. I'm certain of it." Catherine turned and left the room. As she made her way downstairs, the phone rang. Trent hurried after her.

"Hello," Catherine answered. "Yes, he's right here. It's Jason."

"Hello. No, I'm afraid I don't know anything else. The *Houston Chronicle* is running an article in the paper tomorrow and we are hoping it might flush out something. Not every child has a birthmark in the shape of a fish on his chest. I appreciate that, but I'm going to take the family up to the cafe for dinner later. Maybe we can get together tomorrow before I leave for work. Sure. Thanks for calling." Trent hung up the phone and looked at Catherine.

"You're going back to work tomorrow? Like nothing happened?"

"What do you want me to do? I have no more time off. If I lose my job, we'll go through our savings in a matter of years. Do you want that? I can't spend my days moping around here. It's not going to bring Jacob back."

Trent went to the kitchen and grabbed the whiskey bottle from the top shelf. He filled a water glass half full and drank it down without stopping. Refilling the glass, he sat at the table and put his head in his hands. *I have to go back to work. I need to stay busy or I will go crazy.*

Catherine and Trent did their best to stay polite around the children. The tension seemed to ricochet off the walls. By the time Trent pulled his bag from the wardrobe to pack, they were barely speaking to each other. Neither knew what to say to the other.

Catherine was the first to apologize. "I'm so sorry. I'm so sorry I brought that man into our home."

Trent took her into his arms as she cried. "You can't stop bad people from doing bad things, Catherine. I'll try to come home next weekend."

When he got to the train station, he stopped at the small newsstand and purchased a Houston paper. The headline read. "Babies for Sale." The article read more like an editorial warning parents to safeguard their children when they went out. It gave statistics about the number of children in Texas that were missing. In the past year, there had been nine abductions in the south Texas area. Finally, the last paragraph said, "Read more about a recent abduction in Rosenberg, Texas, on page four. He turned to that page and staring back at him was the drawing of Martin Boudreaux. It went into more detail about the abduction and gave a description of Jacob, including the unusual birthmark. At the end it said, "Anyone having information about this should contact the Texas Rangers." A phone number was given.

Trent folded the newspaper and tucked it under his arm. He wanted to believe his son would be found, but he knew the reality of it all was that Jacob was gone forever.

X X X

When Trent got to his apartment in Houston, he took out Steven Morris' business card and looked at it. He picked up the phone and asked the operator to connect him to the number. The phone rang several times before someone picked it up.

"Yeah, he's here. Hold on."

"Morris."

"I wasn't sure you would be there this late on Sunday. It's Trent Matthews."

"I'm glad you called. A body was found in an alley a couple of hours ago. It's at the police station. They called me because they think it could be Martin Boudreaux. Are you up to meeting me at the police station?"

"Yes, I'm in Houston. I'll be there shortly."

Trent left immediately and hopped on a trolley. Morris was waiting in front of the station when Trent walked up to him. The two men entered the building and took the stairs to the basement. They walked down a long hallway and opened a door that said, "Morgue." Morris flashed his badge at a uniformed man and went through another door. A man in a white coat was hovering over a body that was partially draped in a white sheet. The two men approached and again Morris flashed his badge at the coroner.

Trent stared at the face of the man that had prepared his meals, helped him build a fence and a play area for his children, and then stole his son. For a moment he said nothing.

"It's him," he finally said. "What killed him?"

"A single gunshot to the side of his head. Died instantly. Do you know if he has family?"

"No, he doesn't."

"Then who are you?" the coroner inquired.

"I employed him."

"Will you pay his burial expenses?"

"No, he can rot on the side of the road for all I care."

Morris led Trent upstairs into an empty office. Sergeant Max Chambers with the Houston Police Department joined them. "I'm sorry to hear about your son, Mr. Matthews," he said. "I read about it in the paper this morning and Steven has filled me in on some more details. We suspect Martin Boudreaux was robbed. His pockets were turned inside out and he had no wallet or identification. I called Ranger Morris because I recognized him from the picture in the newspaper. The likeness was uncanny."

"I don't suppose you have any information about the couple that might have my son, do you?"

"No, I'm afraid not. We had a few other cases where a man and woman working together may have been involved in some other kidnappings. These folks don't hang around very long after they do their business. They move on to another city where no one knows about them. There's a playground of children out there for the pickin' and these people do their job well. I wish we had answers for you. I know the Texas Rangers are diligent in their efforts and if anyone can catch them, they will."

29

Trent returned to Conroe the next day and found it difficult to concentrate on his work. His boss, Clarence, came in and sat across from him. "Want to talk about it? I was surprised when I read Sunday's newspaper. Frankly, I didn't expect to see you back at work."

Trent sat back in his chair. "The Texas Rangers are doing everything they can to find him. They suggested I get on with my life. Said the chances of getting Jacob back was a hundred to one. They think he is in another state by now. If there was anything I could do, I'd be doing it. Sitting home in Rosenberg won't accomplish anything so I figured here I could get my mind off of it."

"I understand, but I still think taking a few days off might be a good idea. You are caught up with all your important duties here at work and I can spare you for a couple of days. I'm sure Catherine and the children would love to have you. Take a few sick days. It's not a suggestion. It's a direct order."

When Clarence left his office, Trent gathered up his papers and put them away. By the time he arrived back in Houston it was late afternoon, so he went to his apartment and poured himself a stiff drink. He paced the floor, thinking and trying to make some sense of what had happened. He knew he was just as much at fault as Catherine. He, too, enjoyed the luxury of having another man and woman take care of the house and children. He didn't want to believe that Martin might be a thief. Guilt began breaking down his will and this time he poured the drinking glass full with whisky. The bottle had been three-quarters full when he started and an hour later, the bottle was empty.

The next day when Trent woke up, he was spread-eagle on the floor. The pounding in his head was a thunderbolt of pain. He raised himself up on his elbows and immediately fell back down and closed his eyes. Drawing a deep breath, he let it out and then stared up at the ceiling. He lay unmoving for a few minutes and then slowly raised himself up. Feeling nauseated, he crawled into the bathroom and threw up.

A few minutes later he grabbed a washcloth that was laying on the side of the tub, reached over, and wet it under the faucet, and put it to his face. The cool rag momentarily brought him some relief, but he needed something for his headache.

Slowly he got up, opened the medicine cabinet and found the aspirin. He took out three and plopped them into his mouth. He leaned under the faucet and slurped the water, letting it drip down his chin. Drying off his mouth with the washcloth, he rambled into the bedroom and fell on the bed. Feeling as though he had been robbed of his sanity and with every muscle aching in his body, he closed his eyes and fell back asleep.

When he woke, it was mid-afternoon and the phone rang. His headache was better, but he still felt out of sorts as he jaunted toward the telephone. "Hello?"

"It's Morris. Are you all right? You sound terrible."

"I had a little too much to drink last night if you want to know the truth."

"Can't say I blame you. The reason I called was to tell you that Ranger Armstrong just got back from Sugar Land and has completed a sketch from the eyewitnesses; the innkeeper, and waitress. "We have several copies for you to pick up if you want to come by later on."

Trent sighed. "I'll be there shortly."

Trent managed to give himself a quick shave and he splashed water under his arms and then dried them off. He quickly dressed and decided the ten-or fifteen- block walk to the Rangers offices would be good for him. He stopped at a street vendor's wagon and purchased a can of soda and a corned beef sandwich. He gulped it down in several bites and continued walking.

When Trent got to the Ranger's office, Steven introduced him to a couple named Robert and Andrea Summers. "Their one year old daughter was kidnapped four months ago. We think the same couple might be involved. Go ahead, Mrs. Summers."

"Our daughter, Shirley, was in the back of the house playing when this woman came to the door." Mrs. Summers pointed to the picture. "She said she was moving into the neighborhood and asked me questions about the schools and where I shopped. I guess we must have talked about ten minutes. When she left, I called Shirley and she didn't answer so I went to look for her. I heard her cry, 'Mama,' and then I heard a noise outside. I ran out into the street and saw a car disappear around a corner." She wiped her eyes with a handkerchief.

Trent picked up the picture of the man and woman and looked at it.

"Our sources believe these two are responsible for at least four abductions over the last few months." Morris said. "We believe they hang out around parks and playgrounds and zero in on innocent women with a pretty child. They follow them to their homes and watch for an opportunity."

"I've never seen them before." Trent said. "Martin did come to Houston a couple of months ago. Said he heard his uncle moved to Houston and he wanted to visit him. He received a couple of letters after he got back, but there was no return address on them. He left nothing behind when he took Jacob."

"There's no telling how he met up with this couple. We think they skipped town after they took your son. There have been no sightings in the past few days. Sources confirm their names are Ira Gentry and Gilda Perkins. He was originally a professional gambler and played in high stakes games. She was a prostitute."

"He signed the register at the hotel in Sugar Land as Tom Perkins from San Antonio," Trent said.

"I'll send a wire to our San Antonio office tomorrow," Morris added.

"Ma'am, I'm really sorry about your daughter. I know how you must feel. I think about our son every minute of every day," Trent said sadly.

"I'm afraid it never goes away," Mr. Summers said.

After they talked, Morris took Trent aside and gave him several copies of the drawings. Trent thanked him and went directly to the Houston Chronicle.

"Why, Mr. Matthews. It's nice to see you again," Agnes Sweeney said.

"I wanted to thank you for the article you wrote. They found the man who took my son, but someone murdered him last night. I brought you a picture of the couple that left with my son in Sugar Land. There was another couple I met at the Texas Rangers office today. They said this same couple took their one year old daughter six months ago. Summers was their last name."

"Yes, I remember them. I covered their story. Thank you for bringing this to me. It's too late for

Sunday's edition, but I'll get some more details from Mr. Morris and run a nice article the first of the week," Agnes said.

Feeling guilty and wanting to make amends with Catherine, Trent stopped at a small jewelry store before going to the train station. His eyes fixed on a gold chain with the symbol of a fish hanging from it. "I'd like to see this one, please," he said to the salesman.

The salesman took the pendant out and placed it on a black velvet tray. "The symbol of Christianity," the salesman said.

"Yes, I know," he answered back. "I'll take it."

"That will be fifteen dollars. It's solid gold."

"It's a present and I would appreciate it if you could put it in a pretty box."

The salesman left and returned with a gold box tied neatly with a red ribbon around it. Trent handed him a ten and a five. "Thank you," he said.

It was the first time Trent felt anything at all since Jacob was taken. He felt a twinge of excitement. It was confirmation that if his relationship with Catherine was going to improve, he had to be the one that was strong. He had to lead his family out of their grief.

30

The station was empty when Trent arrived, having missed the train leaving for Rosenberg. He had to wait another hour before the next one would leave. His thoughts were on his family. *How could this have happened? Why didn't I pay more attention when the sheriff warned us about Martin?*

It was after eight o'clock when he arrived home to an angry Catherine. "You could have called to let me know you were coming. When I didn't hear from you, I was afraid something happened to you. The children are already in bed." She turned and went upstairs before Trent could defend himself.

Trent set his bag by the staircase and went to the kitchen. He had not eaten since his corned beef sandwich earlier in the day, and he didn't want to argue on an empty stomach. He poured himself a whiskey first and sat down.

"I'm sorry. I'm afraid my nerves are preventing me from thinking straight. I was concerned, that's all." Catherine was standing under the doorway to the kitchen.

Trent got up, walked over to her, and put his arms around her. "Would you like me to pour you a drink?"

"No, I'll just sit here with you. Have you eaten yet?"

"No."

Catherine got up and opened the ice box. "I cooked a ham today."

Trent grabbed her hand and pulled her close to him. "Ham will be fine, but first sit with me for a minute. I have something I want to say to you. I know you are blaming yourself. I'm blaming myself, too. I should have protected my son. But we can blame ourselves all day and it won't bring Jacob back. I don't want this to destroy our marriage. I love you and the children so much it hurts." He brushed a long curl away from Catherine's face. "Look at me. We have to move on." Trent took the small box from inside his vest pocket and handed it to Catherine.

Catherine pulled the string on the ribbon and it fell away. She slowly opened the box and stared at it.

"It's the symbol of Christianity and a symbol of our son." Catherine lifted the chain from the box and Trent placed it around her neck.

"It's beautiful, thank you." She reached over and hugged him. "I really am sorry. I love you."

While Catherine warmed the leftovers for Trent, he told her about the Summers and how their little girl had been kidnapped. "This is a business for these people and they have to be stopped." He showed her the picture of the couple involved in the abduction. "We think this was who Martin was meeting when he came to Houston. They have no idea where they might have met. Maybe Martin knew him before he and Emily moved to Rosenberg." Not wanting to go into more detail, he changed the subject.

"We are close to solving a lot of the problems with the oil wells in Conroe. Clarence was really nice when he heard about Jacob. He told me to take a few days off before my next assignment. I was thinking we might rent one of those houses on the beach in Galveston and take the kids. They would love the water." Catherine smiled for the first time.

"That would be wonderful, but what is this about your next assignment?"

"Don't worry; he assured me that it would be close to Houston."

"What if the Rangers find Jacob? How will they know where we are?"

"I'll let Steven Morris know our plans. Perhaps we could give him Father Jonathan's phone number and let him know where we are staying."

"Yes, I'll call Father Jonathan after we make our plans."

The next day Catherine called the real estate agent managing their house in Galveston and asked if he would find them a weekend rental in the next few weeks. He said he would look into it and get back with her. An hour later he called her and said he reserved a three bedroom house on the beach for the weekend of September 10th. "I got you a very good rate since school has started and the season has come to an end."

Catherine hesitated remembering the storm in September, 1900. "Is that weekend all right?"

"Uh, yes, yes, of course. I was there during the terrible storm a few years ago and I'm sure the weather will be fine. It will probably be a hundred years before we have another one like that, if ever," the agent said."

"Yes, well, we'll see you then."

"Let me know when you plan to arrive. I'll send you the address before you come and I will meet you at the house. I think you will be very satisfied."

"Thank you," she said and hung up.

"Everything set?" Trent asked when he came into the room.

"I'm afraid the soonest he could find something was September 10th. Will that work with your schedule? Daniel will be in school then, but it's over a weekend so he'll just miss Friday."

"I'll make it work." Trent walked over and put his arms around her and kissed her on the neck. "I've missed you. I've missed us."

Catherine reached up and kissed him. "So have I."

After kissing the children goodnight, Trent changed into his nightshirt and slipped under the covers. He was anxious for Catherine to join him. She was helping Sadie give the children their baths. Trent was asleep when Catherine came into their room and took off her clothes. She slid under the covers naked and cuddled next to him. Kissing his neck and moving her hand gently across his chest, he pulled her close to him. "Hmm, what a nice pleasant surprise," he whispered.

"I'm sorry if I woke you," she teased.

"I'm not. I'm going to devour you."

Their kisses became passionate, but Trent could feel Catherine tense when he moved his hand between her legs. She encouraged him to move inside her, but that part of his anatomy wasn't responding. She began caressing him and after a while he pulled away. "I'm sorry," he said. "This has never happened to me before. I guess I'm just tired."

"Don't worry about it. There is always tomorrow morning," Catherine said, encouraging him. When Catherine woke the next morning, she was surprised Trent wasn't in bed. She changed into a housedress and went downstairs. Trent was in the kitchen frying bacon and making breakfast.

"Good morning. Thought I would surprise you and the children by making breakfast."

"Well, you surprised me," she said giving him a precarious look. "Everything all right?

He ignored her comment and began taking plates out of the cabinet.

"What can I do?" she asked.

"Not a thing. I have it all under control."

After breakfast, they played with the children, made a picnic lunch, and ate outside on the porch. The children played outside until naptime and afterwards, Catherine and Trent went to their room.

"Trent, about last night. I know it upset you. It's not uncommon for this to happen to a man after a tragedy."

"Are you playing doctor now?"

"You can call it what you want, but we have to talk about it. This, this thing that happened to our son has affected both of us. I understand you are trying to be strong and it might take some time, but we have to grieve. Like you said, we might never get him back, and I'm trying to deal with that, but I don't want you to shut me out. Talk to me."

Trent looked away and his body began to shake. Tears flowed from his eyes. Catherine went to him, put her arms around him and sat on the bed. They clung to each other out of guilt, desperation, and love. "We're going to get through this darling," Catherine whispered.

Trent hovered over Catherine and the children the remainder of the week. He dreaded going back to work and thought seriously about staying home. "Isn't it time for you to get your things together?" Catherine asked.

"I suppose so. I just hate to leave you and the children."

"Nonsense."

"You trying to get rid of me now?"

"I don't know what's gotten into you, but I've never seen you this way."

"A man wants to be with his wife and children. Is that so bad?" he grinned, teasing her. "All right, I'm going." Trent lazily got off the bed and grabbed some clothing from their wardrobe. "I'll be back in a week. Promise you'll call if you need me."

"I promise."

31

Catherine was home-schooling Sadie while the children played and drew pictures the next morning when a knock on the door interrupted them. "Want me to get it?" Sadie asked.

"No, finish your math problem while I go see who it is."

Alex Cooper was waiting, holding a newspaper under his arm, when Catherine opened the door. "Alex, what a nice surprise." She invited him in to the living room.

"How are you doing, Catherine? I'm so sorry about Jacob. Is there anything I can do?"

Catherine sighed. "I wish there were. Does the whole town know?"

"Well, Lillie at the phone company spares no details. It's the disadvantage of living in a small town. It's been all over the newspapers. Even Rosenberg's small newspaper put it on the front page." Alex handed her both papers.

Catherine opened The Chronicle first and read Agnes Sweeney's article. She stared at the picture of the couple and her eyes filled with tears. The article stated that most of the children taken were rarely reunited with their families.

"I'm so sorry Catherine. I know it's upsetting, but this will help find Jacob. This is the first time they even had a clue as to what these people looked like."

She sniffed and touched a handkerchief to her eyes. "I can't seem to run away from this turbulence that has followed me over these past few years. I thought it was behind me when I married Trent. We've been so happy and he's been a wonderful father to the children. It's really hit him hard. He went back to work today. I suppose if he keeps busy it might take some of the pain away. You've been a very dear friend, Alex, and I appreciate the newspapers. How are your wife and son?"

"We just found out last week that Meredith is with child."

"That's wonderful. The children would love to see you. Do you have time to say hello?"

"Of course."

After Alex left, Adam asked Catherine if God was looking for Jacob, too. "Of course he is," she answered.

"Then why doesn't He find him?"

Catherine tried to smile and had to search for an answer. "I'm sure He will find him soon and bring him back home."

"I hope so. I miss him," Adam said.

"So do I, sweetheart. We all do."

Later that day Catherine picked up the phone to speak with Lillie, their telephone operator. "Lillie, I was wondering if you could help me with a small task."

"I'd be happy to. We're all so sorry about what happened. What can I do?"

"I want to send some letters to some of the large orphanages in San Antonio, Austin, Houston and Dallas. By chance if he is found by the local authorities, that would be a logical place to take him if they don't know who the parents are. I'd like the names and addresses of these agencies."

"What about Galveston, it's so close."

"I have a close friend in Galveston whom I shall also send a letter."

"Yes ma'am, I'll get right on it."

Catherine removed a piece of writing paper from her desk drawer and began composing a letter, leaving space to go back and fill in the name and date. She gave the wording considerable thought

My son was recently kidnapped by this man and woman in the enclosed picture. The authorities believe they steal babies and children and sell them to unsuspecting couples who are unable to have children of their own. My son's name is Jacob Matthews and he is three and a half months old with dark brown hair and brown eyes. He has a distinct birthmark on his chest just to the left of his Adam's apple in the shape of a fish. If you have any knowledge or hear of

*anyone speaking of a recent adoption of a male infant,
please inquire as to his heritage. My phone number is
RB8-2760 in Rosenberg, Texas and you may call me
collect.*

Catherine wrote the same letter six times when
her phone rang. "Hello."

"This is Lillie and I have a list of those
agencies. I'll have little Billie Harrison bring it to you.
His mother is here right now and she said Billie would
be happy to run it over."

"Thank you and tell Mrs. Harrison I said thank
you."

Ten minutes later Billie knocked on Catherine's
door. "Hello Billie. Thank you for bringing this to me.
My, you've grown since I last saw you."

"I'll be fourteen in twelve days," he said
grinning. "I sure hope you find Jacob."

"Thank you, Billie."

Catherine addressed eight envelopes and
finished her letters. She carefully folded the flyer with
the picture and names of the couple and placed it
inside the envelope with the letter. The last letter she
wrote was to Father Jonathan and included copies of
the newspaper articles from the newspapers that she
had saved. When she put her pen down, she prayed
God would bless the letters and that they would find
Jacob. Closing her eyes, she prayed, *Dear Father, I
come to you in this hour of need. Please watch over
Jacob and protect him from harm. Have mercy on us*

dearest Lord Jesus. Please bring him home to us. We'll be waiting for his return. Amen

32

Trent left Conroe early Friday morning and stopped at his apartment to change into some fresh clothes. After spending a few hours in his Houston office, he decided to stop at the Texas Ranger's office before catching the train to Rosenberg.

Steven Morris was out of his office, but expected back before five o'clock. Fifteen minutes later Morris walked through the front door. "Trent. I'm glad you stopped by. Join me in my office." Trent sat in a chair across from Morris's desk.

"After Agnes's article ran in Monday's paper, our phone hasn't stopped ringing. We've received over a hundred calls." Trent perked up and sat forward in his chair.

"I don't want to give you false hope, but there was one call in particular from a woman that said she was an acquaintance of Gilda Perkins. She wanted to know if there was a reward. I told her there might be, but only if it was information we could use to find Jacob. She said she and Gilda used to work the streets together until Gilda met Ira. Said she knew Gilda's real name and where she came from, but wanted a hundred dollars before she gave us any more information. She wants to personally talk to you. Said she would call tomorrow and hung up before I could get her name. I can't promise she'll call back tomorrow, but if she does, it might be a good idea if you stayed in Houston. I'll try to set up a meeting."

A clerk came in and told Steven there was a call from the same woman on the phone.

"This is Steven Morris. "Yes, as a matter of fact, he's sitting right here across from me. Tonight?" Trent nodded his head, yes. Steven picked up a pencil and scribbled some information on a blank piece of paper. Afterwards, he hung up the phone.

"I don't like this." Steven said. "She wants you to come alone. No police or Rangers, she said."

"I'll go by myself. I don't mind."

"I know, but this could just be a scam. I have a new man I'm training and I'll have him in the saloon prior to you getting there. He doesn't look anything like a police man or a Ranger. He looks like a farm boy, but he's twenty-four and pretty sharp. I won't be far away. Whatever you do, don't give her more than a twenty. Tell her she'll get the rest if you can verify her story. You're to meet her at ten o'clock tonight. Said she would be wearing a royal blue gown, a string of pearls and a red plume in her hat. Have you been in any whorehouses in Houston?"

"No, why would you ask me that?"

"She said she met you over a year ago."

Trent stared at him blankly. "She must be mistaken."

X X X

It was late afternoon when Catherine heard the familiar ring of the telephone. She was filled with hope that it was good news. "Hello, Catherine. It's Samuel." There was silence and then he said, "I've read about your son's disappearance. I'm so sorry. How are you doing?"

"Samuel," she said almost in a whisper. "I'm trying to cope." Tears filled her eyes.

"I can't even imagine how you must be feeling. I just wanted you to know I've been thinking about you."

"Remember when I told you that bad things happen to those I love?"

"Catherine, it's not your fault. You can't control other people's actions."

"I know. But I can't seem to escape this unimaginable pain. Ever since I've come to America I've lost my mother, two husbands and now my son. When will it all stop?"

"There are no easy answers, but you must be strong. Your children need you more than ever. Promise you'll call me if you need to talk. I have a strong shoulder."

"Thank you, Samuel. I appreciate your friendship." Catherine hung up without saying goodbye.

Catherine walked to her office when she heard the telephone ring again. Rushing to answer, she stumbled and fell. The phone continued to ring and finally after the sixth ring, she answered.

"Catherine, I've been trying to reach you. Lillie said you were on the phone with some man. What's going on?" Trent demanded.

Still shaken from her fall, she put her hand to her head and then sat in the chair next to the phone. "I, uh, nothing. I'm sorry, I tripped and fell trying to get to the phone."

"Are you all right?"

"Yes, yes, I think so. Just shaken a bit."

"Who were you talking to?"

"An old friend of mine from Houston. I used to work with him at St. Mary's. He was calling to say how sorry he was about Jacob."

"Did you hurt yourself when you fell?"

"No, I'm fine. When will you be home?

"That's why I'm calling. There's a woman that says she knows the couple that was involved in Jacob's kidnapping. She wants to meet later tonight to give us some information. She is expecting some kind of reward and that's why Morris wants me to be available."

"Oh Trent, she might know where we can find Jacob."

"Don't get your hopes up, Catherine. Morris has received dozens of calls and he said most of them don't pan out. I just have to hope that she's not lying and isn't just trying to get money from us."

Catherine bit down hard on her lip, trying to compose herself. "All right, darling. Please be careful."

"I will. The Rangers will be with me. I'll talk to you soon."

33

Trent arrived at the Baxter hotel thirty minutes early and sat at the bar. He immediately saw Thomas Myers, the young man Steven introduced him to at the Rangers' offices. Their eyes met but neither acknowledged the other. Trent ordered a shot of whiskey and drank it down. The bartender filled it again.

"It's nice to see you again, Mr. Matthews," a young woman in her mid-twenties said.

Trent recognized the woman in the blue dress, but couldn't place her.

"I'm Gloria, Gloria Wagner."

"I've seen you before, but you look different."

"It was about a year ago, the train station and then the Roosevelt Hotel. You were meeting a friend as was I. We were both stood up."

Trent got up from his chair and offered her a seat. He could hardly take his eyes off her. She had morphed from a drab moth into a ravishing butterfly. He remembered her as being very plain and homely. Now she was wearing an expensive low-cut gown. Make-up highlighted her high cheekbones and her auburn hair was swept up under a designer hat. The transformation was remarkable.

"We should probably go somewhere more private," Gloria remarked.

Trent paid his bill and stood. "Where are we going?" "I have a small apartment not far from here."

"Wait. I'd rather just find a table in the back and talk here."

Gloria looked around and said, "Fine, but I won't be able to stay here more than a few minutes. I'm supposed to be working and she will expect to be paid."

"How much do you charge? Don't get the wrong idea, I only want to talk."

"Twenty-five dollars for an hour."

"Then start talking."

Gloria acted nervous and looked around the room. "Look, someone may be watching us, but I can stay and have one drink."

Trent motioned to the waitress and she took their order.

"I read about what happened to your son. It wasn't until I read an article about Gilda in the newspaper that I made the connection."

"How did you know it was me? I don't remember an exchange of names when I offered to give you the room?"

"We didn't exchange names. When you reached under the pillow on the bed and took out the box with the necklace in it, your card must have slipped away from the package. I found it on the floor after you left. It was your business card. You wrote a note on the back that said; *I love you, Catherine.* I wore that necklace for a long time until someone stole it."

The waitress returned with their drinks and they stopped talking until she left. "The reason I mentioned a ransom to Ranger Morris was because my madam expects me to work and I have to pay her. I wanted to be sure you brought money."

"Tell me about Gilda. What do you know about her?"

"We met on the street a couple of days after I met you. I only had a few dollars from the ten dollars you so graciously gave me, I guess out of pity. Anyway, she told me what she did and that I could make some easy money. I was desperate, and she made it sound like it was nothing. She said she was originally from Waco, Texas, and followed her boyfriend to Houston, just as I did."

"Do you know this Ira Gentry?"

"Gilda and I worked together for about three months and then she got fed up and said she was leaving. Said she met a professional gambler and they were hooking up. I ran into her awhile back and she was with this man. We only spoke briefly. She looked different. She was wearing more expensive clothes and said that she and Ira had a business together."

"Anything else?"

"Look, I'll tell you the rest at my apartment."

"This isn't a set up to rob me, is it?"

"No. I would never stoop that low."

Trent left some money on the table and they both got up. Concerned that he might be walking into a trap, Trent felt for his gun inside his holster. They walked several blocks, through an alley and up a flight of stairs. The light in the hallway was dim and long shadows followed them to a door with the number, "6-B." When they entered the apartment, several lit candles illuminated the sparsely-furnished small room. Trent sat on a single chair across from the double bed. Gloria sat on the bed across from him.

Trent reached into his pocket, took out his wallet and handed her a ten. "I'll give you the rest when you tell me where they have taken my son."

"I don't know anything about that. I only know what I've told you and what is being said on the street."

"What are they saying on the street?"

"A man who is a solicitor has been offering money for small children, more for babies. He arranges adoptions for families who are barren and want children. Many are willing to pay large sums for these babies."

"Go on. Do you know his name?"

"Beauregard, Beauregard Tyson, but I can't be sure. I've never met the man. I overheard some of the other girls talking; that's all."

"Can you give me the names of these girls?"

"No, I'm sorry. That's all I can tell you. I've taken a big chance telling you what I've already told you. If word got out that I was a snitch, my life would be in danger." She looked at the clock and got up.

Gloria gave Trent a seductive look. "You are a very attractive man, Trent. Why don't you lie down with me? You wouldn't regret it."

Trent stood, took fifteen more dollars from his wallet and laid it on the bed. "You may contact me through Ranger Morris. You've been very helpful."

Once outside, Trent walked the length of the dark alley and met up with Texas Rangers, Myers and Morris. "Are you all right?" Morris asked.

"I'm good. I did meet her over a year ago, but she wasn't selling her goods then. We hardly exchanged names, but she later found my business card. I think she's telling the truth. Said Gilda offered to help her get back on her feet and she agreed out of desperation to become a prostitute." The men continued to talk as they went into a small cafe for coffee. After filling in the two men on the remainder of his evening with Gloria, Trent said. "I think she is telling me the truth."

Morris was writing in his notebook. "So this Beauregard Tyson; he is the front man for this string of baby snatchings?"

"Apparently. Have you heard of him?" Trent asked.

"No, we'll check police records and have our research department find out what they can. You did good, Trent. Give us some time and we'll catch these bastards. It doesn't really matter now, but I did promise you a report on Martin Boudreaux's background."

Trent's body grew rigid at the sound of the name. "Go on."

"He was detained in New Orleans because he was caught picking pockets. They were going to send him back to Liverpool, but he managed to get away. The authorities didn't pursue him since there were so many people arriving there. They informed the police, but apparently he left New Orleans and the authorities didn't pursue it. It was unfortunate for you and your family. I'm sorry."

"They must have taken the train to Rosenberg. They were working for Catherine when I met and married her. She didn't know a lot about them and I didn't press it. They put up a nice charade and on the outside appeared to be trustworthy. He was very dominant toward Emily and I figured it was none of my business, so I said nothing. How stupid was that?"

"You were newly married with four children. I must admit, I'm not sure I would have done anything different," Morris added.

"Catherine and I thought we might take the children to Galveston next weekend. The children have been very upset about this, and we thought it might get their minds off Jacob."

"As long as we can get in touch with you, that won't be a problem," Morris concluded.

"If that's everything, I'm going to try and catch the last train to Rosenberg tonight."

"We've got your numbers, just don't go too far away from the phone."

34

Ranger Morris, his team of Rangers, and the Houston police department spent days on the streets talking to their snitches, arresting prostitutes, madams, and anyone else that looked suspicious. Gloria Wagner waited for her turn outside one of the interrogation rooms at the Rangers' office. She wondered why she had been dropped off there instead of going in the paddy wagon to the police station. Two other prostitutes accompanied her. Once inside the small dark office, she waited on a hard wooden chair and wondered what was going to happen to her.

"Gloria Wagner?" the tall stern man asked.

Gloria looked around the room, scared and confused, unable to speak at first.

Clearing her throat, she said, "yes."

"I'm Ranger Steven Morris. I spoke to you when you first called in. You need to tell me everything you know about this kidnapping."

Gloria said nothing and stared around the room. Steven slammed his fist onto the table, creating a noise so loud it was as if a clap of thunder had penetrated the walls. Gloria jumped and put her hands over her mouth to hush a small cry. Steven stared at her. "We can do this the easy way or you can sit in jail until you rot."

Gloria sat up and pulled her shoulders back. Taking in a deep breath, she finally spoke. "I had nothing to do with that baby's kidnapping. I've only known Gilda for a short time; only met her boyfriend, Ira, maybe once or twice."

"Go on."

"If I tell you everything I know, will you let me go? I don't want to go to jail."

"The sooner you tell me, the sooner you can get out of here."

"There's one more thing."

"What is it?"

"If anyone finds out I was the one that told you this, my life would be in danger. I'll need to leave. My parents have no idea what has happened to me, and I want to return to my home in San Antonio." Gloria took a deep breath and let it out. "Perhaps Mr. Matthews could afford to do that. He helped me before when I first arrived in Houston."

Morris thought for a few minutes. "Tell me everything you know and I'll see you get back to your family in San Antonio."

Gloria collected her thoughts. "There is a young Indian man. They call him Riddle. He speaks Cherokee and broken English. People say Beauregard Tyson took him off the streets when Riddle was fourteen. He is Tyson's bodyguard and errand boy now and is in his mid- twenties. They say he makes all the deliveries for Tyson. Sometimes he travels by train and other times he rides his Paint. If you can catch him and get him to talk, you might find Tyson."

"Do you know where Tyson lives?"

"Tyson does not have an address. He moves around living in hotels, sometimes staying in one of the brothels. I heard he destroys all the paperwork once a transaction is finished so there is no evidence."

"I have a sketch here that we've put together from other witnesses." Morris turned a picture over and slid it across the table for Gloria to look at.

It was a likeness of Beauregard Tyson. Studying it closely, she said. "His jaw is square and eyebrows much thicker, kind of bushy."

Morris got up and left the room. He returned with the sketch artist and asked Gloria to repeat what she just said. The artist took his pencil and began making corrections on the sketch. When he finished he turned it around so Gloria could take a look.

"That's really a good likeness."

"Want me to get it to the newspaper?" the man asked turning to Morris.

"No, not yet. If he sees it in the newspapers he'll make a run for it." Morris turned his attention back to Gloria. "Have you ever seen this Indian, Riddle?"

"No, maybe from a distance, but I guess he looks like all the other Indians. His dark hair is shoulder-length and he keeps it tied in back with a leather strap, I think. Maybe it's some kind of twine. Like I said, I've never seen him up close. May I leave now?"

"No, I'm going to move you to another room in back; mainly for your protection. Once we verify your story, you'll be on your way to San Antonio."

After putting Gloria in a small cell, Morris called a meeting of Rangers and included Detective Max Chambers from the police department.

Morris used a blackboard to compile all the information the investigators had regarding Tyson and Riddle. One man reported Riddle's Indian name was White Eagle because his mother was a white woman. "He's also known as John Smith," another man answered. Someone else reported that Riddle had a wife and lived on a small Indian reservation southwest of Houston.

Almost no information was reported about Tyson. No bank accounts were discovered at the major banks and he had no permanent address.

Two hours later the men left with their assignments and they were to meet back in twenty-four hours.

35

The next day White Eagle and Beauregard Tyson met at a small brothel in southwest Houston. "There has been too much publicity in the newspapers and I've decided to head north. I want you to go with me," Tyson said.

White Eagle frowned and bit down hard on his lower lip. "You have been like father to me. I'm a grown man and have my own family. I will not leave my wife and son."

"Then I suggest you stay close to them on the reservation. Stay away from the city for a while." Tyson took his wallet from his vest pocket. He counted out five hundred dollars and handed it to White Eagle.

He shook his head. "Don't need money. We live from the land."

"Take it. Educate your son with it, Eagle. Put it in an account at Wells Fargo. Hell. Don't be a fool, take it." He placed the money in Riddle's hand and closed his fingers around it. "I doubt I'll ever return to Houston. You be safe now." The two men hugged.

White Eagle took a leather band from his arm and handed to Tyson. "The bear's tooth hidden inside the leather will ward off evil spirits. Keep it close to you." The two men shook hands and each went their separate ways.

Several hours later, White Eagle was inside his family's tepee when he heard a commotion outside. Looking out of his tent, he saw a young boy running up to him out of breath. "Go. White men looking for you."

White Eagle grabbed his gun and ran towards the corral for his horse. A rope circled his body and jerked him to the ground, causing him to drop his rifle. Stunned, he tried to reach for it, but the rifle was kicked away as the rope tightened around his body, dragging him several yards.

"You White Eagle?" a man asked.

When there was no response, another man jerked him up and pulled his arms behind him binding them with a pair of handcuffs. "What's your name?" the man asked again.

"Tie him up good," the mounted Ranger said. "Make sure the rope is secure and tight."

White Eagle looked around and saw six men on horseback. Without another word, one Ranger tied the end of the rope to the horn on his saddle.

"Someone get his horse." The man shouted to another Ranger as he clicked his tongue, moving the horse forward.

Following behind two mounted Rangers, White Eagle began running to keep up with the horse's pace.

Ranger Steven Morris and four other men began a search through the reservation for White Eagle's wife. Several minutes later, an Indian squaw holding a small child came out of a tent. "What do you want of my husband?"

Another Ranger joined them with White Eagles' horse. "You need to come with us, ma'am"

"My name is Eve. Evening Dove."

The Ranger walked the palomino horse up to her and she handed her son to another woman. "Look after him as if he is yours," she said to the woman.

"Not so fast," Morris said stopping the woman from leaving. "The boy comes with you."

Once on top of the horse, the woman handed her the boy. Eve swung the boy onto her back and wrapped him in a shawl another Indian woman handed her. Tying the ends together she looked up at Morris. "My son does not pay for his father's sins."

"Let's go." Morris and his men surrounded Eve and they rode off toward Houston.

Thirty minutes later they caught up with the two men leading an out-of-breath White Eagle. "Stop for a few minutes," Morris said. "We need him alive, not dead. Give him a rest."

White Eagle sunk to his knees and heaved trying to catch his breath. Eve watched in horror.

Morris got off his horse and took his canteen from his saddle. He walked over to White Eagle and lifted his head. Removing the top of the canteen, he poured water into Eagle's mouth as he gulped it down and coughed.

"Where is Beauregard Tyson?" Morris asked.

White Eagle said nothing.

"Get the woman down. She can run with White Eagle." Eve was pulled from her horse as the child began to wail.

Her hands were tied in front of her and her frightened eyes stared at White Eagle. He did not look at her. Her child was still in the sling on her back.

After getting back on his horse, Morris said, "Have it your way."

The Rangers started at a slow pace and then began to speed up.

Eve began crying, "Husband, husband."

While Eagle refused to look at her. A half mile later, the Rangers stopped when Eve stumbled and was dragged several yards on her belly. She had passed out.

"Take the child from her back and put her across the Paint," Morris said. "We'll make camp over by those trees."

Two ropes were swung over a large limb of a towering oak tree. Eagle and Eve's hands were tied tightly with rope. Two men pulled on the ropes, lifting Eagle and Eve off the ground leaving them hanging several feet in the air. Arms over her head and feet dangling, Eve woke up and began crying. Eagle stared blankly into the fading evening sky.

"What's the kid's name?" Morris asked.

He reached up and hit the back of Eagle's knee causing him to scream in pain.

Eve cried out. "Bear, his name is Bear."

"Now we are getting somewhere," Morris said, as he walked over and untied the rope that was holding Eve off the ground. He lowered her to the ground and she slumped over. "Look I really don't want to hurt you or your son, but unless you talk, I'll pull you back up."

Bear sat off to the side, crying, "Mama, mama."

"He is hungry and needs his mother's milk."

"Tell us what you know about Tyson, and then he can eat."

Eve looked at Eagle, who refused to look at her. "Mr. Tyson employs my husband. I do not know what they do. He goes into town sometimes and works for him. He tells me nothing of the business."

"Did you know your husband takes babies away from their mothers and gives them away?"

Again Eve searched White Eagle's face for answers. "No, no. The men on the reservation tell their wives nothing. Now can I feed my son?"

Morris nodded at one of his men who was tying a small noose together. The man got up and walked over to the child who was sitting in the dirt still crying. He picked him up and began putting a noose around his neck. Eve screamed. "No, Eagle. Do something, say something."

Eagle looked over at his son, fear raging from his face. "Stop!"

Everyone looked. "I tell you everything, but you must promise to let my wife and son go back home."

"Go on," Morris said.

Eagle tried to take a deep breath, but found it difficult. He coughed and his shallow breathing caused him to speak in short breaths. "Tyson is gone. North, he said. Will not be back."

"Tell us where he took the boy. The one with the birthmark."

"A few days ago I go to Austin and meet business man. He gave me briefcase and I gave him letter. I came back and gave to Mr. Tyson."

"Where did you meet this businessman?" Morris asked.

"Train station." Eagle grimaced from the pain that was shooting up is his arms and his knee.

"Where?"

"Austin."

What did he look like?"

"White man. Older, like you."

"Did he give a name?"

"No."

"Then how did you know who to give the briefcase to?"

"He come up to me and called me Riddle. No other man would know that and he gave me briefcase. You can kill me, but my son and my wife know nothing. I tell her nothing."

"Give the woman her son," Morris said.

Another Ranger came up to Morris. "Sir. Are we going to let her go?"

"In the morning. I want to sleep on it." He turned to the other Rangers. "Let him down and tie him to the tree."

After Eve nursed her son, they cuffed her leg to a tree so she could hold her son. The men took turns throughout the night keeping watch over their captives.

XXX

Small whimpers seeped into the silence of the morning breaking open its stillness. Eve awoke as her small child hungrily searched her breast. She looked around at the now empty camp. Moving her legs and adjusting her body so she could nurse her child, the reality that the men had left sometime during night, haunted her. She untied her leather strap below her neck and pulled down her smock exposing her nipple.

257

Bear found it immediately and began suckling. Tears swelled in her eyes. White Eagle was gone and somehow she knew she would never see him again. It was then she noticed that she was no longer cuffed to the tree limb and the palomino was tied to a tree nearby. They had spared her and her child and she was thankful for that.

36

Trent returned to Rosenberg for the weekend. His work no longer interested him and there was nothing he could do to aid in the search for his son. The guilt had grown inside him like poison ivy and his family needed him now more than ever.

Breakfast was finished and Sadie took the children outside to play. Catherine poured Trent a third cup of coffee and poured hot water in her cup for tea. She bent down and kissed his cheek. "You didn't get in until late last night. How did things go with your meetings?"

Trent put a scoop of sugar in his coffee and sat back in his chair. "The Rangers have taken an interest in our case. According to them, we are not the only ones who have lost children, and they have formed a special group of Rangers to do nothing but find who is taking them. They now have some new leads and are following through on them."

"Did he say we had a chance of finding our son?"

Trent reached over and took Catherine's hand. The look of hope in her eyes was painful for him to look at. "They aren't making any promises. Most likely the children abducted are relocated in other cities, possibly other states. It's like finding a needle in a haystack. I can't say, Catherine, but for now our immediate family needs us to be as normal as possible."

When Catherine's eyes filled with tears, Trent went to her and pulled her into his arms. "It's not going to be easy, Catherine. I'll give my notice to Clarence so he can find someone else to take my place. I'll find something here to supplement our income and if you want to re-open the clinic, I'll help with that. Daniel will start school next month and Sadie should be able to take care of the other children."

"Yes, that would probably be best. What about Galveston next weekend? Should we still go?"

"I think it would be good for both of us and the children. We may not get another vacation for a while. I need to finish out the week at my job and I'll be home Thursday evening to help get things together for our trip. It's not going to be easy for either of us, but as long as we are together, that's what is important."

"I know it will take some time. Right now I just feel numb, but I will do my best around the children," Catherine said almost in a whisper. "You mean everything to me. Thank you."

They held each other for a long time hoping their combined energy would sustain them.

While Catherine worked in the house, Trent joined Sadie and the children outside. He wandered into the stables and saw some leftover fencing wood in the corner. Carefully selecting the best pieces, he decided to build a porch swing.

"Need some help with that?" Jason asked as he held a small dog on top of his horse.

"What do you have there?" Trent asked putting his saw down.

"My hound fathered six puppies and I thought the children might like to have one."

Trent reached up and took the dog and then looked over at the children who were busy with their toys in the sandbox. "Children," he yelled. Squealing and running towards them, Trent knelt down so the children could take a good look at the puppy.

"Can we have him?" Daniel asked.

"If your mom says so." Adam ran into the house, returning with Catherine.

"Can we have him? Please Mama, please." There was a chorus of, "please!"

Catherine laughed and bent down to take a closer look. "If it's all right with your father, it's fine with me."

"I guess so," Trent remarked and turned to Jason. "We are taking a trip to Galveston next weekend and I'll need someone to look after him. Think you could help me out with that?"

"Sure. He can stay here until then and I'll bring him back to my house. You can pick him up when you return."

When things settled down, Catherine returned to the house and the children took turns holding the puppy and picking out names.

"Any news?" Jason asked Trent when the men were alone.

"I wish there was. Thanks for the dog. It will keep the kids occupied."

Jason bent down and picked up the hammer. "Let me help you with this."

While there was almost a ten-year span between the two men, they had formed a special bond "I'm not sure I ever thanked you for helping me track down Martin. The Ranger told me it increased our chances of finding Jacob. They are pursuing a number of leads right now and they might be closing in on the ringleader. I haven't told Catherine, because I don't want to get her hopes up."

"You would have done the same for me. I just wish we would have been able to catch them before Jacob was handed off."

"So do I. If Catherine and I had stayed in Houston, we would have had a much earlier start finding them."

"You can't blame yourself. Obviously Martin had this planned for some time."

"Not sure I told you, but Martin was murdered in Houston the next day. The Rangers said he was robbed. Guess he got what was coming."

"You said there were some other leads?"

"Yes, once the articles turned up in the newspaper, and an alert was given to the public, one person in particular came forward with some information that restarted the investigation. I'm hoping to hear something soon."

"Papa?" Emma interrupted. "Is our puppy a boy or girl?"

"It's a boy," Jason said.

Daniel joined in. "Everyone has a different name."

"Can you and Adam pick out a name and I'll have the girls pick a name. Then I'll toss a coin in the air."

Several minutes later they all crowded around. "Adam and I want to call him Rover," Daniel said.

"Isabelle and I want to call him Honey," Emma said.

"All right then, heads for Rover and tails for Honey." The coin was flipped. "Looks like his new name is Honey.

X X X

Trent left after lunch on Sunday so he could go by Ranger Morris' office and check on their progress.

"Glad you stopped by," Morris said. "Could you sketch out on this paper what the birthmark looks like and where it is on his body? I've spoken with Agnes at the newspaper and she will see that the article is circulated throughout the other large cities in Texas. It's a long shot, but it could give us another lead."

Trent stared down at the drawing of a human torso. He took the pencil from Morris and began outlining the shape of a small fish that was placed three inches down from the Adam's apple on the drawing. He shaded it, leaving a small "v" on top. "It's almost a perfect fish, but the open area with the "v" is not shaded in. I think it's close enough."

Morris studied it. "You said he is three months, and two weeks old, has about half an inch of hair and it's brown?"

"Yes, his birthday was July 12, 1906."

"This should help."

"Are there any new leads?"

"We found the Indian, but he isn't saying much. It's possible your son was handed over to a couple at a train station outside of Austin, but they could have arrived from any number of places."

"That's at least something."

"We're doing everything we can."

"What about the Indian?"

"We've turned him over to the police. They are to call me if he tells them anything else. Don't think he will tell them much. Said the man who was his boss moved on and didn't tell him where he was going. The ringleader didn't keep an address and moved around a lot. We have found no trace of him, and the Indian never laid eyes on your son."

"I'll be at work through Thursday and I'll check in with you then. You have my number in Humble, Texas, where you can reach me this week if you find him."

Morris nodded his head and shook hands with Trent.

37

Catherine struggled over the next few days trying to stay busy. She altered the children's clothing to make bathing suits for them to wear in Galveston. She even took Emma and Isabelle to the thrift store in town and found suitable outfits for them to wear at the beach. While she sewed, she frequently had to stop to wipe her tearing eyes. She should be used to tragedies by now, but with every disappointment came sorrow and grief.

While she was in town, everyone she knew stopped her on the street and asked if Jacob had been found. The loss followed her everywhere, but it was the sinking hole in her heart that seemed to drain the life from her. Jacob was Trent's only biological son and there was always a possibility she couldn't get pregnant again. Trent's physical rejection haunted her every waking hour. It was as though the joy of their lovemaking had been ripped away from his body. Surely, over time, the joy and desire would return, but what if it didn't? *I have to stop thinking this way or I'll go crazy.*

X X X

Buddy and his father were always busy doing chores on the dairy farm and there was little to talk about except the mundane yarns. After milking, it was Buddy's job to deliver the milk to the local townsfolk.

The conversation at supper time was about the couple that bought milk for their baby. His father told his son about the unusual birthmark and that it looked like a fish. Buddy didn't think much of it and was more interested in talking about the automobile and what made it move. On his deliveries, he would often pick up old magazines from the ranchers and farmers' burn barrels. He had to quit school the previous year after his mother died to help his father on the farm. He took the old magazines and newspapers home to read so he could keep up with current events.

The Tompkins's ranch was his favorite place to stop. Mrs. Tompkins always tied her magazines and newspapers in a bundle for him every few days and left them at the door for him to pick up. Wednesdays always included the Houston newspaper and he looked forward to reading it when he finished his chores. Mr. Tompkins was originally from Houston and frequently went there on business. Buddy liked to read the Sunday comics, but saved them until last.

The Sunday before last, he was intrigued by the story about the child abductions. He wondered about the couple that stopped for milk, and tried to talk to his father about them at the supper table. His father quieted him quickly. "Don't go getting yourself mixed up in something that don't concern you, boy. We're just plain folks. That's a whole 'nother world out there and it will just git you in trouble. Don't like you readin' that propaganda. Half of it ain't true anyway."

Buddy yawned as he crawled into his bed. The windows stood wide open, but the stillness of the night did not allow any cross ventilation in his room. He untied the string around the bundle of paper, took a section of the newspaper and began fanning himself. He reached over and turned up his oil lamp to give him better light. He used the end of his bed-sheet to whip away the sweat that had formed on his brow and then he opened up the newspaper to the front page.

He leaned closer to the oil lamp and looked at a picture of a man and woman. In a smaller picture below the article was a picture of the baby's birthmark. His mouth was dry and he found it hard to swallow. The picture looked just like the couple that drove up in the automobile. He read the entire article and then read it again. He got up and opened his door slowly, and then crept to his father's door. He could hear his father's snoring and knew he would be angry if he were awakened.

Buddy quickly went back to his room and read the article one more time. His heart was racing and he took a pencil and paper from the drawer on the side table. After writing down the phone number and contact name, he double-checked it for accuracy and then put the paper in his drawer.

Buddy's thoughts went to his father and what his reaction would be when Buddy told him about the newspaper article. *He will be madder than a hornet. Not at the couple, but at me.*

Buddy was an only child and his parents had him late in life. His father was now in his fifties and set in his ways. Prior to her death, Buddy's mother insisted that he attend the local school. She wanted Buddy to be more than just a farmer; but not his father. He was from the old school where you worked your fingers to the bone day in and day out. Buddy loved and respected his dad, but he, too, wanted to be more than just a farmer.

Buddy tossed and turned most of the night and a loud crow from the rooster made him sit straight up in bed the next morning. A few moments later, he heard his father in the kitchen. Dressing in the clothes he'd worn the day before, he grabbed the newspaper and went into the kitchen. Placing the newspaper beside his father's coffee cup, he poured some dry oats into a bowl and took out a bottle of milk from the icebox.

"What's this?" his father demanded.

"That couple, the one with the baby last week. I think they stole him."

Staring down at the pictures, his father picked it up and read the headlines. He read a few paragraphs and then walked over and threw it in the trash.

"We have to call someone, Papa. That baby wasn't theirs."

"What have I told you about getting into other people's business?"

Buddy knew better than to argue with his father. Somehow he would have to figure out a way to notify the authorities. The farmer and his son ate in silence and then went outside to do the milking.

The next morning when Buddy made his milk deliveries, Mrs. Tompkins was on the front porch of her home, watering her flowers.

"Good morning, Mrs. Tompkins."

"Well, good morning, Buddy. I see you have been picking up my old magazines and newspapers. Thank you."

"No, thank you. It's the only way I can keep up with the news. My dad needs me at the dairy and I'm not going back to school."

"I'm sorry to hear that."

"Um, Mrs. Tompkins, do you ever read the newspaper?"

"Yes, when my husband gets through reading it, I like to keep up with the fashions and read the news."

"Have you been reading about the children and babies that are being taken away from their families and then sold to couples who want to adopt them?"

"Yes, and I think that is appalling. Why do you ask?"

"Well, that couple, the ones that had their pictures in the paper last Sunday. Well, they stopped by our farm last week and bought some milk from us. The baby had that fish birthmark on his chest. I didn't see it, but Pops did."

"Are you for certain about that?"

"Oh, yes ma'am. It was them. Came drivin' up in one of those fancy automobiles.

"You need to go tell the sheriff."

"I would, but Pops will whup me. He told me not to say anything. I have the number of the Ranger's office in Houston. Maybe you could call for me, but you can't give them my name. Maybe you could just tell them that you heard it from a neighbor and can't give them the name or something like that."

"Let me think about it and I'll see what I can do. Do you have the number with you?"

Buddy searched his pants pocket and brought out the piece of paper he had placed in his pocket when he dressed. "Here," he said handing it to her.

Mrs. Tompkins looked at the number and turned to Buddy. "Don't you mind about it anymore, Buddy. You did the right thing givin' this to me."

38

Ranger Morris was sitting at his desk when one of the clerks told him a woman was calling about the couple that took the baby. He got up and walked over to the main phone. "This is Ranger Morris."

"Yes, well I can't give you my name, but I have some information about that man and woman that stole that baby."

"What kind of information?"

"Well, several days ago that man and woman, you know, their pictures were in the Houston paper. Anyway they had a baby and stopped at one of our dairy farms and asked to buy some milk for him. The farmer took a careful look at the child and the baby had a birthmark on his chest; the one that looked like a fish."

"And how did you come by this information?"

"I promised the young man who told me that I wouldn't give you his name. His paw wouldn't like it. People 'round these parts don't want nothin' to do with the law."

"Could you at least tell me the whereabouts of this farm?"

"It's just off the main road to Brenham, about eight or nine miles south of town."

"Would that be the road from Houston to Brenham?"

"Yes, it would.

"Can you tell me anything else?"

"I think I better hang up now."

Ranger Morris stared into the receiver. He clicked down the hook on top of the phone several times and the operator answered.

"May I help you?" she asked

"Francis, this is Ranger Morris. Do you know where that call came from?"

"The operator on the other end said it was a long distance call through the Brenham switchboard."

"Do you think you could call her back for me? I need to talk with her."

Morris waited by the phone and it rang several minutes later.

"Morris."

"I have the Brenham operator on the telephone. Go ahead."

"This is Ranger Morris at the Texas Rangers' office in Houston, Texas. A few minutes ago a woman made a long distance call from your end and I need to know her name."

"That would be Mrs. Roger Tompkins."

"Is she a reliable individual?"

"Oh, yes sir. Her husband is a big rancher in these parts."

"Thank you. You've been a big help."

"There is one more thing, Mr. Morris."

"Yes, what is it?"

"Being a switchboard operator, we hear all kinds of stuff."

"Like what?"

"Well, we don't get too many of those fancy automobiles around here, so when that man and woman with the baby came through, everyone noticed."

"Go on."

"Well, they stayed at the Palmer Hotel downtown. The man met up with another couple who came in on the train from Austin, Texas. They were all dressed up in those fancy clothes. Anyway, the couple from Austin came back an hour later and boarded a train back to Austin. Oh, and they had a baby with them. Didn't come here with one."

"The man and woman in the fancy automobile, do you know when they left?"

"Sure do. They left early the next morning and were headed north."

"You have been a big help, ma'am. Thank you."

"I sure hope that you find that little baby and get him back to his mama."

When Morris hung up the telephone, Thomas Myers walked up to him. "Get your things together; we're taking the next train to Brenham, Texas." Morris said.

XXX

Trent made every effort to concentrate on his work, but his mind was on Jacob and Catherine. Thursday morning, he decided it was time to clean out his desk and give his final notice to his boss, Clarence. He tossed most of the old scraps of paper and unimportant things into the wastebasket, gathered up his files, and went down the hall to Clarence's office.

"I was wondering when I'd see you. I can tell by the look on your face that you're going home," Clarence said with a grim face. "Can't say I blame you. You've been through a lot."

Trent sat down in a chair across from Clarence and placed his files on Clarence's desk. "These are all the drilling reports I've been working on. I've enjoyed working with you."

"So, you're not coming back?"

"No. My family needs me more than ever. I'll find something local to do. Sam Shepherd is familiar with my work and I think he will be the best man to take it over."

"I appreciate that information. You've been a great employee, Trent. I sure hate to lose you. Why don't we leave the door open?"

"I don't want to give you false hope. I'm not planning to come back. I've enjoyed working with you more than you know. You've been a really good friend."

After getting his briefcase and saddlebags, Trent left to catch the next train back to Houston. It was two in the afternoon when he arrived and he took a trolley to the Rangers' offices.

"I'd like to see Ranger Morris, please," Trent said to the receptionist.

"I'm sorry, but Ranger Morris left a little while ago."

"Will he be back today?"

"Oh no, I'm afraid not. Can someone else help you?"

"What about Thomas Myers?"

"They are both out of town."

"Can you tell me where they went?"

"I'm sorry, but I'm not allowed to."

"Would you give him this note and ask him to call Trent Matthews if he has any news for me? My contact information is on this paper."

Yes sir," she answered, taking the note. "I'll make sure he reads it."

Trent went back to his apartment for a fresh change of clothes. He filled the tub with hot water, poured a glass of whiskey and stripped off his clothes. His thoughts were on Jacob. He was mad that Morris had left town without calling him and giving him an update. Trent wondered if Morris was pursuing a lead in the investigation. He was also having second thoughts about going to Galveston. He soaked in the tub for a while, finished his drink, and then washed. When he got out, he looked at his scruffy three day old beard and quickly shaved.

A fresh change of clothes made him feel better, but only for a brief moment. Trent sat on the bed and began to cry. His life had made a one hundred and eighty degree turn from being a happily married man and father to a grief stricken old man. He felt he had aged ten years. Trent looked around the small apartment, and then packed up the remainder of his clothes in the suitcase he stored in the closet. He grabbed the few remaining clothes Catherine had left and then emptied the icebox. He made a quick trip to the trashcan in the alley and then stopped at his landlord's door.

"I'm returning the key to the apartment. I won't need it anymore. I'm leaving all the furniture and bedding. You can keep it or sell it. Use the twenty dollar deposit to clean up the place and if I owe you anything else, you can send the bill to my Rosenberg address."

"You've been a good tenant, Mr. Matthews. I'm sorry about what happened to your son and I hope you find him soon."

"Thanks. I hope so, too."

Trent barely made the six o'clock train. Staring out the window, he felt as if the weight of the world was on his shoulders and he hoped he would be able to be a good enough actor to hide his misery. *Pray, he needed to pray.*

X X X

Catherine heard the train whistle from a mile away and she prayed this was the train Trent was on. It was half-past seven in the evening and she left dinner warming on the stove before going upstairs.

Anxious, Catherine picked up her brush and pulled it through her hair several times. After taking off her apron and hanging it on the doorknob, she made her way downstairs. Several minutes later, she saw Trent approaching as she waited on the front porch. When he got closer, Catherine ran down the stairs and into his loving arms. "Oh, how I've missed you, my darling."

"I've missed you, too," Trent said pulling her close and kissing her. They walked hand in hand back to the house.

While the children were upstairs taking their baths, Trent and Catherine sat in the kitchen while he ate his dinner. "I stopped by the Rangers' offices before I came here. I'm afraid there is no news. I left all the contact information about our whereabouts over the next few days in case they needed to contact us. I'll call him again in the morning before we leave for Galveston."

Catherine put her hand on top of Trent's. "They are going to find him. I know they are," she said softly and smiled at him.

"I know they are working hard on it. Oh, I cleaned out the apartment and returned the key to the landlord. I've packed all our stuff in that one suitcase I brought home."

"So, you aren't planning to go back to work, ever?"

Trent put his last bite of supper in his mouth and chewed before swallowing. "I'm not planning to go back to Humble. If we stay here, I'll find something. I've been thinking about Galveston. I might have better odds of getting a decent-paying job there. We could move into your Galveston property when the tenants move out."

"Our property," Catherine corrected. "It's yours, too."

Trent smiled. Let's just enjoy our little vacation and worry about tomorrow, tomorrow."

279

Their privacy was interrupted when the children joined them. Each child attempted to gain Trent's attention. "Hold on now, just be patient. Let me finish my discussion with your mother and then I'll read you a story."

"Take them into the playroom please, Sadie, we'll join you shortly," Catherine said.

When the children were gone, Catherine moved around the table circling Trent's neck with her arms. "Thank you for putting your family before your job. I know it's been difficult for you. We're going to get through this together." She bent down and kissed his cheek. Trent turned and gently pulled her into his lap.

"Everything I do is for us; you, the children, our future. I'm probably going to smother everyone. I may never let you out of my sight." They kissed each other for a long moment and Catherine got up.

"I'll never grow tired of you. Why don't you go read them a story and I'll finish up in the kitchen?"

39

The Santa Fe pulled into the Brenham train station at four-thirty and the two Rangers quickly made their way inside. "Which direction is the sheriff's office?" Morris flashed his badge at the clerk.

"Left out the door, go six blocks, turn right till you get to Main Street. Take another right and it's in the middle of the block. Can't miss it."

"Ever been to Brenham?" Thomas asked Steve.

"Can't say I have. Looks like any other railroad town."

Fifteen minutes later the two men walked into the sheriff's office and asked the deputy if the sheriff was in. The deputy hesitated for a minute and then stood when Morris flashed his badge. Several minutes later they were sitting in a small office with Sheriff Willard Townsend.

Morris proceeded to explain why they were there and asked Townsend if he had heard the rumors the telephone operator had relayed to him.

"Been expecting you," the sheriff said. "You boys don't let any grass grow under your feet."

"Tell us what you've heard."

"Pretty much the same thing Edith Jones, the switchboard operator, told you. She came in to see me right after she got off work a while ago. I've been doing some checking around. That couple with the baby stayed at the Palmer Hotel up the street. You might want to talk to Milton Palmer. If you got a picture, he can confirm if it was them."

"What about the clerk at the depot? Did you ask him anything?"

"Said he was pretty busy selling tickets but he noticed 'em."

"Think he could give us a description of the couple that left with the baby?"

"You'll need to talk to him about that. Gets pretty busy at the depot with trains coming and goin'. Oh, he did say the couple got to the station early and had to wait before their train left. He probably got a good look at them."

"Do you mind taking a walk with us over to the Palmer Hotel? Mr. Palmer might be a more reliable witness if you were along."

"Let me get my hat."

The three men were at the Palmer Hotel ten minutes later. After introductions, Mr. Palmer invited them into an adjoining parlor and asked his wife to get some lemonade.

"We'd appreciate your giving us any information you might remember about these two people." Morris handed Mr. Palmer the front page of the recent Houston paper. Palmer studied it for a moment.

"That's them. For sure it's him. I didn't see too much of her. Kept her head down and held the baby close; looked like the baby was asleep. They went upstairs to their room and about thirty minutes later the man left."

"He left alone?"

"Yes. He was gone about an hour and then came back with another man and woman. Came in through those doors and walked right past me. Didn't say nothin."

"Can you describe them?"

Palmer scratched his scrubby beard. "Nice-looking couple. Not from around here. He looked like he might be a banker. All dressed up wearing a black hat. Expensive looking suit; it fit him like a glove. She, on the other hand, walked like a real lady. You know what I mean. She glided across the floor and walked up the stairs like she had a book on her head. I'd say they were both in their late twenties, maybe early thirties."

"Did either of them say anything? Think hard. It's important."

"Nobody said anything."

"How long did the couple stay upstairs?"

Mrs. Palmer came in the room and served the lemonade. Palmer took in a deep breath and blew it out, took a sip of the lemonade, and then winked at his wife. "Delicious, my sweets. You make the best lemonade." He turned back to Morris. "I'd guess they were all up in room 210 ' bout forty, maybe fifty minutes. I heard the baby crying and then he stopped. A while later, the two strangers came down the stairs and the Mrs. was carrying the baby. Funny thing, the man had a nice briefcase when he went upstairs and when he came down he was only carrying the woman's carpetbag. That just occurred to me."

"After the first couple left, how did they leave the room? Was it in a mess? Did they leave anything?"

"Fannie, my wife, she cleans up after they vacate. Said they left several dirty diapers; two empty baby bottles and some wet baby shirts. Guess the couple didn't want them. Oh, and she found a wadded-up hundred dollar bill on the floor. Not many people leave a hundred dollar bill. I told Fannie she could buy herself some nice clothes with the money."

"You've been a big help and we appreciate your time," Morris said. "If you think of anything else you might have forgotten to tell us, you can get in touch with the sheriff."

The Sheriff followed the men to the train station and introduced them to Charlie Weaver, the clerk at the train station.

Morris showed Charlie Weaver the newspaper with Ira's and Gilda's picture. "I need you to think real hard about this." Pointing at Ira's picture, Morris asked, "This man met another couple here a few days ago and I wondered if you remember the couple he met."

"Sure, I got a good look at them. I thought it was strange that they were met by that man in the picture and when they came back an hour and a half later, they had a baby with them."

"Do you remember their destination?"

Charlie twisted his mouth and then spit out a wad of chew into a spittoon. "They took the four o'clock that goes through to Austin. They had a return ticket so they didn't buy one from me. Wait a minute. Let me ask Tucker. He punches the tickets." Charlie left and returned with another man and introduced him as Tucker Burton.

After introductions, Morris asked if he could remember seeing this man with another couple.

"I remember them. The couple came in on one train and left a couple hours later on another train and had a baby with them. She was cooing all over the baby and kept saying. 'Isn't he the most beautiful baby in the world?' Said that to her husband and he agreed with her. Wait a minute." Tucker looked up at the ceiling as though thinking about something. "Yes, she said, 'Nathan;"she called the man, 'Nathan."

"That's great. Do you know what destination was on the ticket?"Charlie thought again. Then shaking his head, he said. "I believe it was Austin. Yes, pretty sure it was Austin."

"Was there anything distinctive about the man or woman?"

"Other than being part of the upper class, can't say I do. No, wish I could be of more help."

"You've been very helpful."

Morris turned to Charlie and the Sheriff. "If I have a sketch artist here tomorrow, Sheriff, do you think you could get the three witnesses together and come up with some pictures?"

"Sure thing."

"Good." Morris turned to Charlie. "I need to send a telegram to my Houston office. Do you have time to do that for me?"

"Sure thing."

Morris wrote out a short note. "To: Ranger Marcus Davidson. Need your help in Brenham. How soon can you come? Steven Morris."

Morris and Thomas waited for the telegram to be sent and paid Charlie for the wire. Thirty minutes later a reply was received. "To: Steven Morris. Davidson in Beaumont on assignment. Back in three days."

Morris turned to the sheriff and Charlie. "Looks like it will be a couple of days before Ranger Davidson will be available. He not only is a good Ranger, but he has a real knack for drawing people. I guess we'll head back to Houston on the next train. Appreciate all the help."

"Next train to Houston arrives in about fifteen minutes. Just get on and flash your badges to the conductor. You don't need a ticket."

Steven Morris thanked everyone and told them he would be back in touch.

After the men boarded the train, Thomas looked at Morris. "I'm beginning to think we might find Trent Matthew's son," Thomas said.

"If he doesn't get sold a second time, you could be right. I'm afraid this couple could be part of this ring and if they are, the baby could end up anywhere."

"Do you ever think about quitting the Rangers?" Thomas asked.

"Everyday."

"Then why stay?"

"'Cause someone has to do it. I've been with the Rangers over six years now and except for the traveling, I've enjoyed it."

"What about your wife?"

"What about her? She knew I was a Ranger when we married."

"She doesn't get mad when you have to leave town?"

"I'm married to a great girl and she rarely complains. That's why I married her. Why all the questions, anyway?"

"I've been dating this girl for a while and I'm thinking about asking her to get married."

"Be sure she understands what your job is. Does she know about the traveling?"

"Yes, she is close to her family and she told me that if we got married and I was gone, she would probably stay at her folk's house."

"Looks like you are already committed."

"Yeah, I guess I am."

40

The next morning Catherine and Trent got up early to finish preparations for their trip to Galveston. They were almost through putting their last minute items in the suitcase when Catherine held up what looked to be a cut-off pair of men's underwear. "I made you some swimming trunks."

Trent stared at them. "Do men really swim in those?"

Catherine laughed. "Yes. I think you will look quite handsome in them."

"If you say so. What will you wear?"

Catherine picked up a stripped pink and purple top, and bloomers. "This is mine."

Trent smiled. "Not sure I want you to wear that in public."

"Nonsense. It's the latest beach fashion."

Catherine's smile slowly turned serious. "We are making the right decision, aren't we? I mean leaving town and going off like nothing has happened?"

Trent walked over and put his hands on her shoulders. "I'm just as concerned and worried as you are. Morris knows how to reach us if they find him.

We will only be an hour away. I told him I'd call his office each day, person to person. He said to call collect and if he had nothing to report, he wouldn't accept the charges. It will be good for all of us. If you don't mind, I may spend some time visiting some survey companies in town to see if there might be work for me in Galveston." Trent was interrupted when the phone rang. "I'll get it."

Moving quickly down the stairs, Trent picked up the phone on the fourth ring. "Hello."

"Good morning Trent. This is Ranger Morris. My office said you called yesterday and I knew you would be leaving for your trip today. We are following up some leads and it's going to take some time to sort them all out. I wish I could tell you more, but I don't want to give you false hope."

"Are you sure it will be all right for us to go? I left contact names and numbers with your agent at the front desk."

"There is no need to sit around and be depressed. Take your family and get your mind off of this. I know it's easy for me to say that. I'm following up some leads and I will be in and out of my office. If we come up with anything, I'll find you. Have a nice trip."

Trent hung up the phone and turned when he felt Catherine behind him. He shook his head and grimaced. "Nothing new. Morris said he was following up on some leads. Said he would find us if there was any news about Jacob."

Catherine put her arms around him. "It's in God's hands."

Trent kissed her lightly on the cheek. "I wish He would hurry up."

Moments later the children were standing on the stairs watching their parents. "Are we still going to Galveston?" Daniel asked.

"We certainly are," Trent said. "But first, we need to have some breakfast." Scurrying to the kitchen, each child took their usual seat while Catherine took out a fresh bowl of fruit and scooped several spoonsful on each plate.

"I believe its Isabelle's turn to say grace," Catherine said looking at her."

"Bless this food, Lord, and keep us safe on our twip. Oh, and please find Jacob for us. We myth him."

"Thank you Isabelle. Now, please eat your fruit while I make some oatmeal," Catherine said.

"How long will it take us to get to Galston?" Adam asked.

"The train leaves at noon. After we board, if you take your naps, we should be there by the time you wake up."

"Will we go swimmin' when we get there?"

Catherine looked at Adam. "We will all go swimming after we get settled in our rooms. Now let's eat our breakfast and then you can get dressed."

X X X

While Morris was waiting on a phone call from Davidson, he was called to the phone. "I think it's that newspaper lady at the Houston paper. Want me to tell her you are busy?" the clerk asked.

"Naw. I'll take it."

"This is Ranger Morris."

"Good morning, Ranger Morris. I was wondering if you had any more news on the kidnappings."

"If I give you some information, when would it appear in the newspaper?"

"Well, if we hurry, I could slip it in to a column Sunday."

"What if I didn't want it run until Monday? I haven't given this information to the Matthews and I don't want them to read about it before I tell them."

"I would be happy to hold it until Monday."

Morris proceeded to update Gladys on his leads. "Please understand that the only reason why I'm telling you this is because it might shake out some more witnesses. Do you think someone in Austin would print this in the Austin paper?"

"I have a friend that works at the Austin paper. We went to journalism school together at the University of Texas. She's always looking for a good story and I think this will pique her interest."

"That would be great. I really appreciate you helping us catch these villains. They need to be stopped."

"Always happy to help the law." Agnes hung up the receiver, put a sheet of paper in her typewriter and began pecking away at the keys:

On Trail of Kidnappers

Ranger Steven Morris with the Houston Rangers' office has confirmed sightings of the malicious pair that stole baby Jacob Matthews. After arriving in Brenham, Texas, several days ago, baby Jacob was handed off to a couple that may be from Austin, Texas. The couple returned to Austin with baby Jacob that same day. The man and woman are described as being approximately thirty years old, well dressed, and the man was addressed as Nathan by his companion.

The scoundrels that originally kidnapped baby Jacob are identified as Ira Gentry and Gilda Perkins. Their whereabouts are unknown as they are traveling in an automobile that has been identified as a three-horsepower, curved dash Oldsmobile. If anyone has knowledge of these scoundrels or know the whereabouts of baby Jacob Matthews, please contact Steven Morris at the Texas Rangers' offices in Houston, Texas.

After finishing her article, Gladys picked up the telephone and called her friend in Austin. When she came to the telephone, Gladys introduced herself and read the article to her friend. She read it again at a much slower pace as she could hear the typewriter on the other end tapping away. Afterwards, the two ladies visited a while longer about the incident.

"I've been keeping up with these abductions, Gladys, and I'm just as concerned as you are. Let's stay in touch and I'll let you know if I hear anything locally about this. Knowing the man's first name is important," her friend said. "A new baby in a family where the father's name is Nathan will be hard to cover up. That is, unless they were part of the gang that took him. I'll do what I can."

"I really appreciate it," Agnes said and hung up the phone.

41

Trent, Catherine, Sadie and the four children settled into their seats on the train; Trent on one side with Emma and Isabelle while Catherine sat across on another bench facing them with Daniel, Adam and Sadie. As they had hoped, the children were fast asleep fifteen minutes into the trip. Trent caught Catherine's eyes and mouthed, "I love you." She did the same and they both smiled. An hour later, Daniel woke and stared out the window at the bayou. He had never seen this amount of water. The Brazos River was wide, but it was nothing compared to this. Seconds later the other children woke and did the same.

"Are we almost there?" Emma asked.

"Yes, we should be there soon."

"It's not gonna rain, is it?" Adam asked.

"No. I think we are going to have a nice sunny weekend for swimming," Catherine answered. Several minutes later, they pulled into the Galveston train station.

After retrieving their luggage, Trent hailed a large carriage. "We need a ride to this address," Trent said handing a piece of paper to the driver. The driver got down and helped put the luggage on the back of the carriage. The children were surprisingly good as they rode through the streets towards the gulf. As they approached the seawall, the seagulls kept them entertained as they watched them collect fish from the water.

"Do they bite?" Adam asked.

"No," Trent said laughing. "Only if you are a fish."

When the driver stopped at the address, Mark Graham, the real estate agent, was waiting in front of the property. "It's good to see you," he said. "Hope you had a nice trip over."

"It was great," Catherine said and made the introductions. The agent left after giving Trent the keys. The children ran upstairs and out to the balcony. "Look, I see a ship," Daniel said. Trent and Catherine followed with the luggage and unlocked the door.

"This house looks funny. There is nothing underneath it." Adam commented.

"It's built up on stilts so if the water rises, the rooms won't get wet."

Sadie and the two girls shared one bedroom and the two boys took the one across the hall. Catherine and Trent settled into the large master suite that had a panoramic view of the gulf. The living room and kitchen were at the back of the house. After unpacking, Catherine helped the children into their swimsuits. Trent changed into his and looked in the mirror. "I look like a clown."

Catherine laughed. "You'll look just like all the men in bathing suits."

"That bad, huh?"

"I didn't mean it that way. You look right handsome."

"What about me?" she asked as she posed.

"Beautiful."

Catherine grabbed the carpetbag she had filled with towels, a mixture of olive oil and Aloe Vera lotion and some dry cereal. "Let's gather the children and head for the sun."

The beach house they rented was in walking distance to Murdock's bathhouse, which made it very convenient for food and necessities. Trent rented a locker to put their valuables in and pinned the key to his bathing suit. They also rented a large umbrella and settled their things underneath its cover. When given the go-ahead, the children ran screaming into the splashing waves. Sadie splashed in the water with the children and after some coaxing, Catherine and Trent joined in the fun.

"One, two, three, four, one two three, four. Catherine was sitting back under the umbrella with her eyes glued to her four children. They were further out into the water and even with Trent and Sadie close by she couldn't help but count over and over. After an hour, she finally got up and walked to the water's edge. "Trent. Trent," she said louder. He turned and looked at her.

"Gather the children and bring them in. I don't want them to get sunburned."

As they dried each child with a towel, the four children begged to stay in the water longer. "I'm afraid that's it for the day. You are getting sunburned."

"What's sunburned, Mommy?" Emma asked.

"The sun's rays will cook your skin and make it turn very red. It will hurt a lot."

Tired and slightly sunburned, they gathered up their things, retuned to Murdock's and stood under the showers to remove the sand. Trent left to return the umbrella and retrieve their things from the locker. Together they walked up the steps and across the street toward the beach house.

"What are we going to do now, Mommy?" Adam asked.

"We are going to get dressed and take a ride around the island."

"I'm hungry," Isabelle said.

"I think we should stop over there by the ice cream man and get them a treat," Trent suggested.

"Yea," the children replied.

42

Nathan Armstrong and his wife, Trudy, had been home for almost two weeks with Jacob on their ranch, just south of Austin, Texas. It was a magnificent piece of land with a creek running through the center of it. Nathan was a business man with holdings in several oil companies. A herd of over one hundred fifty cattle grazed the land that surrounded his five thousand square foot two-story home. It had been three years since their only son, eight year old Brian, had fallen from his horse and broken his neck. His mother, Trudy, never recovered from the loss of her son and frequently went on drinking binges.

Nathan was thirty-four years old and Trudy was thirty-one. She had been unable to conceive another child and after losing Brian, her depression never left her. It was Nathan's idea to adopt a child. At first Trudy didn't want to, but slowly Nathan convinced her it was the only way she could get better. After trying several agencies in the Austin area, the process was slow and they were told that younger couples had priority. After six months of waiting, Nathan was told by a friend's brother about Beauregard Tyson.

"I've heard he only arranges babies for the upper class and that the babies go through a screening process, the man assured him."

Nathan asked his attorney, Rodney Horton, to get in touch with Mr. Tyson on his behalf.

"I'm not sure about these solicitors that charge extra fees for these babies. Are you sure you want to spend that kind of money?" his attorney asked.

"Trudy hasn't been herself since Bryan died. The regular adoption agencies think we are too old and don't want to fool with us. I'll do whatever it takes to get a child."

"Hmm," his attorney said, looking over the name and address of Beauregard Tyson. It's a general delivery address with a drawer number. If he is well respected, I wonder why he doesn't have an office."

"I asked that same thing. My brother's friend said Mr. Tyson kept his matters very confidential and he didn't want people to be able to find him if they changed their minds after signing the papers. It made sense to me."

"Yes, I can understand that. I've only handled a few adoptions, but none of them have come back to me because they changed their minds. Of course, they sign a statement that all the information is confidential and they are not allowed to know where their child might be living now. Yes, that could be the reason. All right, then, I'll send him a letter."

"No, send him a wire. Whatever it costs, you know I'm good for it."

The next day, Nathan received a call from his attorney. He was astounded when his attorney received a wire back saying that the fee would be five thousand dollars and that there may be a child available the second week of May. A quick reply was requested in order to secure their being first in line, if the child was healthy when it was born. Mr. Tyson assured the attorney the parents had been through a background check and the baby would have a medical examination prior to the adoption. If the offer was accepted Mr. Tyson would wire the necessary steps for them to adopt the baby.

The five thousand dollars was a mere drop in the bucket for multi-millionaire Nathan Armstrong, but he was not a man to throw away money if he didn't have to.

"We need to wire him a confirmation today or he will go to the next couple in line behind you," the attorney told Nathan.

"Let's do it. Make the arrangements and keep me informed," Nathan said.

While the Armstrongs waited for the arrival of their new baby, Brian's old room was turned into a nursery. Trudy spared no expense buying imported lace curtains for the windows and having a mural of colorful animals painted on the nursery wall. She promised Nathan she would stop drinking, but she continued to indulge behind his back. *I'll give it up when the baby comes.*

As promised, the call was made to Nathan's attorney with the instructions for the Armstrongs to meet Ira Gentry in Brenham, Texas, to pick up their new son.

A nanny was employed to help Trudy take care of their new baby. Agnes Johnson was a spinster, thirty-six years old and the eldest of ten children. She had raised her siblings and after the youngest married a month earlier, she heard through a friend that the Armstrongs were looking for a nanny.

When Nathan and Trudy came home with their new son, whom they named Ryan, Trudy handed him to Agnes and told her she had a bad headache and was going to bed. Over the next few days, Agnes saw to all the needs of Ryan and fell instantly in love with him. It didn't bother her that Trudy would not change a diaper and rarely held him. Trudy made lots of excuses and Agnes knew Trudy was drinking, but kept it to herself.

Mr. Armstrong traveled a lot during the week and usually came home on the weekends. On Sunday, Agnes was in the living room and sat down in the rocking chair to feed Ryan his afternoon bottle. Mr. Armstrong came in and sat on the divan. "How is my son doing?"

"He's a really good baby and hardly ever cries. You are so very lucky to have him as your son."

"And how is Trudy around him? I never see her tending to him."

"Well, she's faring well," she lied, not wanting to get involved in a marital dispute.

"Good, I'm glad to hear that. By the way, Trudy tells me you are doing a wonderful job. I guess with so many brothers and sisters in your family, it's second nature to you."

"I played mother after Mom died when I was twelve. Daddy worked all the time and it was my job to take care of my brothers and sisters. We were all very close."

"That's good to know."

After Nathan left the room, Agnes put the bottle in Ryan's mouth and began rocking him in her arms and humming a soft tune. She loved putting him to sleep for his afternoon naps. She did wonder who his real parents were. *Ryan is so beautiful, I can't believe anyone would just up and abandon him. He's mine now. I don't think the Armstrongs really want you, but don't you worry, little child, I'll raise you myself.*

After Ryan finished his bottle, Agnes continued to rock him, humming quietly. When someone rang the bell at the front door, she looked up and saw Nathan open the door.

43

The weather in Galveston couldn't have been more perfect. The morning breeze swept across the gulf and filled the beach house with the promise of a beautiful day. Trent woke first and was sitting on the veranda in a wooden lawn chair, sipping his coffee when Catherine joined him.

"Isn't it beautiful?"

"Absolutely. I know now why you are so infatuated with this place."

"Still think we could make this our home?"

"As long as I'm with you and the children, nothing else matters."

Trent took Catherine's hand and pulled her onto his lap.

"You look beautiful in the mornings."

Catherine snuggled up next to him and they lay together on the lawn chair.

"Would you mind if I went downtown and checked in with a few land companies? I want to touch base with the Rangers' offices too. I should be back before noon."

"By all means. The children are anxious to ride on one of the trolleys and it will be a great way to show them the island. Sadie and I can handle it."

Trent went back inside and dressed while Catherine went to the kitchen to prepare breakfast. "Don't worry about me. I'll get something later," Trent said as he put his arms around her and kissed her.

Trent found that most of the land offices were closed on Saturday and as he made his way down the Strand, he saw a sign that said, Land Sales, Mark Graham, and Conveyor of land. The door was unlocked and he went in. Mark was sitting at a desk and looked up. "Is everything all right Mr. Matthews?" Mark asked.

"Yes, we are very pleased with the house we rented. I was wondering if I could make a person to person phone call. I'll pay for the costs."

"Yes." Mark turned the phone around and told Trent to have a seat in the chair beside his desk. While Trent spoke with the operator, Mark left and walked down a hall to a back office. When he returned a few minutes later he asked if everything was all right.

"Yes, my party wasn't there so I'll try back another time. Do you mind if I ask you a few questions about some of the land offices? What do they do exactly?"

"Several are owned by lawyers that solicit business for real estate. Some have architectural and survey backgrounds, and make drawings for houses.

Others are like me. They find buyers and sellers of real estate."

"It's a small island. Is there much business?"

"You'd be surprised. Since the flood wiped out half its population in 1900, it's done nothing but grow. There is a lot of undeveloped land back to the west and we have land developers coming in by the dozens. Some Galveston businessmen are in the process of looking at some land on the Seawall to build a five star hotel."

"Well, I appreciate your time, Mark. I've left your phone number with someone as a contact. If they happen to call, I'd be obliged if you would send a message to us."

"Yes, I'd be happy to."

Trent left and continued walking down the Strand until he reached Broadway and then took the trolley back to the beach. By the time he reached the beach house, he was beginning to feel the heat of the afternoon sun. He had picked up a copy of the Galveston Gazette while he was in town and was reading it when he heard Catherine and the children coming upstairs.

"Oh, you're home." She walked over and kissed him on the cheek. "I picked up some hot dogs and buns at the market and thought we could roast them over the fire-pit downstairs."

"Sounds good to me," Trent answered as he got up to help her.

Sadie found some long metal skewers in a drawer and helped put the hot dogs on the end. Trent went downstairs to start a fire in the pit. Wood and kindling were stored underneath the house and Trent grabbed what he needed and carried it over to the fire pit. A few minutes later, everyone was gathered round the fire watching the hot dogs roast. When they were finished, Catherine used a hot pad to place the skewers in a large pan and carry them upstairs.

"I believe these are the best hot dogs I've ever eaten," Sadie said and everyone agreed. After their feast, the children were put down for their naps while Trent and Catherine sat in the bedroom and talked.

"I suppose there was no news," Catherine said sighing.

"Morris wasn't in his office and there was no message for me so, I guess not."

"How was your morning?"

"Interesting. Most of the land offices I saw were closed. However, Mark was in his real estate office and I stopped in there to use his phone and ask him a few questions. He was very positive about the real estate market and said housing prices were continuing to go up."

"Yes, he told me our house was definitely going up in value. Do you have any thoughts what you might do if we moved here?"

"It's hard to say right now. I figured I could learn all I need to learn about Galveston in about a month and then I might just open up my own company. There are rumors that a huge hotel is going to be built not far from here by some local businessmen. I'd say my chances of opening up a surveying company could be a possibility."

"I think that's a great idea." Catherine yawned and put her head on Trent's shoulder. They both napped for a while and were awakened by the screaming and laughing of their four children. "Guess we have to get up now."

Trent yawned. "Are you sure? I thought we were on vacation."

"Did I forget to tell you parents never get to go on vacation?"

The family made their last trip to Murdock's beach. Catherine insisted she put the oil on the children before they went swimming. When they finished, the well-oiled children ran ahead to the water's edge and waited for their parents to join them. Trent arrived first and said, "Last one in is a rotten egg." Screaming, they all went out to the first wave.

Catherine watched from the water's edge, counting heads as she had done the day before. After some coercing, she joined them in the water to splash in the waves. They had been in and out of the water for almost two hours when Trent suggested they had had enough.

"Let us ride just one more wave," Daniel pleaded.

"All right, but try and stay together." Trent said as everyone ran back into the water.

A large wave approached followed close by an even larger one separating Adam from Trent and Sadie. Catherine screamed, "Adam, come back."

"Look at me, Mommy," Adam shouted back.

Catherine swam after him, grabbed his arm just as another large wave passed over them and pulled them further back from the beach. Trent looked up just as they disappeared. He dove immediately into the wave and swam after them. Sadie was holding Isabelle's and Emma's hands and pulled them back to shore. Daniel was a stronger swimmer and followed the girls back. It seemed like forever before Trent pulled Catherine and Adam back to shore. They were coughing and breathing hard.

"Mommy, Papa, are you all right?" Daniel asked.

"Everyone is fine," Trent said.

"Wow, that was a huge wave," Sadie said.

"Yes, but we are fine. Just a bit shaken," Catherine answered.

"I think we have all had enough swimming for the day," Trent said.

"Can we go swimming again tomorrow?" Adam asked.

"Tomorrow we go home," Catherine said. "But we will be back soon, I promise."

The children were unusually quiet the next morning as the train passed over the bayou.

"Can we go get Honey from Jason when we get home?" Isabelle asked.

"I think it would easier if Jason brought Honey to the house," Catherine said. "You can spend the rest of the day with him after your naps." She smiled up at Trent and he took her hand and kissed it.

"I guess I will need to check with the blacksmith and see about buying another mare and wagon on Monday. Jason said he would help me pick out a new mare."

Catherine smiled at Trent. "You'll need a new saddle, too. I know you like to ride."

They arrived at the Rosenberg train station at eleven-forty-five and Trent saw a stack of newspapers that were still tied in a bundle. He walked over and looked at them and then went back to the clerk. "Did the Sunday *Houston Chronicle* just get here?"

"Yes, about thirty minutes ago. Haven't had time to get them on the stand."

"Mind if I get one?"

"Help yourself."

Trent put a nickel on the counter, took out his pocket knife and cut the string. He put the paper under his arm, walked back over to his family, and gathered up the luggage. Trent and Catherine walked slowly with the children to their home. Catherine had given

Sadie some money and asked her to go by the market and pick up some bread, cold cuts, and milk for their lunch.

Once home, Trent dropped the three pieces of luggage and walked over to the divan. He began scanning the newspaper and turned the page. He stopped short when he read the headline: *On Trail of Kidnapper*. After reading the article, he immediately went to the phone and called Ranger Morris.

"This is Ranger Morris."

"Steven, what's this article in the newspaper all about? Why haven't you told me about this couple in Austin?"

"I'm sorry Trent. That article wasn't supposed to run until tomorrow. I was going to call you when you got home tonight from Galveston. We are hoping someone will come forward with more information about the couple in Austin. The article is also running in the *Austin Statesman*. We don't know if they were the adoptive parents or part of the snatching scheme. We're making progress. Just hang tight,"

Catherine helped Sadie put the groceries away and make sandwiches for the children. Once the children said grace, she got up and went to Trent. She could see the stress and concern in his face. "What is it? Have they found Jacob?"

Trent handed her the article and she read it. "They are getting close."

"Morris said they could be closing in. We just have to wait and hope someone comes forward. The article is also running in Austin's Sunday paper today."

44

When Nathan and Trudy brought Ryan back to Austin, Nathan's brother, Eli and his wife were there to greet them. Nathan and Eli were very close and it wasn't unusual for Eli to stop by on the weekends.

When Eli arrived Sunday morning at Nathan's house, he had a folded newspaper under his arm. Nathan answered the door and they shook hands, giving each other a brotherly hug. "I want to show you something. Let's sit on the porch so we will have some privacy," Eli suggested.

Agnes was sitting in a rocking chair with Ryan in the living room and couldn't resist going to the window and peeking from behind the curtain. Nathan and Eli sat in the chairs outside the window and even though their voices were low, Agnes could clearly hear their conversation.

"Have you read the Sunday paper this morning?"

"Just the business section. Why? What did I miss?"

Eli turned took the Austin paper from under his arm and opened it. "You need to read this."

Nathan looked at the headline. "Where is Baby Jacob?" He looked up at his brother.

"What does this have to do with me?"

"Ryan might be the kidnapped baby that was taken from his crib in the middle of the night two weeks ago."

"What makes you think that?" Nathan began reading the article. His color turned ashen as he read.

"The description matches Ryan perfectly including the fish birthmark."

"Oh my God. This will kill Trudy."

"Who else knows about Ryan's birthmark besides us?"

"The nanny. She bathes him and tends to him on a daily basis."

Nathan continued to read. "For Christ's sake, his mother is a doctor and they live in Rosenberg." Nathan ran his hand through his hair and began pacing.

He stopped and turned to his brother. "What should I do?"

"I guess you better call your lawyer and get his advice. He's the one that set it up. I think you better hide that newspaper if you don't want Trudy to see it."

Nathan and Eli went back inside and Agnes rushed back to the rocking chair barely sitting in it before they came back in. Nathan and his brother walked through the living room and down a hall where Nathan kept a small office.

Agnes jerked when she heard the door slam. She stared down at the sleeping Ryan. Almost in a whisper, Agnes said, "I'll put you in your crib for now. I need to pray about this."

A while later Trudy found Agnes asleep in a chair by Ryan's crib. She decided to go downstairs and look for her husband. As she approached his study, she heard her brother-in-law's voice. "You have to do the right thing, Nathan. If Ryan was taken illegally from his parents, you have to return him."

Trudy abruptly opened the door without knocking and glared at her husband. She looked down at the newspaper article on his desk and picked it up. Her eyes began to tear as she read the article. She looked up at her husband. "You are not taking my son."

Nathan walked over to her and put his arms around her. "We have no proof of anything right now. We'll fight it. I have a call into our attorney."

Trudy turned and ran back upstairs to her room.

"Oh, God. She's probably going to get drunk now."

"I thought she quit," Eli said.

"I thought she had, too, but she sneaks around and thinks I don't know. I haven't seen her holding Ryan since the day we got back. I guess getting her a baby wasn't such a good idea. Maybe this is for the best."

Nathan was walking Eli to the front door when they heard the explosion of a gun going off. The two men looked at each other and ran upstairs. They first looked in Ryan's room and saw Agnes holding a crying Ryan. Nathan turned and ran down the hall to his bedroom. Eli was right behind him when Nathan opened the door and stopped. Eli walked around Nathan and over to Trudy's bed. Blood splatters of dark red adorned the mahogany headboard and expensive white French linen bedspread. Her head rested on a pillow aligned with the finality of death. The gun still rested in her right hand. Black soot from the gunshot marked its presence and Eli turned to his brother shaking his head.

"You don't want to see this up close," Eli said taking Nathan out the door. They passed Agnes as she stood in the doorway of Ryan's room. The expression on their faces was verification enough that Trudy had done the unthinkable. She had committed suicide.

45

In the two weeks Agnes cared for Ryan, his presence had secured a permanent place in her heart. She paced the floor in Ryan's room mumbling to herself, and talking to Ryan. "Don't worry my precious darling, I won't leave you. I promise. I won't leave you."

She heard more voices downstairs and she looked out the window into the front gardens. Several horses were tied to posts and Eli's automobile was parked in the circular driveway. She had only ridden in Nathan's automobile when he picked her up and she didn't think it was that hard to maneuver. She recalled him pulling a knob and then a lever before the automobile started, but beyond that, she couldn't remember. It was at least twelve miles into Austin and even though she had learned to ride a horse at an early age, she wasn't sure she could mount a horse if she were carrying Ryan.

Agnes continued to walk the floor and Ryan began to get fussy. "It's going to be fine, my precious. I'm your new mother now." Her thoughts were interrupted by a knock on the door.

It was Eli. "You need to bring Ryan downstairs." Agnes hesitated. "Now," he said firmly. He turned and waited for Agnes to go first. Once downstairs, Nathan walked over and took Ryan from her. Ryan immediately began fretting.

"He's hungry. Give him back to me and I'll go feed him." Nathan ignored her and walked over to the settee, and laid him down. He unbuttoned Ryan's shirt and pulled his tiny tee shirt over his head. Ryan was fretting and kicking his feet.

Agnes grabbed him up in her arms. "Why he could roll off this settee," she shouted. Two men walked forward and took a closer look at Ryan's chest.

Ryan began crying when one of the men touched the spot where his birthmark was."

"Have you seen enough?" Nathan said to the man.

"Yes, we'll contact his real parents."

"No, no, you can't do that. He belongs to Mr. Armstrong. I'm his nanny and will take care of him." Agnes was backing away with Ryan.

"Calm down, Agnes. You can go feed him now," Nathan said. "Go with her, Eli." Nathan continued talking with the sheriff and a man from the Texas Rangers' office in Austin.

Texas Ranger Gerald Connelly addressed Nathan. "Can your nanny be trusted?"

"I think she is just shaken up by Trudy's death." Nathan closed his eyes and looked away. He was still in shock and just saying Trudy's name caused him to break down. He turned and walked over to a chair and sat down with his head in his hands.

Eli watched as Agnes went back upstairs with a crying Ryan and fresh baby bottle filled with milk. He turned and walked over to the sheriff.

"I hope the coroner gets here soon. My wife will be here shortly and we will take Ryan to our house until this mess is sorted out. I don't trust the nanny."

"I think that would be a good idea. I need your address," Ranger Connelly said.

"That's easy. I live two miles up the road behind the red brick wall and iron gate on the right.

A while later, the coroner and two attendants arrived along with Eli's wife, Clarice. Eli was sitting in a chair next to Nathan and said, "When the sheriff and the Ranger get through with their questions, Clarice and I want you and Ryan to come back to our house and stay until all of this gets sorted out. Do I have your permission to give Agnes her notice?"

Nathan reached into his vest pocket and took out his wallet. He counted out fifty dollars and handed it to Eli. "Tell her to pack her things and go. This will take care of her wages plus some severance. Will you see she gets back into town? She can go to her sister's house."

Eli followed Clarice upstairs to Ryan's room.

"No, I won't let you take him," Agnes screamed.

Eli walked out to the top of the stairs and motioned for the Sheriff to come up. Agnes was crying as she backed into a corner with Ryan in her arms.

The sheriff was calm when he spoke to her. "Agnes, I've known you and your family a long time and I know you want to do the right thing. Give the baby to Clarice and gather your things. I'll see you get back to your sister's house." Clarice walked over and took Ryan from Agnes. She fell to the floor sobbing.

46

Nathan refused to leave the house until Trudy's body was removed by the undertaker. Eli and Clarice left earlier with Ryan and a while later he walked back to Nathan's house. The house was empty when Eli entered and searched the house for Nathan.

Nathan was sitting in a chair with a drink in his hand when Eli walked into the master bedroom. Eli looked at his brother who appeared to be in shock. Nathan's eyes were fixed on the blood-stained bed.

"I didn't know she knew how to shoot a gun. I always left my gun and holster hanging over my chair. Who would have thought she had the nerve. I did this. It's my fault she's dead. She was the love of my life." Tears filled his eyes as he stood up and threw his empty whiskey glass against the wall, shattering pieces of glass onto their bed.

He turned and looked at his brother. "I don't ever want to see that baby again. Send him back to his parents."

Eli left and went downstairs to use the phone. He returned to Nathan a few minutes later. "The sheriff said it would be tomorrow before the parents could be notified. I'll stay here with you tonight." Their conversation was interrupted by the telephone.

"I'll go see who it is," Eli said and went back downstairs. "Hello."

"This is Rodney Horton. May I speak to Nathan?"

"This is Eli, we've got a real problem and you need to get over to Nathan's house right away." Eli hung up the phone before Rodney could say anything.

Thirty minutes later Rodney drove through the cattle guard and parked in front of the house. Eli met him at the door. "What's so urgent that you call me out on a Sunday afternoon? My wife's not happy." Eli and Rodney went into the living room as Nathan walked stoned-faced down the stairs.

Rodney looked at Eli. "What's going on?"

Eli picked up the newspaper and handed it to Rodney. Rodney started reading the article.

"Trudy shot herself in the head," Nathan said casually. "She just took my gun and shot herself. Can you believe that?" He walked over to the window and looked out.

Rodney looked first at Nathan and then at Eli. "Oh, my God."

Eli walked over to the bar and poured whiskey into three glasses. He handed one to Rodney and then walked over to Nathan and put it in his hand. Nathan finally walked away from the window and sat down on the settee.

Eli was the first to speak. "What's my brother's liability in this kidnapping?" Rodney looked dumbfounded.

"I don't think he has any as long as Ryan is returned to his parents."

"And the five thousand dollars?" Eli asked.

"I'm afraid it's gone. You can't expect Ryan's real parents to pay it back. They were victims, too."

"Screw the money," Nathan yelled. "I don't want to hear any more about it. Trudy's gone and nothing will bring her back."

"Where is Ryan?" Rodney asked.

"We took him to our house. Clarice is looking after him now. I wanted Nathan to come back to our house, but he doesn't want to see Ryan. Why don't you take him home with you?"

"Me? Cindy would murder me. We have four kids of our own and she can't take care of another one."

Eli looked at his brother. "Will you be all right if I stay here with you tonight?"

"If you don't mind sleeping upstairs, I'll sleep in the guest room downstairs." Nathan finished off his drink and walked to the bar to pour another.

"I'm going to see Rodney out. I'll ride along with him so he can drop me off at my house. Clarice is cooking dinner and I'll bring you back something to eat. I'll be back soon."

Nathan didn't answer as he took another drink of whiskey. After he downed the last drop, he poured another and took it with him upstairs. He stopped at the entrance to Ryan's room. He stared into the room for a few minutes and then went over to the window. It was half-open and he raised it. He reared back with his foot and kicked the screen out. He chugalugged the remainder of whiskey in his glass and threw the glass out the window. Jerking the French linen curtains from the window, he threw them outside. He did the same with all the curtains and then proceeded to remove everything from the crib, throwing them outside. Yanking and kicking at the crib, it gave way to his boot and fell into pieces. He gathered up everything, the wood slats, the rocking chair, and finally the drawers that held Ryan's clothes. He watched as it all fell to the ground.

He was panting as he turned and went to his bedroom. Gathering up the bed linens, pillows and blanket, he returned to Ryan's room and threw them all out the same window. He closed his eyes and inhaled, holding it in for a second, and then blew it out. *That's it, Trudy. That's it.*

He turned and raced downstairs and into the kitchen grabbing a box of matches. When he got outside, he made several trips to a burn barrel twenty-five yards away. When it was full, he picked up a can with kerosene and poured it onto the pile. Nathan struck a match and threw it into the barrel. It exploded into a huge ball of fire. He stepped back and watched.

A few minutes after the fire died down, he went back to pick up another pile of linens.

Clarice was at her sink washing dishes when she first saw a large black cloud of smoke appear down the road. The window she was looking through overlooked the pasture between their house and Nathan's. The smoke appeared to be coming from the back of Nathan's house.

"Eli," she screamed. "Eli."

"What's wrong?" he said, looking at her.

"Look!"

Eli raced to the window and looked out.

Eli ran outside and started his automobile. He drove over some hedges before he reached the back of Nathan's house. When he stopped, he saw Nathan filling the burn barrel. His heart was racing and he put his head down on the steering wheel, relieved Nathan was all right.

When he finally exited his car, he walked over to Nathan. "Want some help?"

"Grab the rest of that crib and break it up with your boot." Eli did as he was told. Nathan picked up the pieces and returned to the burn barrel. When the last piece was put in, Nathan turned to Eli. "I need a drink."

After three more drinks, Nathan passed out on the divan. Eli went to the phone and called Clarice.

"Everything all right?"

"Yes, the children are all asleep. Is everything all right there?"

"Nathan decided to burn everything in the burn barrel. The blood stained linens, Ryan's curtains, the crib, everything. I guess it made him feel better. I don't know. He's passed out on the divan. He killed the whiskey bottle. Sorry to run out on you like I did."

"It hasn't been too bad. Mom came over to help with the children. Ryan is a very pleasant baby. As long as he is dry and fed, he's happy. I'm afraid you are the one with your hands full."

"Yeah, it's going to be a tough week."

47

Morris left his office at two o'clock Sunday afternoon. His in-laws were coming to dinner and he promised his wife he would be home early. He told the clerk not to bother him at home unless it was an emergency. The Rangers' offices were officially closed on Sunday, but Morris often worked when he was on a big case. There was usually a clerk there to answer the phone, but he was often away in another part of the building.

The clerk went to the back of the building to catch up on some filing when he heard the phone ring in the front office. He looked at his pocket watch. It was after 4:25 in the afternoon and he shook his head. He stopped what he was doing and slowly made his way to the front. "Rangers' offices."

"I need to speak with Ranger Morris."

"Sorry. Won't be back till tomorrow. Call back then." The clerk hung up and returned to his filing. He was several steps away when the phone rang again.

Irritated, he answered. "Rangers' offices."

"Look, I need to speak with Ranger Morris. I'm Texas Ranger McAllister in Austin, Texas, and I need to talk with him. Could you please get in touch with him and ask him to call me at GR7-8776?"

The clerk took down the number and hung up. He didn't think the call was urgent, so he walked over and put the piece of paper over a spike that was used for messages on Morris' desk.

X X X

Sunday afternoon while the children napped, Trent helped Catherine unpack the two suitcases and carried things to the laundry room off the porch. "Thanks for helping me with all this. The children had a great time and so did I."

"Are you sure about that? I was really concerned when you and Adam were separated from us in the water. That part wasn't fun." He stopped and took her in his arms. "I don't know what I would have done if something happened to you, Catherine."

"Nothing happened and I'm fine. Adam and I were just a bit shaken up."

Trent frowned.

"Why are you frowning?"

"I just feel like I should be doing something. If Jacob is in Austin, maybe I should take a train up there in the morning. If the same article ran in Austin's paper that was in the *Houston Chronicle*, somebody would know something. If that Nathan fella and his wife were there to adopt him and the man is a businessman, well. . . wouldn't he want to do the right thing if he read that Jacob was taken illegally?"

"I know we are going to get him back. If you go running off on a wild goose chase and Morris calls to tell us they found him, wouldn't it be better if you were here and not somewhere we couldn't find you?"

He sighed. "You're right. You are always right."

"I just think it's better to talk things through. Logic is usually the best answer."

"I know. I just think I'll go crazy if they don't find him soon."

"Tomorrow is a new day with new hopes and answered prayers. We have to put it in God's hands."

Trent hugged Catherine. "Oh, my darling, just keep reminding me of that."

"I need to go into the kitchen and see if I can find something to fix for dinner. The cupboards are pretty bare."

"What are the choices?"

"Eggs, biscuits and gravy."

"Sounds good to me. I'll help."

Trent opened the icebox. "Think the bacon is edible?"

Catherine took it from his hand. "It still feels cold and it's cured so I think we can fry it up. I know the children will be hungry when they wake up. I'll prepare an early dinner. If you feel like it, you can clean and cut up those ripe peaches Mrs. Johnson brought by last Thursday, I'll make us a peach cobbler."

Trent carried the bowl of peaches to the sink to wash. "You just want me to stay busy, don't you?"

Catherine smiled. "Sometimes you are like a cat on a hot tin roof. You cannot sit still."

Trent laughed. "You know me too well."

While Trent went to work on the peaches, Catherine prepared the biscuit dough. Trent was sitting at the kitchen table with an apron wrapped around his waist cutting up peaches.

Daniel walked in and sat in a chair next to him. "Can I watch, Papa?"

Trent smiled at him. "You sure can. Are your sisters and brother still napping?"

Daniel yawned and said. "Yes, sir." He placed his elbows on the table and propped his chin on top, occasionally looking up at Trent.

"What's on your mind, young man?"

"I was just thinking about how brave you were when mama and Adam almost drowned."

Trent stopped cutting the peaches and wiped his hands on his apron. He pulled Daniel into his lap. "I know it frightened you. It scared me a little, too. But I think your mama was the hero. She was closer to him than I was and she grabbed him first. I was just along to make sure they made it."

Daniel got down and ran over to his mother and hugged her. "Thanks, mama. You're the best." He turned and ran upstairs.

Catherine laughed. "So, you made me the hero."

Trent grinned up at her. "Moms can be heroes, too." He shrugged.

Catherine bent down and kissed him. "You are my hero."

48

Morris was anxious to get to work Monday morning. He stopped to pick up a cup of coffee at a cafe across the street. Fumbling, he put the key in the lock and grimaced when he tilted the cup, spilling coffee on his hands. *Damn that's hot.* Before he could open the door, Thomas came up behind him. "Let me get that."

"I see you couldn't sleep either," Morris snapped.

"Nope. Guess it comes with the job."

Steven sat at his desk and sipped his coffee. Thomas sat down in a chair beside him. "Looks like you have a message," he said looking over at the spike.

Steven removed the slip and looked at it. He sat straight up in his chair and looked up at the clock. It was six-forty-five.

"What is it?" Thomas asked.

"It's a call from a Texas Ranger in Austin. Came in yesterday sometime after I left."

"I wonder if they are open yet." Steven went to the front where the telephones were kept and picked up the receiver. After giving the number to the operator, he waited as he heard the phone ring several times.

"I'm sorry, but there is no answer."

Morris hung up and returned to his desk. "Guess no one has come in yet."

"Maybe he got a new lead," Thomas suggested.

"Maybe so. We'll just have to wait and see."

Fifteen minutes later, the phone rang and Steven went to the front to answer.

"I wasn't sure you would be up this early," Trent said. "Do you know anything yet?"

"Working on something and I'm waiting on some calls myself. I'll let you know as soon as I hear. Stay close to your phone."

Thomas looked at Steven. "Jacob's father. If I don't find his son soon, I think he might move in with me." Thomas roared with laughter.

"I wish it was a laughing matter. I can't imagine what he must be feeling right now."

Thomas's grin turned into concern. "Think the Austin Ranger might be on to something?"

"I hope so." They were interrupted once more by the phone.

"Rangers' offices,"

This is Ranger Sidney McAllister and I need to speak to Ranger Morris."

"This is Morris."

"Finally. I think we've found the Matthews' baby."

"Where is he?"

"A couple living south of Austin were planning to adopt him. The man's brother called the sheriff on another matter and the sheriff called me here at the Rangers' office. I went out to their house to see the baby and I'm fairly positive it's the right boy - birthmark and all."

"Where is the baby now? Does the couple still have him and are they willing to give him up?"

"I don't think that's a problem anymore."

"Why not?"

"When Mrs. Armstrong was told by her husband that the baby was taken illegally, she went crazy. Ran upstairs to her bedroom and shot herself in the head with her husband's gun."

"Oh, God. Where is Jacob now?"

"When I left them yesterday Mr. Armstrong's brother, who lives down the road from their house, took Jacob to their house. Someone needs to come get him."

"I think it would be a good idea if you went back there and stayed until I get there. We need to make sure nothing happens to him. Can you hold for a minute?" Morris put his hand over the phone and looked up at Thomas.

"Thomas, bring me that train schedule on the corner of my desk."

Thomas picked it up and took it to Morris. As he read the schedule, Morris spoke into the receiver. "The next train, Houston to Austin, leaves at nine fifteen. I should be at the Austin station at eleven-forty-five. Give or take a few minutes. Can you have someone meet me there and take me to the Armstrong's house?"

"Sure thing."

Morris tapped down on the receiver disconnecting their call and tapped it again. "Yes, I need you to call a number for me."

Trent answered on the second ring. "How soon can you meet me in Houston?"

"I can make the eight o'clock to Houston."

"Good, I'll be waiting." When Trent hung up the phone, he looked up and saw Catherine.

"I'm going with you," Catherine said, standing in the doorway.

"Be quick. We have to make the eight o'clock train. I'm calling Jason."

Ten minutes later Catherine had changed her clothes and was back downstairs with a satchel.

"Jason and Shelby are on their way," Trent said as Catherine turned to Sadie.

"Go, I'll be fine with the children. Just bring Jacob back," Sadie said.

Trent grabbed the satchel and led Catherine quickly to the station. They were halfway there when the whistle blew indicating its arrival.

By the time they bought their tickets and boarded the train, the reality of the moment set in.

"Tell me what Morris said."

"He asked how soon I could meet him in Houston. I didn't get a chance to ask him a lot of questions. There was just an urgency in his voice. I guess we'll find out when we get there. How were you able to pack so quickly?"

"When we got back from Galveston, I had a premonition. Something inside told me to have a bag prepared. It's something new mothers do when they know they might have to drop everything and rush to the hospital. It's kind of a mother thing, I guess. I didn't pack a lot; a change of underclothes, a clean night shirt for both of us and of course, things Jacob would need to come home."

Trent's mouth dropped open and he looked at her incredulously. "You're unbelievable. I would never have thought of that. Let's go to the dining car and get some coffee."

Forty-five minutes later they pulled up at the Houston train station. Morris was waiting with his arms folded across his chest looking grim.

When they got off the train, Morris approached them. "We won't be going far. The next train will be here in fifteen minutes to take us to Austin. I'll tell you what is going on when we get settled." They walked over to the clerk and purchased two round trip tickets.

As soon as the train arrived, they moved to a back Pullman car with a private suite. "Do you always travel this way?" Catherine asked, trying to break the ice.

Morris laughed. "Sometimes, if the suite is not booked, we get to use it for special meetings and such, free of charge." The porter knocked on the door and Morris said, "Come in."

"I will be serving Danish and coffee shortly unless you prefer something else."

Morris looked at Trent and Catherine. Catherine asked if he could serve her hot tea instead of coffee.

"Add some orange juice to that, please," Morris said.

When the porter left, Morris sat back on the cushioned bench. "I've been informed by our Austin office that an infant boy matching Jacob's description has been found. Without a family member being there, you will have to make the positive identification before we can bring him back. Understand, there is the chance that it's not your son, so I hope we aren't on a wild goose chase."

Catherine spoke first. "Did they say he had a birthmark in the shape of a fish?"

Morris shook his head and bit his top lip. "Yes, but it's third party. Sometimes people get excited and think they see things just because they read it in the newspaper."

"Was your source reliable?" Trent asked.

"I think so. I guess I'm trying to prepare you in the event we get there and it's not him."

"We understand," Catherine said. "We know you have to say these things. It's your job, but I know in my heart, it's him."

They stopped talking when the porter returned with the refreshments. After he left they continued their conversation.

Morris smiled. "There is something I need to tell you, and it won't change anything, but there has been an incident."

"With Jacob?" Trent asked, moving forward in his seat.

"No, not exactly. When the woman's husband told her about the article in the paper and that Jacob might have been taken illegally, she became hysterical. She apparently went to their bedroom and shot herself with her husband's gun."

"Oh my word," Catherine said almost in a whisper."

"Was Jacob hurt?"

"No, he was with the nanny in the nursery."

"Oh, thank goodness."

"Where is Jacob now?"

"Mr. Armstrong's brother lives close by. He and his wife are caring for Jacob until we arrive. Mr. Armstrong is not fairing very well. He blames himself for his wife's suicide."

"So if it is Jacob, will we be allowed to bring him home with us?" Trent asked.

"I don't see why not. There are any number of things that could prevent that."

"Like what?" Catherine asked.

"I'm not expecting this to happen, but Mr. Armstrong could stop it if he were to obtain a court order."

"Can he do that?" Trent asked. "Our son was stolen from our home."

"Like I said, I'm not anticipating that will happen, but sometimes people change their minds. He has no legal right to keep him from you. I think you should prepare yourselves for the worst and hope for the best."

Trent reached over and squeezed Catherine's hand. "If it is Jacob, I will not leave without him," Catherine said. "Law or no law."

Morris did not argue with her and instead picked up a Danish and took a big bite.

49

Two hours later, the train pulled into the Austin train station. Morris had his Ranger badge pinned to the lapel of his suit. When they got off the train, a man approached. "Are you Ranger Morris?"

"I am."

"I'm Jud Patterson and I am a clerk at the Ranger station. I have been given instructions to take you to a property just south of Austin. Follow me, please."

He led them outside to a covered carriage and helped them in. "We should be there in about thirty or so minutes."

Trent put his arm around Catherine as they took off and held her hand with the other.

"What if it's not him?" she asked Trent.

"You've been praying, haven't you?"

"Every minute of every day."

"It's him. I don't think Morris would have invited us to come along unless he was pretty sure it's Jacob."

The carriage ride seemed to take longer than the suggested time, but eventually they turned between two brick walls and crossed over a cattle guard. Morris exited first, then Trent and Catherine. "I think you should wait here until I speak to the family," Morris said.

They stood outside holding hands for what seemed a lifetime. Soon, the door opened and Morris motioned for them to come in. "This is Eli and Clarice Armstrong."

"It's nice to meet you," Trent said. "This is my wife, Catherine and I'm Trent Matthews." The silence was awkward and they were interrupted by an older woman joining them.

"This is my mother, Ester Rawlings. She's been looking after Ryan," Clarice said.

"Who is Ryan?" Catherine asked.

"I'm sorry. That's the name my brother gave the infant," Eli said.

"The child is asleep upstairs. You are welcome to come up and take a look," Mrs. Rawlings said and turned. Everyone followed her upstairs. When Mrs. Rawlings got to the door, she stopped and turned. "Why don't we let Mr. and Mrs. Matthews have the first look?"

Catherine walked in first, followed by Trent. When they got to the crib and looked down at his tiny body, Catherine put her hand over her mouth. She looked up at Trent and they hugged each other. Catherine turned, grateful tears flowing down her cheek, and nodded her approval. There were smiles on everyone's faces. Catherine spun around and walked back to Steven Morris, wrapping her arms around him and kissing his cheek. "Thank you," she whispered as she turned and went back to the crib. She looked up at Trent, who was wiping his tear-filled eyes with his handkerchief.

They were joined by Mrs. Rawlings. "He's been asleep for over an hour; you're his mother and it's up to you if you want to wake him up." Catherine hugged her and turned. She gently picked up Jacob as he stretched and yawned. When he opened his eyes, a huge smile creviced his cheeks, confirming that he recognized his mother.

Trent wrapped his arms around both Jacob and Catherine. When they turned around, the room was empty.

"He needs his diaper changed," Catherine said to Trent. "Would you get my satchel and I'll change him."

Fifteen minutes later Catherine, Trent and Jacob were saying goodbye to everyone. "Thank you for everything," Catherine said. "You've taken good care of him."

Trent turned to Eli. "We're very sorry for your loss. Please tell your brother how thankful we are that he has returned our son to us. We will be forever grateful."

Steven Morris rode back to the train station with them, but did not leave on the train. "I've got some business to take care of here. I'm very happy we were able to find your son, Trent. He would be gone forever if not for your quick thinking. You are the one that brought your boy back home. Everything you did brought us one step closer. We will probably never find the couple that took him, but I think Houston is rid of them both for good. Have a safe trip."

They took turns holding Jacob on their way back to Houston. When one was holding him, the other would be holding Jacob's hand with his tiny fingers clutching his parents. They changed trains in Houston and finally arrived in Rosenberg at three in the afternoon.

"The children should be waking up from their naps by now," Catherine said.

"Looks like Jason's wagon is at our house. I'm not sure what we would do if we didn't have him and Shelby as our friends," Trent said.

The room filled with screams and laughter when they walked through the front door. Jacobs' eyes opened wide, followed by a huge smile, as his brothers and sisters surrounded him, smothering him with kisses. Sadie stood to the side as tears dribbled down her high cheek-bones. Catherine went to her and hugged her. "He's fine. We are all fine. God has answered our prayers."

Later that evening, Trent received a call from Agnes. She wanted to know if she and a photographer could come to Rosenberg and get a picture of the family. She wanted to do a follow-up story in the upcoming edition of the *Houston Chronicle*.

Trent met Agnes and the photographer at the train station at eleven o'clock the next day. He drove them back to his house in their new covered carriage. Catherine had lunch ready in the formal dining room. After everyone was seated, Trent got up and made a toast. "To Agnes and our friends at the newspaper; your journalism skills were instrumental in bringing home our son and we are forever grateful and thankful for the work you do in our community. Good job."

The next Sunday, Trent walked to the train station to purchase a *Houston Chronicle*. He turned to page four. He couldn't help but giggle when he saw the adorable picture of Honey. The caption read: *New Puppy Welcomes Home Baby Jacob. In order to maintain the family's privacy, it was their desire not to have a family picture in the paper. They wish to thank the Texas Rangers and the Houston Chronicle for their diligent search and recovery of their son. Baby Jacob is now home and safe with his loving family.*